Misfits, Inc.

Holly Copella

ISBN: 0986441694
ISBN-13: 978-0986441691

To my very own mystic warriors,
Daniela & Anthony

ACKNOWLEDGMENTS

Copella Books: First Paperback Edition 2015
Cover Artist: Shardel
SelfPubBookCovers.com/Shardel
Printed by CreateSpace, An Amazon.com Company

PUBLISHER'S NOTE

Chapter One

*S*muggler's Bay Hotel was an impressive resort along the white, sandy beach of the secluded, tropical island. The luxurious hotel was twenty stories high with private balconies facing the scenic ocean. Ivy climbed the sides of the building, giving it an old-world charm and added to its tropical appeal. A young attractive woman in her mid-twenties, Hailey Aramis, walked along the empty, moonlit beach. The moon glistening off the dark ocean was the most romantic image she'd ever seen. Small waves gently crashed to shore then pulled back into the ocean leaving behind hidden treasures, mostly broken seashells. The only thing missing from her romantic, moonlit walk was a handsome man by her side. It wasn't that she didn't find the time for romance and relationships. Time was all she had. It wasn't as if she wasn't an attractive, young woman. She was more than attractive enough to gain plenty of male attention. Hailey just didn't feel that heart pounding attraction toward any man. She desperately wanted to fall in love; she wanted to feel the way others felt, but she just didn't.

The man of her dreams was out there, she was positive. She even knew what he looked like--sort of. She'd met him once in a dream when she was a young teenager. She fell in love with him, or perhaps with the idea of this perfect man. A few years later, she'd had the most erotic dream with the same man. There was a pond surround by flowers with a gorgeous, tropical waterfall, and they'd made love in the glacier blue water alongside the falls. It was a romantic illusion, but it was one she enjoyed and kept with her the last few years. She allowed the surf to rush past her bare feet and enjoyed feeling the wet sand between her toes. Hailey drifted off into her own world. She wanted to meet the love of her life. She wanted to be with him so badly; she could almost will him to join her on the beach at that very moment. Hailey suddenly felt compelled to look toward the hotel.

The dark silhouette of a man could be seen near the dimly lit poolside cabana. Although she couldn't make out his features, he was a lean man, possibly built athletic. He had his hands casually in his pants pockets and watched her in the distance. Could it be him? Could this really be the man of her dreams? As she stared at him, a thousand inappropriate thoughts raced through her mind. It was then that a woman's shrill scream shattered her fantasy. The woman's scream was somehow familiar to her. Hailey turned in the wet sand and looked toward the nearby path in the woods, but she didn't see anyone. She felt concerned for the woman and slowly walked closer to the path.

A young woman ran from the woods and stopped when she saw Hailey on the beach not far from her. The woman looked familiar, but she couldn't place her face. Her nightclub dress was dirty and torn. Hailey could almost make out the tears streaking her face. She was terrified by something she'd seen. That's when Hailey saw the blood covering the woman's hands. Hailey took a step toward her, attempting to think of something comforting to say. A strange snarling sound was barely heard behind the woman causing Hailey to stop in her tracks. The woman was suddenly thrown face down on the sand where she once stood. She screamed while clutching and clawing at the sand as she was dragged back into the dark woods by her ankles. In a split second, she was gone. Hailey stared at the empty path with horror on her face as the woman's screams trailed off. She turned toward the man standing near the poolside cabana to see if he'd help. His hands were now out of his pockets and hung by his sides.

"Help her!"

The man, although she couldn't make out his face, appeared more interested and possibly alarmed by something behind her. Hailey heard a strange rumbling sound from the ocean. She slowly turned and looked behind her. A large wave had built up in the ocean and now rushed toward her. Hailey screamed as the wave crashed down upon her, engulfing her in a powerful rush of water. She gasped for air but only inhaled salty ocean water. She floundered within the water, but there was no way to reach the surface.

†

*H*ailey suddenly woke with a gasp and jumped upright on the leather bench seat in the back of the helicopter. She attempted to catch her breath, still tasting the saltwater in her throat, and quickly looked around with disorientation. The loud thumping of the helicopter's rotor blades was almost hypnotic. She could feel the seat vibrating beneath her, reminding her that they were still in the air and she hadn't drown. She looked at the woman sitting alongside her in the back. Her young companion was also her friend and co-worker, Melana Thayer. Mel stared at her with a look that conveyed surprise and possible concern to her sudden outburst. Hailey slowly straightened in her seat and attempted to shake her dream while putting on a false smile.

"Guess I dozed off," Hailey said timidly.

A moderately attractive woman in her late thirties with plump, red lips stared back at Hailey from her position in the front. Both women shared the same expression. Obviously, Hailey had made enough noise to startle her boss, Lucinda, as well. Considering the noise from the helicopter, she must have been quite loud.

"Really, Hailey," Lucinda huffed. "I'm starting to think I hired a basket case for an assistant."

"Just a bad dream," Hailey gently informed her as she slowly looked around. She couldn't admit just how much the dream had bothered her, at least not to her boss. She couldn't shake the sensation of drowning she had felt. It seemed so real. "I'm just not used to flying."

Hailey hated lying to her boss, but she wasn't going to admit just how frequent her nightmares were. She hadn't worked for Lucinda Keenan long enough to share such personal details. It was true; she didn't want her boss to think she'd hired a basket case. Lucinda remained turned in the front seat while staring at them and played with an old, stone pendant necklace she wore. It mostly looked like a polished rock, but she cherished the thing. Her look conveyed moderate concern. She possibly wasn't buying the 'flying' story. She finally smiled and appeared to brush off her concerns.

"A few fruity drinks will cure that," Lucinda announced cheerfully. "You'll have the afternoon to unwind before our meeting with Nevin Brody." The chain on Lucinda's necklace suddenly snapped and the pendant fell onto her lap. Her boss seemed horrified that her treasured, flea market necklace had fallen off. Her attention immediately shifted to Mel, and a hint of their less forgiving boss surfaced. "I thought I told you to get the clasp fixed, Melana. Do you have any idea how valuable this stone is?"

"The jeweler said it was fixed," Mel protested.

Hailey slouched slightly in her seat and hoped Lucinda's verbal lashing would be short-lived. The thought of her cheap necklace being valuable was almost humorous to Hailey, but that didn't mean Lucinda wouldn't berate her personal maid for the remainder of their journey.

"Did you want to bring her in for a landing, Ms. Keenan?" their pilot asked almost as if swooping in to save Mel from her verbal lashing.

Lucinda's foul mood immediately disappeared and glee filled her face as she turned forward in her seat. "I've always wanted to try a rooftop landing." She eagerly took the controls before her.

Hailey and Mel were both relieved by the pilot's timely save, whether intentional or not. Mel shifted uncomfortably in her seat and tightened her safety harness.

"Brace yourself," Mel muttered to her friend.

Hailey smiled and laughed softly. Mel finally eyed Hailey and appeared curious while possibly attempting to get her mind off their boss crashing the helicopter while landing it.

"Which nightmare was it this time?" Mel asked. "The one with the snakes in the cave? That one is nasty."

"No, the enormous tidal wave," Hailey replied and again shifted in her seat. She didn't even want to think about it.

"You know what you need?"

Hailey rolled her eyes and avoided looking at her young friend. "Here we go--"

"You need to meet some bronzed cabana boy with rippling muscles," Mel announced while grinning lustfully at her own thoughts. "Life is too short--"

The helicopter suddenly jerked and jolted downward. Hailey was immediately reminded of that time Mel had gotten her to ride the mechanical bull at a nightclub. Mel and Hailey clutched their seats and held back their startled gasps.

Mel looked at Hailey with concern evident in her eyes. "Literally too short."

The helicopter was nearly upon the hotel's rooftop landing pad at the island resort. Mel and Hailey again gripped their seats while witnessing Lucinda bringing the massive, flying machine closer to the roof for a landing. It was a terrifying view from the backseat, making Hailey's nightmare almost the lesser of two evils.

"Wee!" Lucinda giddily squawked from behind the helicopter controls.

Chapter Two

*T*he elegant resort lobby was a massive marvel of carved wood, marble, and glass. Countless leather sofas and overstuffed chairs welcomed guests to hang out in the lobby with its open doorways to the outside, allowing the sounds of the ocean to fill the area. The cathedral ceiling was two stories high with an inside balcony to the second floor rooms. A massive, carved staircase towered up to the second floor. For those less adventurous, the elevators were off to the side of the lobby near the gift shop. The front desk was a breathtaking work of art in itself. It encompassed half the back wall and consisted mainly of marble and stone. A perky blonde woman dressed in business attire stood behind the large front desk and handed the last of the afternoon arrivals the electronic keycards to their guestrooms. As the last couple approached the elevators and marveled at the grand staircase, the perky blonde desk clerk, Cass, frowned and looked impatiently at her watch.

A lanky man in his late twenties, Skyler DeMorris, appeared from a connecting hallway toward the rear of the lobby. He was clearly out of sorts as he approached and hurried behind the desk to join her. Cass glared at him with disapproval. He caught her glare, looked away, and immediately fidgeted.

"I know; I'm late," he quickly announced and fumbled around behind the desk.

"Again," she snapped then shook her head with annoyance. "I don't know why Talbert hasn't fired your ass."

Skyler seemed average in every way imaginable. Average looks, average height, and possibly average intelligence. What set him apart was his above average personality and explosive energy. He resembled a teenager jacked up on caffeine. Skyler avoided looking at his moderately attractive co-worker and hastily straightened his gold nametag on his official resort jacket.

"I'm sorry, really," he fumbled over his own words. Attempting to slow his speech was one of his many main issues. When he became overly excited, which was often, he tended to speak faster than most could understand. "I don't sleep for days, and when I finally do, I can't wake up."

"You and your sleep disorders," Cass huffed and rolled her eyes at him for good measure. "I can't believe they don't have a pill for what's wrong with you."

"I wish they did," he remarked while attempting to straighten his tie, although his efforts seemed to make it worse. His hands seemed to move faster than his thoughts, making his movements uncoordinated and jerky. "Drugs don't affect me."

His attractive co-worker obviously had little use for him and made it known by the way she cast scathing looks at him. "Save it for someone who cares, Skyler. Ms. Keenan's helicopter was heard approaching," Cass informed him in a tone firmer than necessary. "I sent Merle to the roof with the luggage cart. If she kept her keycard to the penthouse, she won't have any reason to come down here before this evening." Even the staff attempted to avoid the resort owner. "I tried paging Talbert, but I didn't get a response. I'd like to believe he's helping security search for that girl who wandered off last night, but I think he's just avoiding the boss."

"Ms. Keenan's here?" Skyler questioned then ran his fingers nervously through his hair. His rising anxiety was evident. "I'd forgotten she was arriving today."

The look on Cass's face conveyed her annoyance. "What else is new?" she muttered.

Skyler frowned, obviously ashamed of his current condition. He cast a sheepish look at his coworker.

"What's this about a guest wandering off last night?" he nervously asked.

"More of the usual," Cass scoffed. "Some girl hooks up with some stud, slips off with him for a few days, and everyone immediately assumes she's missing."

Skyler fidgeted and cast a strange look at the woman alongside him. "What did this girl look like?"

"It doesn't matter, Skyler," Cass snapped at him with annoyance. "She'll show up soon enough. You have enough of your own work to do, and no one needs your toxic, runaway imagination added to the mix."

As the elevator dinged, Skyler jumped and immediately looked across the lobby. The elevator doors opened as if on command to reveal Lucinda in her full glory. She walked straight and with purpose in her formfitting dress and daringly high stiletto heels across the lobby and toward the front desk. Hailey and Mel followed behind in less of a hurry and marveled at the lobby with amazement. Skyler immediately went to work in an attempt to appear busy and possibly go unnoticed. Cass sprang to attention and offered her best, professional smile while Skyler did his best to remain invisible to the hotel owner.

"Ms. Keenan, welcome back," Cass announced cheerfully. "Your penthouse suite has been freshened for your arrival. I'm sorry Talbert wasn't on the roof to greet you personally. He was momentarily detained."

Lucinda allowed a throaty laugh to escape. "Tell Talbert he could have smoked his nasty cigars on the roof while he waited," she announced while grinning knowingly. "Cass, this is my new assistant, Miss Aramis. I trust you've given her a suite on the nineteenth floor with an ocean view."

"Yes, absolutely," Cass replied.

"Lucinda--" came a male voice from across the lobby.

All three turned and looked in the direction of the voice. Talbert Jenkin, the hotel manager, approached them with possibly the worst false smile Hailey had ever seen. Despite Lucinda's beauty and perfect body, most men went out of their way to avoid her. Men and women within her circle fondly referred to her as 'the barracuda'. Talbert cupped Lucinda's hand in his and suavely kissed it. Talbert was a charming man in his fifties and most women forty and over would consider him handsome in a vintage sort of way.

"I wasn't expecting you for another three hours," he announced cheerfully. His lack of response to his page indicated he was possibly avoiding the rooftop greeting with the barracuda, prolonging their meeting to the last possible moment.

"Talbert, darling," she announced in a tone that was meant to convey insincerity. "I'd like you to meet my new assistant, Hailey Aramis."

Talbert was quick to cast his eyes upon Hailey and took in her body with a sweeping glance that immediately made her feel uncomfortable.

"It's a pleasure, Miss Aramis."

"Treat her well," Lucinda announced firmly. "I simply can't live without her."

He again eyed Hailey and grinned with an attempt at charm that came off instead as moderately creepy. "I can see why." His attention immediately returned to Lucinda and the insincerities continued. "I'll escort you lovely ladies to your rooms."

Talbert extended his arm to Lucinda, who immediately linked onto him like an old flame. Hailey found the exchange entertaining; especially considering Mel's gossiping indicated Lucinda couldn't stand Talbert. Hailey got the distinct impression the feeling was mutual. He guided her toward the elevator with Mel obediently following behind them. Hailey was about to follow then remembered her earlier assignment and turned to Cass behind the desk. She caught the perky desk clerk gazing after Lucinda with a hard to read expression on her face. It would seem Lucinda wasn't popular in any circle, something that was becoming apparent to Hailey the longer she worked for the barracuda. Cass focused her attention back on Hailey and her pleasant smile appeared on command.

"I'm expecting an important document," Hailey said politely to the desk clerk not much older than herself. "Could you notify me when it arrives?"

"My shift is nearly over, but Skyler will be at the desk all evening," Cass announced cheerfully in response and casually indicated Skyler, who busily worked.

Skyler didn't even seem to realize his name had been mentioned. Cass waited a second then cleared her throat. Skyler still didn't react.

"Skyler--"

Skyler snapped out of his trance and looked at Cass dumbfounded. She indicated Hailey across the desk from him. Skyler turned and met Hailey's gaze. His expression suddenly dropped as his lips parted, unable to speak. His look was baffling and almost distant as he stared at her.

"Miss Aramis would like to be notified when her documents arrive," Cass recapped the conversation.

Skyler continued to stare at Hailey, frozen in the same position. The fact that he hadn't even blinked was almost disturbing. Cass saw his look and appeared embarrassed.

"Skyler?"

Skyler still didn't react or take his eyes off Hailey. Hailey was feeling uncomfortable by his strange, distant stare obviously directed at her, but it was almost as if he was staring through her.

"Skyler!"

Skyler snapped out of his trance, twitched with surprise, and knocked a pile of blank keycards from the counter. The pile scattered onto the floor by his feet. Both women watched as he fumbled in high speed to pick them up. He straightened with a handful of keycards and hit his head on the marble counter. He clutched his head and dropped the keycards. While attempting to catch the falling plastic cards, he knocked over a container of pens. The pens flew across the desk.

Cass's expression never changed. She casually looked at Hailey and offered a reassuring smile. "Clumsiness is a side effect of the gifted--or so he says. I assure you, he's on top of it."

Hailey offered a tiny smile, although she wasn't convinced, and headed for the elevator. Skyler straightened with a fistful of pens and stared after Hailey, his mouth hanging open and the same fixated look on his face. Cass turned to face him and smacked his arm, startling him.

"What's wrong with you?" she demanded.

Skyler replaced the pens with trembling hands. None wanted to go back into the holder. "Nothing," he chirped in a pitch higher than normal while avoiding looking at her. "It was *nothing*."

Her eyes suddenly turned demanding. "Don't start with that psychic crap again," Cass threatened. "It freaks out the guests and gives me the creeps."

Chapter Three

*T*he beautiful, tropical beach was alive with hotel guests tanning and relaxing in the sun under large umbrellas. Other, more adventurous guests surfed with boogie boards on moderately tame waves. Further out in the water, guests rode the waves on jet skis. Since it was the beginning of off-season, the beach wasn't nearly as crowded as it was at its busiest and made for a relaxing atmosphere. Maximum capacity for the hotel was one thousand guests, but there were no more than two hundred guests during the slow season. Mel and Hailey walked along the beach carrying their large, fruity drinks with the standard, colorful umbrella straws. Mel had changed into proper beach attire, which included a conservative bikini and sarong. Despite their visit being work related, Hailey was certain Mel intended to make the most of her free time, which would undoubtedly include finding her own bronzed cabana boy. Hailey remained dressed in her business skirt suit, looking out of place among the beach dwellers. Mel was obviously disappointed with her friend's choice in beachside attire.

"I wish you'd reconsider lying on the beach with me," Mel pouted. "I need to work on my tan, and I hate not having someone to talk to."

"I'm far too tense for something so relaxing," Hailey replied. Unlike her friend, Hailey had business matters with which to attend and couldn't take the rest of the afternoon off. "We'll worship the sun all afternoon tomorrow, I promise."

"I'm holding you to that."

Hailey suddenly stopped and stared at the woods' edge across the beach. There was a trail leading into the forest, which oddly reminded her of the path in her dream on their journey to the island. Mel was talking to her, but she no longer heard her friend. She listened to the sound of her own heart beating as the nightmare returned to her in full horror. She could almost hear the woman's scream. The sound of a woman's scream startled Hailey from her daze. A young woman wearing a flashy, tropical bikini bodysurfed out of control on a boogie board and nearly collided with them. Hailey and Mel jumped out of her path just in time to avoid being run down. The young, bikini clad woman, Desi, flipped the board near them, taking more wet sand than ocean into her ample cleavage. She laughed as she dizzily stood and eyed the pair with which she nearly collided.

"Sorry," Desi announced cheerfully. "I didn't mean to nearly wipe out on you. These things have a mind of their own."

Mel eyed the short board Desi picked up from the sand. "That looks like fun," she remarked.

"Complimentary from the surf shack," an out of breath Desi announced.

Two more women also in their early twenties, Amy and Penny, approached them. Amy, a short blonde-haired girl, wore a more conservative tankini swimsuit with a swim skirt, while Penny, a tall auburn-haired beauty, wore a slightly more revealing bikini in hot pink. Hailey wasn't positive from the front, but she was almost certain Penny was wearing a thong bottom.

Desi looked at her approaching friends then back to Hailey and Mel. "I'm Desi and these are my friends, Amy and Penny."

"Mel and Hailey," Mel announced, her eyes automatically drawn to Amy's black rose tattoo creeping out of her bikini top on her left breast. "We just arrived." She indicated the tattoo. "That's an interesting tattoo."

Amy looked at her tattoo peeking out from her bathing suit then met Mel's gaze and grinned. "My boyfriend wanted me to get a yellow rose," she announced then casually indicated the black rose.

"After I dumped his sorry ass, I had the artist change it to a black rose."

"Acht," Desi loudly announced and pointed a warning finger, "we're not discussing ex-boyfriends on this trip. We're here to have fun and do our own prowling."

Amy looked at Hailey and Mel with enthusiasm on her face. "Oh, you have to join us tonight in the lounge," she chimed in. "After the piano man retires, the old fogies go to bed, and they crank the dance music. It's a total stud-fest."

"Yeah, come out with us tonight," Desi announced in response. "It'll be so much fun. Last night, we didn't get to bed until nearly sunrise."

"We'd love to," Mel quickly replied and clutched Hailey's arm before she could open her mouth.

"Great," Desi announced cheerfully. "We'll meet you in the lounge around ten."

The three women waved and left. Hailey couldn't resist taking a peek at the back of Penny's bikini. She'd been correct; she was wearing a thong bottom. Once her curiosity was satisfied, Hailey glanced back at Mel.

"You know I have that meeting tonight," Hailey reminded her friend.

Mel waved her off. "Boss lady always turns in before the witching hour," she boldly teased. Her look turned serious. "You're going to have fun this week even if it kills me."

t

*I*t was early evening and not long until Hailey and Lucinda's scheduled meeting with the all-important Nevin Brody. Hailey stepped out of her suite on the nineteenth floor and entered the brightly lit, elegant corridor. Her floor contained several of the hotel's finest suites for its most important guests. She was certain Nevin Brody's suite was somewhere on her floor. She'd never met the man, so she had no idea if she'd even seen him around the hotel. Lucinda's meeting with the wealthy businessman was extremely important to her and the future of her company. If Lucinda wanted to expand, she needed a wealthy investor, and Nevin Brody was her best bet. Hailey preferred that version to the rumor going around back at the office. Some speculated Lucinda had overextended her credit and was falling into financial ruin. If that were the case, she certainly didn't let a little thing like going broke curb her spending. The elevator dinged as the doors opened.

Lucinda stepped out wearing an expensive, moderately revealing evening dress with a plunging neckline and a slit up her thigh that would have revealed her panties, had she actually been wearing any. She was a beautiful woman even younger women would envy. Her god-awful stone pendant necklace was the only thing keeping her from looking perfect. Hailey didn't know why she insisted on wearing the thing as if it were the Crown Jewels. Lucinda approached while smiling brightly beyond plump, red lips. Her excessively full lips, particularly in that shade of red lipstick, were always the first thing anyone saw of the barracuda. The second thing they saw was that hideous necklace drawing attention to her awe-inspiring cleavage, which was usually attempting to break free from her plunging neckline. Lucinda gave her a quick once over.

"My God, you're not even dressed yet!" Lucinda proclaimed. "Have you considered what you're going to wear tonight?"

Hailey hesitated and uncertainly looked over her conservative business skirt suit. She met Lucinda's gaze with a dumbfounded look but feared to admit she was already dressed for dinner. Lucinda's smile immediately faded.

"Oh, really, Hailey!" Lucinda shook her head with disapproval. "You're not going to the most important business meeting of my life looking like, well, a businesswoman." She nodded her toward the elevator.

Hailey was already confused.

"Come on," Lucinda commanded. "We'll find you something suitable to wear in my closet. Lucky for you, I have an entire wardrobe of sexy dresses I keep here."

She had to be kidding! Hailey couldn't even imagine wearing one of Lucinda's most conservative dresses let alone whatever her boss was thinking of stuffing her within.

"I really don't--" Hailey attempted to protest.

"Have you ever heard of fun, Hailey?" Lucinda asked and raised her perfectly sculpted brow. "It's what attractive, young women like us enjoy having in our lives. You really need to try it. Show off a little boob." Lucinda gestured, jiggling invisible boobs with her hands. "Kick your granny panties to the curb." She grinned deviously. "Try it; you might like it." Lucinda commanded her to the elevator with a carefully manicured finger. "Upstairs, young lady!"

Hailey attempted to hold back her groan and obediently headed for the elevator. Lucinda followed after her and grinned mischievously.

"This is going to be fun," Lucinda announced as she giggled. "Wait until I introduce you to your cleavage and the joy of going commando. Very liberating--" Her devious smile returned. "--and just a tiny bit breezy."

"My underwear are fine just where they are," Hailey announced firmly as they entered the elevator.

"Uh, huh," Lucinda teased then winked at her. "We'll see about that."

As the elevator doors closed, Hailey feared it was going to be a long night. It never dawned on her that she'd have to worry about a female boss trying to get her out of her underwear.

Chapter Four

*I*t was nearly six o'clock that evening and guests were spilling into the lobby from their day on the beach or, in some cases, their adventures touring the island's interior. Skyler stood behind the front desk and watched the last of the guests make their way into the elevators. Most were on their way to change for dinner and evening entertainment in the lounge. Apart from the nightlife in and around the resort, there was little to do on the island itself, since the resort was the only known civilization on the island. Once the lobby cleared, Skyler leaned on the desk and rubbed his temples. The heavy knitting of his brows suggested he had a migraine headache. A sturdy built, rugged looking man in his late thirties, Marcus Sherwood, approached the desk with a mission. Skyler straightened the moment he saw him, but he obviously wasn't pleased to see the man. Despite his expensive suit, Marcus was far from gentlemanly, and judging by his stern expression, Skyler had reason to react with concern.

"Skyler," Marcus demanded in a gruff tone before even reaching the desk. "Why wasn't I notified when Nevin Brody arrived?"

Skyler weakly fumbled with an explanation. "I, uh, told Delaney--"

Marcus obviously wanted none of Skyler's excuses. He stopped before the desk and stared down the meek man. It was a look most feared from the tough man.

"Delaney isn't in charge of security," he launched back. He pounded the desk with his index finger, never taking his eyes from Skyler's eyes. "I expect to be kept informed of our VIP guests, especially those traveling with personal attack dogs."

"You mean Rafe--"

"You know damned well I mean Rafe!"

Skyler appeared scolded, although it seemed to be a normal state for the downtrodden man. He attempted to hold his head up and make direct eye contact with the head of security, but Marcus was far too intimidating. Skyler finally had to look down with shame. The dinging of the elevator stopped the verbal assault, since Marcus wasn't about to berate the staff in front of guests. Hailey stepped off the elevator wearing a revealing black evening dress in true Lucinda fashion. She was insecure about her exposed cleavage and the high slit up her leg. It was too much skin for a business dinner, but Lucinda refused to listen to such nonsense. Mel entered the lobby from the beach entrance, saw Hailey in the lobby, and stopped to stare. Hailey caught her friend's stunned look and immediately frowned.

"Don't even--" Hailey growled softly.

Mel suddenly grinned and placed her hand to her mouth to suppress her giggle. She attempted a more serious look as she approached then stopped in front of her and gave her a quick once over.

"I'm assuming boss lady dressed you for dinner," Mel teased then ogled her exposed cleavage.

"What gave that away?" Hailey snarled, lacking her friend's humor.

Mel gave her another once over, eyed the healthy slit up her thigh, and couldn't contain her grin any longer. "Please tell me you're not going commando as well."

"Don't be ridiculous," Hailey scoffed and looked away as her cheeks reddened.

Her friend's eyes widened and a gasp immediately followed. "Are you wearing one of Lucinda's thongs?" she softly cried out with surprise.

Hailey sneered and avoided looking at Mel, hoping the men at the desk hadn't heard the question. She knew her cheeks were bright red and gave away the answer. Mel burst out laughing.

"Shut up," Hailey snarled and headed toward the front desk, nearly stumbling in the high heels she wore.

Mel obediently followed and took in an eyeful of her from the back. "My God, you're really rocking that dress." She giggled. "And no unsightly panty lines."

She ignored her former friend and paused before the front desk not far from Marcus. Marcus saw both women and immediately smiled, officially ending his interrogation of Skyler.

"You must be Ms. Keenan's new assistant, Miss Aramis," Marcus announced cheerfully and extended his hand. "I'm Marcus Sherwood, Head of Hotel Security."

Despite her feelings of vulnerability in the revealing dress and being sexually assaulted in Lucinda's *barely there* thong, she managed a smile and shook his hand.

"It's a pleasure, Marcus."

His ruggedness aside, she found Marcus oddly attractive, and he smelled exceptionally nice with just the right amount of expensive cologne. Beyond his suit, she could tell he was built sturdy and tough. She didn't doubt his arms were made of steel. His handshake was firm, possibly too firm for greeting a woman, but she couldn't deny he was intimidating with the way his look pierced into her eyes. His smile conveyed there was more beyond that ordinary smile. She felt as if he were attempting to read her thoughts with the way he stared at her.

"If you need anything at all, don't hesitate to call me," he announced.

Marcus gave both women a polite nod then left. If nothing else, he had been polite enough not to stare at her cleavage. Of course, with the amount of time he'd spent in Lucinda's company, he was probably immune to breasts thrust in his face. Hailey shifted her attention to Skyler while attempting to ignore her physical discomfort. Skyler's eyes were locked on her with a similar expression from their earlier arrival. There was something unusual about the way he stared at her. She couldn't quite describe it. Hailey felt uncomfortable by the way he stared, but for some odd reason, she didn't feel he meant any real harm.

She gently cleared her throat and shifted slightly. "Did that letter arrive for Ms. Keenan?"

Skyler suddenly snapped to attention and began a frantic search of the desk. "Oh, I was supposed to notify you," Skyler fumbled and rummaged quickly through papers and envelopes. "I'm terribly sorry. It's--" Everything scattered from his trembling hands. "It's, uh, it's here--somewhere."

Skyler dumped the penholder again and subconsciously placed his hand to his temple in response. He couldn't seem to touch anything without knocking it over. Hailey watched him practically destroy the desk while frantically searching it. She almost felt sorry for him. Mel simply rolled her eyes and walked away from the desk.

"Skyler--" Hailey announced.

Skyler immediately froze and stared into her eyes, almost as if obediently commanded by her voice.

"It's okay, really," she announced gently in an attempt to calm him before he gave himself a stroke.

His brain seemed to function on its own as realization hit him. "I, uh, just remembered; Talbert took it to Ms. Keenan's suite."

Hailey found the strange desk clerk oddly adorable. She wasn't sure what it was about him, but she decided she liked the awkward, bumbling man.

"I know what it's like to have one of those days," she assured him. "I have them frequently."

He seemed to relax to the comment. "Mine is never ending," he announced while softly exhaling. "Even my dream world shows little mercy."

"I hear you," she groaned softly. "Mine too."

Skyler suddenly became excited by her comment and nearly jumped across the desk as his eyes lit up. "Really? Are you a vivid dreamer?"

Although his question surprised her, she was intrigued. Few people ever asked her about her dreams. She was usually too ashamed even to discuss them.

"A little too vivid," she replied. "Most people think I'm nutty."

"I'd settle for nutty," he remarked and attempted a wry smile. "I'm considered a freak."

She couldn't help but smile at him. Skyler relaxed, possibly for the first time, and laughed at himself. Talbert was crossing the lobby, saw Hailey at the desk, and switched direction, approaching them with a curious look.

"Is everything okay, Miss Aramis?"

She glanced at the distinguished looking general manager. "Yes, everything is fine."

Talbert casually placed his arm around her shoulder and guided Hailey away from the desk. Skyler's shoulders sagged with disappointment. Mel hurried to join them.

"I hope Skyler didn't say anything to upset you," Talbert remarked just loud enough for her to hear. "He means well, but he's a little *different*."

She found it odd that Talbert would share that sort of information with a guest regarding an employee. It was also in poor taste, almost as much as the peek he stole at her cleavage. She assumed she couldn't blame him; after all, Lucinda did force her to put them on display. It would be difficult for any man not to notice her breasts.

"No, he was very polite," she assured him.

"I'm glad to hear that."

Hailey was actually wishing he'd take his hand off her bare shoulder. Considering she felt nearly naked as it was, his touch was making her uncomfortable. The scent of his expensive cologne was almost overwhelming in such close confines. As she thought of an excuse to pull away from him, Hailey glanced across the lobby and saw a ruggedly handsome man in his early thirties heading toward the elevator. She found herself staring helplessly at the well-built man in the expensive, black suit. His presence was almost commanding, and her heart rate elevated in response. He had short dark hair, which was just the perfect length for running fingers through. She'd never seen such a handsome man before.

As the handsome man looked across the lobby, their eyes met briefly. Her heart skipped a beat the brief moment their eyes connected, and for the first time, she felt a burning passion in places she'd never imagined. Of course, that could have had something to do with the thong underwear. The man showed no reaction, not even a smile, and continued toward the elevators. She was almost disappointed that he didn't at least offer a smile or take in an eyeful of her revealing dress. Although, she hadn't offered a come-hither smile either. She felt her cheeks immediately redden. Mel and Talbert noticed her stare. She didn't even realize they were standing alongside her. Hailey couldn't take her eyes off the man crossing the lobby. The handsome man paused before the elevator, briefly glanced back at Hailey, and then entered the elevator. Hailey continued to stare at the closed elevator after he was gone. She couldn't seem to tear her eyes away from the spot he once stood even after the doors closed. Mel stared at Hailey with her mouth partially open and a look of surprise on her face.

"I know that look, but I've never seen it on you," Mel announced. A grin suddenly crossed her face. "You may have fun this week after all."

"Not with that one," Talbert firmly informed them. "Trust me; you'll want to stay far away from that man."

Both women looked at Talbert with shared surprise and question in their eyes.

"Why's that?" Mel was first to ask.

"That's Brody's attack dog, Rafe," Talbert remarked.

"Attack dog?" Hailey suddenly questioned, wondering what he meant by the comment.

Talbert shook his head with disgust. "Nevin claims he's his assistant, but I've met friendlier hitmen," he announced. "Nevertheless, you'll want to stay far away from him. There are bad boys and then there's Rafe."

Hailey wasn't sure what to think. Could Talbert be exaggerating? Was there some resentment between the two men, causing him to berate him? She couldn't get Rafe out of her head, despite Talbert's warning. He couldn't be *that* bad; could he?

Chapter Five

*T*he cozy lounge was dimly lit with small, round tables containing elegant lights on each, giving off a romantic glow. A rustic bar encompassed nearly half the back wall with large mirrors and shelves of expensive liquor. A tough looking, yet professionally dressed woman, Tam, tended bar. She was attractive enough to gain the attention of male guests who liked the biker chick look. She wore a sleeveless, button shirt, which revealed some cleavage, her amazingly toned arms, and a tattoo spilling off her shoulder and onto her arm. Guests were already filtering into the lounge to secure drinks before heading to the dining room for a late dinner. Romantic, live piano music seemed to fill the lounge without being too loud for guests to hold a conversation. A large, teddy bear of a man in his late twenties, Logan Holbrook, played the soft, romantic tune on the expensive grand piano. Considering his large size, the tune almost seemed out of place coming from his fingers striking the keys.

Lucinda and Hailey entered the lounge and checked out the scene before approaching the bar. Lucinda set her designer briefcase and clutch purse on the bar then took the available seat. Tam was quick to tend to them, knowing the attractive woman was the hotel owner. Despite her 'girl gone wild' look, Tam wasn't above kissing the boss's ass with the best of them.

"Good evening, Ms. Keenan," Tam announced in an unusually cheerful tone. "Your usual?"

Lucinda always seemed pleased when her subjects fawned over her. "Yes, and make something *special* for Hailey. She's too tense for someone her age."

Tam grinned and nodded. "I have just the thing for that." She began creating drinks for both women, tossing bottles around with amazing style and flare.

"I'd prefer to conduct this meeting sober," Hailey informed her boss.

Lucinda grinned through her plump, red lips. "That's a novel idea, but I doubt it'll catch on."

The piano music continued to fill the lounge, entrancing Hailey. She looked across the dimly lit room to the grand piano and studied the large, African-American man playing so beautifully. The boyish grin on his face told her he loved his work. He never looked down, indicating there was no sheet music.

"He plays wonderfully," Hailey said aloud even if she hadn't meant to.

Tam placed their drinks on the bar before them, glanced at Logan playing piano, and then grinned slyly. "That man puts more women in the mood than all the booze I serve."

"Makes a small fortune in tips too," Lucinda added without looking and sipped her drink. She smiled her approval to the tough bartender.

"Must get a lot of girls," Hailey remarked without taking her eyes off the large teddy bear of a man.

"Logan?" Tam remarked then allowed a throaty laugh to escape. "He's a Boy Scout."

As more customers approached the bar, Tam tended to them, humoring them with her overboard, tough girl personality. Hailey sipped her drink and made a face. It was almost too strong, although she assumed that was by design. Hailey refrained from gagging on what must certainly have been tabasco sauce. Lucinda casually looked around the room while sitting perfectly posed on her barstool. Her bare leg found its way outside the lengthy slit and daintily crossed over her other leg. It was no secret that Hailey's boss enjoyed the company of men. She was a terrible flirt, but from stories Mel had told, it went beyond flirting on many occasions. Hailey hadn't personally witnessed Lucinda in full prowling mode, so this business trip could be quite the eye-opener.

"This trip is only ten percent business," Lucinda informed her then suddenly stared across the lounge. She grinned with a lustful look Hailey had never seen before. "And the other ninety percent just walked through the door."

Hailey looked across the lounge to see the man who'd commanded her boss's undivided attention. An amazingly handsome man with flowing, golden brown hair crossed the room as if he owned it. The man in his early thirties was built more athletic than muscular and dressed in expensive, stylish, hand tailored clothing. He gained the attention of every woman and seemed to know it. He offered the most charming, magnificent smile at each woman he passed. They all seemed helpless to his charm and good looks. Just about every woman in the room kept their eyes on the handsome man. Even Hailey couldn't deny the man was beyond words, yet as she watched him, her thoughts strayed to the forbidden man from the lobby. The handsome man approached the bar and casually posed at it like a male model from a magazine cover. It seemed to come naturally to him. Even Lucinda seemed helpless to his charm. Although, Hailey wasn't about to rule out the wonderful scent of his cologne as a factor. Tam leaned on the bar, thrusting her cleavage forward, and stared at him with the same lustful look as every other woman in the lounge.

"Hi, darling," Tam announced in a slightly higher voice than normal while grinning. "What can I get you?"

"Cognac, if you please," Vance replied.

Tam straightened, grinned, and raised her brows lustfully. "I please." She flipped the bottle of expensive alcohol without taking her eyes off him, poured his drink, and set it before him.

Lucinda allowed her eyes to sweep over his body then settled on his eyes as he met her gaze. "I haven't seen you around before," she remarked.

Vance cast his smile upon Lucinda and suavely extended his hand. "I just arrived this morning. Vance Colten."

Lucinda eagerly accepted his hand with promise of never letting go. "Lucinda Keenan. I own this resort."

His brows raised in response. Hailey swore she heard a cash register ding to his increasing interest.

"Oh?" he replied and maintained his boyish grin. "I'm charmed to make your acquaintance."

Vance suavely kissed her hand. Hailey had to admit, it was almost erotic to watch. Lucinda turned giddy, something Hailey hadn't expected from the barracuda. There was a chance her boss may even have blushed.

Lucinda then indicated Hailey. "This is my lovely assistant, Hailey."

Vance smiled casually at Hailey while avoiding looking her in the eyes and appeared almost disinterested. "It's a pleasure." He immediately returned his attention to Lucinda. "You have a very charming hotel. I'm captivated by the overwhelming beauty everywhere."

Lucinda giggled again. She transformed from Hailey's barracuda of a boss into a little girl right before her eyes. Hailey groaned her displeasure and made an unannounced escape. She couldn't watch what was about to unfold, especially considering the giddy schoolgirl was her boss. Hailey crossed the lounge and found herself drawn to the man playing piano. Logan smiled, revealing charming dimples, as she sat at the piano. He had adorable, chubby cheeks, which complemented his shiny, clean-shaven head. Something about the way he smiled at her immediately put her at ease. Although, the music and the strong drink may have helped.

"That's beautiful," Hailey said warmly.

"I call that one 'untitled 327'," he announced while maintaining his grin.

She couldn't help feeling surprised by the comment. "You write your own songs?"

"Sort of," he replied. "I make them up as I go." Without looking away from Hailey, he gave a general nod toward the bar. "Who's the pretty boy sniffing around Ms. Keenan?"

"Vance Colten," Hailey offered and immediately regretted having rolled her eyes. She didn't know this man, but she felt compelled to open up, which wasn't like her. "He's a real charmer," she muttered.

Logan appeared almost humored. "If he's looking for a gravy train, he'd better move to another station."

She attempted to hold back her laugh, but it felt good to let it out. "Mr. Charming flirted his way across the entire room but blew me off like I wasn't even there. Not that he impresses me any, but it doesn't help a girl's ego." She leaned her elbow on the piano and held her chin in her hand. "Guess I'm not rich enough," she playfully pouted.

Hailey cast a quick glance downward and realized her cleavage was spilling out of her dress. Surprisingly, Logan hadn't looked. Tam may have not been exaggerating about the man being a Boy Scout. She straightened subconsciously and tugged on the neckline to help conceal her breasts. Her action caused his eyes to momentarily stray, but he didn't linger.

"Reminds me of the Charmer in the fable "The Gift"," he casually remarked. "The Charmer possessed the gift to charm all creatures, but if he gazed into the eyes of pure beauty, he would be rendered impotent." Logan appeared humored while staring at her. "He has no power over you."

Hailey felt her cheeks redden slightly while she attempted to hide her smile. "My ego just recovered. You're quite charming yourself," she replied gently then took a more serious tone. "I hadn't heard "The Gift" mentioned in over five years. I loved that fable."

Logan curiously studied her without missing a key. She smiled and sank into her own childhood fantasy.

"A lonely little girl with the burden to protect her father's kingdom, and the power to create her council of mystic warriors to assist her on her journey," Hailey announced with a sigh. "Out of all the creatures, she picks the least likely heroes." She returned to reality and straightened. "Quite moving."

"I appreciate that," Logan announced cheerfully. "I wrote that when I was in college."

Hailey's expression dropped to his admission. "You're Logan Holbrook?"

Logan smiled and nodded.

"What a small world," she almost gasped then attempted to reel in her childish fascination. "I only ever saw that one copy. Did you sell many?"

"Enough to live off the royalties quite comfortably," he replied then grinned. "Would you like a copy? I have two hundred in my closet."

Chapter Six

*T*he dining room was elegant yet had a tropical appeal. There was a wall of glass overlooking the terrace with more intimate seating. The classy, wicker chairs along with the high, faux thatch ceiling gave the room an added tropical feel. Intimate booths lined the side walls and live palm trees appeared to be growing from the marble floor. The charming room was filled with men and women dining by romantic candlelight while soft music created a soothing backdrop. Lucinda and Hailey followed the properly dressed host to an elegant table with the most stunning ocean view. As they approached the table, they were greeted by a man in his mid-fifties already seated at the table. Nevin Brody was probably the richest man Hailey would ever meet. He certainly had more money than Lucinda had, but he was known to be fairly cheap. She couldn't help but feel that his expensive suit and gold watch supported a different version of that story.

Brody was far from attractive, at least in Hailey's opinion. His hair plugs were painfully obvious and the color was excessively dark for a man his age. His grooming screamed he was attempting to hold onto a youth that no longer wanted any part of him. Physically, he seemed to be in excellent shape, undoubtedly exercising religiously. Hailey couldn't help but wonder if his tuxedo cost more than what she made in a year. As he took two quick steps to greet them, Hailey noticed the second man at the table, who'd been standing behind him. She took in an eyeful of Rafe. From only a few feet away, she marveled at how handsome he actually was. Despite Talbert's warning, she couldn't contain her attraction toward this man. Unlike Brody, he didn't bother dressing in his finest tuxedo. His expensive, signature suit was more than adequate. Hailey was so caught up in his straight stance and mildly muscular build; she hadn't even realized he showed no emotion to their approach.

"Lucinda, you look absolutely stunning," Brody announced cheerfully while taking both her hands in his and kissed her warmly on the cheek.

Whether she liked him or not, she greeted him with enthusiasm and grace. "Charming as always, Nevin, dear." She pulled away and indicated Hailey alongside her. "This is Hailey Aramis, my new assistant."

Brody was quick to sweep a glance over Hailey, almost certainly admiring her revealing dress into which Lucinda so graciously stuffed her. "It's a pleasure, Hailey," he announced politely. "You can call me Nevin." He then indicated the serious man remaining at the table. "This is my personal assistant, Rafe."

Hailey eagerly took in another eyeful of Rafe, excited finally for an introduction. He stared back at her with a cold expression and showed no reaction. His complete lack of response baffled her. If she couldn't gain his attention in Lucinda's borrowed dress, she should probably give up. Hailey managed a smile but found it difficult without any emotion from him. Lucinda guided Hailey to the window seat across from Rafe. Brody was quick to pull their chairs out for them. If nothing else, Brody was gentlemanly. As Brody took his seat, Lucinda placed her hand on Hailey's lower arm and casually indicated Rafe across from her.

"Despite his poor manners, Rafe rarely bites," Lucinda informed her. She turned her attention to Brody once he was comfortably seated and sipping his expensive drink. "Let's get business out of the way, shall we."

"Not so fast. First we dance," Brody announced, surprising both, and looked at Lucinda while extending his hand across the table to her. "My dear?"

Lucinda managed a smile but appeared put off by the diversion. She accepted his hand and both stood from their seats. Lucinda reluctantly joined him on his side of the table.

Brody looked at Hailey and offered a slightly devious smile. "You're next, my dear." He then glared at Rafe and turned stern. "You; behave."

Brody guided Lucinda to the dance floor. Hailey watched him pull her a little closer than necessary as they slow danced. She had to admit; she wasn't looking forward to her turn and wondered what the dance conversation would entail. When she looked back, she realized Rafe was staring at her from across the table. She tried to ignore the wonderful scent of his cologne wafting her way. Rafe casually leaned back in his wicker chair and sipped his expensive glass of brandy. With his expression remaining unchanged, she couldn't help but wonder what was going through his handsome head. At this point, she was almost certain it had nothing to do with her.

"Do you know why you're here?" he suddenly asked, void of emotion.

She was slightly surprised by the question. It wasn't exactly the conversation she had hoped to have with the handsome man. Hailey shifted in her wicker chair and attempted to make the best of the conversation she was given.

"Ms. Keenan wants Nevin Brody to invest in her hotel," she casually replied.

"That's why *she's* here," he replied dryly. "You're here as her sexual sacrifice to Brody."

His candor and bully mentality surprised her, but she attempted to show no reaction. "You're certainly offensive," she snapped then cocked her head to the side. "Is intimidation a service you offer, or are you just amusing yourself?"

"Just making an observation."

He was so casual with the conversation; it irritated her to no end. She should have taken the high road and ignored him, but she felt cheated, having been so attracted to him just to find out Talbert had been correct. He was a prick.

"Sounds like you're calling me a high priced whore," Hailey scoffed.

He didn't take his eyes off her and offered no emotion. "I doubt Lucinda pays you that much."

She could barely believe his nerve! Anything she'd found attractive about the man was immediately gone. Her eyes narrowed while glaring at him.

"Shut up and drink your brandy before you're wearing it," she growled lowly.

Rafe suddenly grinned, appearing pleased with her response. "And she has claws--"

Hailey glared at him. She'd never wanted to hit a man before, but she entertained a fantasy where her fist found his mouth. She wanted to wipe that smug smile from his face. It seemed a long time before Lucinda and Brody finally returned to the table. Both were laughing at something the other had said. Brody boldly took the seat alongside Hailey, forcing Lucinda to sit next to Rafe. Hailey could tell by her expression, Lucinda wasn't pleased. Brody placed his arm on the back of Hailey's chair and smiled at her.

"Are you and Rafe getting along?" he asked.

She glared at Rafe and offered a twisted smirk. "He's an absolute angel."

Brody suddenly chuckled. "I somehow doubt that." He straightened and looked at Lucinda across the table. "Why don't we have a look at the proposal before I steal your assistant away for a dance?"

Hailey handed him the folder from the briefcase between the wall and her chair. Brody halfheartedly browsed through the papers with one hand and kept the other on the back of her chair. His hand caressed the bare skin on her back. Hailey was immediately uncomfortable by his touch. Brody returned the folder to Hailey after barely skimming it.

"Pretty detailed," he remarked with little emotion. "Why don't you bring these to my suite later tonight around nine? We'll go over them there where it's quieter."

Hailey stared at him with surprise to the suggestion. Lucinda's expression almost matched Hailey's expression. Lucinda suddenly forced a smile and shifted in her seat.

"It's been a long day," Lucinda announced a little too quickly while casting feral glances from Brody to Hailey. Her eyes finally settled on Brody. "Why don't we get together for brunch tomorrow and discuss the proposal then?"

Lucinda collected her purse and stood without awaiting a response. Hailey collected the folder and briefcase, standing as well. Both men stood respectfully. Rafe's expression never changed, but Hailey could feel his eyes mocking her. Although disappointed, Brody managed a polite smile.

"Yes, brunch," he announced. "Say ten?"

"That will be fine," Lucinda chirped while grabbing Hailey's arm and hurried her from the table.

Hailey had never been so happy to leave a restaurant in her life. She had a difficult time keeping up with Lucinda's long strides. How the woman walked so fast in her high heels was a mystery to Hailey.

Her boss slowed once they entered the corridor just outside the dining room. Lucinda seemed flushed from the experience.

"I appreciate that timely save," Hailey announced and was finally able to relax.

"Men can be so difficult," Lucinda scoffed while defiantly shaking her head. They walked along the elegant corridor a moment in silence. Lucinda finally spoke while glancing at her assistant. "This investment is extremely important, you know that. If you could indulge Brody and get him to sign the contract, I'll promise you one hell of a promotion."

Hailey suddenly stopped short of the lobby and stared at Lucinda. Lucinda realized Hailey was no longer walking alongside her and turned to look back.

"Are you suggesting I sleep with him?" Hailey suddenly demanded in a tone louder than she had anticipated.

Lucinda fidgeted and moved closer to her while attempting a timid smile. "No, of course not," she announced and gently brushed a stray lock of hair from Hailey's face. "Just a little harmless flirting, that's all."

Despite what she *wasn't* suggesting, Hailey felt the color drain from her face. "I doubt that's what he has in mind."

Her boss straightened and held her head up proudly. "Hailey, this is a multimillion-dollar investment. You have to be ambitious," she announced firmly. "What you do and how you do it doesn't matter to me. I need Brody to agree to a partnership in this hotel. Without his name and funding, I could lose everything." Her look turned slightly venomous. "And if I lose everything, I certainly won't have any need for an assistant, will I?"

Lucinda snatched the briefcase from Hailey and continued into the lobby. Hailey followed more slowly. Her mind was cluttered with the possible threat of being fired if she didn't play by Brody's rules. Lucinda didn't seem to care that Hailey was no longer behind her. She entered the elevator, leaving Hailey practically alone in the empty lobby. She suddenly lost the will to approach the elevator. Apparently, her job opportunity of a lifetime wasn't as great as it had originally sounded.

Hailey heard a stern, scolding voice across the lobby. As she looked toward the front desk at the opposite end, a man whom she could only assume to be a security guard argued with Skyler behind the desk. The security guard, Delaney, was an arrogant looking man in his late twenties. He was built solid like his boss, Marcus, although not nearly as handsome a man. Delaney was giving Skyler a healthy verbal lashing, and Skyler seemed to be taking it like someone who'd been bullied all his life, tail firmly between his legs.

"You're a major screw-up," Delaney barked at Skyler, who was barely able to look up at the intimidating man. "If Talbert didn't feel sorry for you, you'd have been fired years ago."

"I'm sorry, Delaney," Skyler replied timidly. "I just thought maybe I could help find that missing--"

Delaney slammed his index finger on the front desk with frustration. "There is no missing girl," he lurched. "They always show up, and they always give the same excuse. Stop making something out of nothing! It upsets the guests!"

"I never said anything in front of--"

"Enough, Skyler," Delaney snapped hotly. "Just give the town crier act a rest. No one wants to hear it, especially me!" He pointed his warning finger at him. "I don't want any more trouble out of you, understand?"

Skyler frowned, lowered his head, and nodded gently. Delaney turned and stormed away from the desk in the direction of the staff wing. Skyler leaned on the desk while holding his head and rubbed his temples. Hailey felt bad for the desk clerk. He was possibly having a worse day than she was. She considered continuing on her way and leaving him to his misery, but her sympathetic side told her she should talk to him. After all, she wasn't the only one with problems in the world. Hailey approached the desk. Despite the clopping of her uncoordinated heels on the stone floor, Skyler didn't even notice her presence. As she paused before the desk, he still didn't look up, but instead rubbed his temples, digging deeper into his skin.

"Pretty quiet out here tonight," she finally spoke aloud.

Although not entirely startled, he jerked slightly and sprang to attention. He stared at her only a moment in silence this time before finally responding.

"Free cocktails in the lounge," Skyler replied casually then attempted a smile. "Did you have a nice dinner?"

"We barely got past drinks," she replied with a dreary sigh. "I've never been in such bad company before."

"I wish I could have warned you," he replied then seemed to relax to her presence.

He again returned to messaging his temples with added vigor. She watched him only a moment and feared he'd tear the skin from his head at the rate he was going.

"Headache?"

He managed a tiny smile. "My usual month long migraine. Drugs don't have any effect on me."

Hailey studied him a moment longer and considered her next move carefully. She couldn't allow the man to suffer more than he already had at the hands of his superiors, much like herself, but she also didn't want to give the wrong impression. He was, after all, a stranger to her.

"I can take care of that for you," she gently informed him then added a tense smile. "My track record is unbroken."

Skyler gave her a slightly dumbfounded stare then finally shrugged with a look of defeat. He obviously had his doubts to her ability. He walked out from behind the desk and reluctantly approached her. His cautiousness was baffling to her. Was he afraid to let her touch him? He was a mystery to her. Most men she understood, whether good or bad. Skyler posed a big question mark. As Hailey placed her hands to his face, Skyler immediately tensed. She rubbed his temples a few times then pulled back and met his gaze. Skyler appeared surprised while staring at her. He apprehensively touched his temples.

"I don't believe it," he finally gasped without taking his eyes from her. "How did you do that?"

She grinned in response. "It's a gift."

Chapter Seven

*I*t was a little after midnight. The secluded beach was partially lit from exterior hotel lights around the empty pool and the moon glistening off the ocean. It was another warm night with a slight breeze coming off the water. Hailey and Skyler sat on a large, round wicker lounge bed not far from the surf. Sounds from the lounge, now turned into a party hot spot, could faintly be heard. Hailey could only guess the sort of night Mel was already having. She just hoped her friend would be alert enough in the morning to cater to their boss lady. After the scene Hailey had made in the corridor, she was certain Lucinda was going to wake in an exceptionally foul mood, and Mel would be the first person with which she came into contact. Skyler hugged his knees to his chest with his cheek on his knees and studied Hailey in silence while she told him about her evening from hell. Once she finished, he straightened his legs on the leather padding over the lounge bed before him and stared at the moon above the ocean.

"Brody and Rafe have been to the resort six times in fourteen months," he announced casually. "In all those times, I've never even heard Rafe speak."

"Consider yourself lucky," she muttered.

Hailey attempted to make herself comfortable on the lounge bed but found herself tugging on either the cleavage of her dress or the slit up her thigh. If Skyler had been stealing peeks, she hadn't caught him. Her feelings toward Skyler were unlike any other she'd felt before. She wasn't uncomfortable around him, yet his odd personality dictated she should have been. She felt as if they were old childhood friends reunited. He again hugged his knees to his chest and gave her an innocent look.

"What do you intend to do about Brody?"

"Nothing. Lucinda can fire me," she remarked firmly.

Hailey considered her own remarks and frowned having heard them spoken aloud. She took a deep breath and glanced at Skyler. She marveled at the innocent way he stared at her, almost with a childlike fascination. He seemed to cling to every word she said, but she was convinced his attention had nothing to do with sexual desire. That in itself was almost creepy. She shifted slightly then offered a tiny smile.

"I've told you all about my boss pimping me out to her investors," Hailey announced. "Why don't you tell me what's bothering you?"

He avoided looking at her and became unusually uncomfortable. "My life is a utopia of disaster. When I'm honest with people, they tend to think I'm a freak."

She felt compelled to stare at him. Something was clearly wrong with him. She could almost feel it. For some reason, it was suddenly important that he open up to her.

"You'll just have to trust me."

He continued to stare out toward the ocean a moment longer, but it was obvious his mind was racing for a response. He shifted several times before finally looking at her. His look was oddly serious and almost concerning to her.

"I'm psychic and connected to the spiritual world," he boldly announced, spilling his entire odd existence as quickly as it would come out of his mouth. "I've seen people in my dreams before they came to the hotel. I know things about them." He hesitated and again shifted, once more slowing his words. "It tends to alarm people, so I've learned not to discuss it."

She stared at him in silence as if attempting to read his eyes. He looked away and refused to meet her gaze. She knew there was something more he wasn't telling her, but she wasn't sure what it was. It then hit her.

"You had a dream about me, didn't you?" she suddenly asked and straightened. "Tell me about it."

"I'd rather not," he replied a little too quickly and refused to look at her.

"That's hardly fair."

He was silent a long moment before taking a deep breath. He finally looked at her. "You were in danger. I tried to save you, but there were all these bats surrounding me. That's when the quake woke me."

"An earthquake on the island?"

"Yeah, things were scattered all over my room," he replied then frowned. "Cass denied there was a quake, but she enjoys playing with my head." He seemed reluctant to continue. "There's, uh, something else. I, uh, see ghosts. They appear as little spots of light randomly around the hotel." His look was serious. "They've all collected around you."

She stared back at him with surprise but attempted to conceal it. "I have ghosts hanging around me?"

He nodded. "Yeah, sixteen to be precise."

Hailey hesitantly looked around her. She wasn't actually expecting to see them, but she found the thought fascinating all the same.

"I've never seen them drawn to anyone before," he informed her then fell silent while staring. "You think I'm crazy."

"Of course not," she replied without hesitation. "I believe in ghosts."

Skyler appeared stunned by her admission whether or not she said it just to make him feel better. Relief swept over him and he seemed to relax for the first time.

"I knew there was something special about you the moment I saw you with your little ghost colony."

†

It was nearing one o'clock in the morning, and the dance party was still going strong in the lounge. There was no end in sight as the over twenty-one crowd drank and danced to the loud, pulsating club music. Despite the small dance floor, the partygoers crowded it, forcing them to dance even closer than they did in most fancy clubs in the big cities. Mel danced with her three new friends from the beach. All four wore club wear, which consisted of short, tight dresses barely able to contain jiggling breasts attempting to make their escape from low necklines. Penny was moderately drunk and brushed against several men throughout the endless club music. She was flirting with just about every man on the dance floor, bumping and grinding with them as if they stood a chance with her. A few of the men she pressed against seemed enthusiastic with their chances of taking the 'ripe for the pickin' woman back to his room. There were going to be some disappointed men.

Amy had her own admirer working his charm on her. She danced with a fairly handsome man in his mid to late twenties. Daniel had some fancy moves and easily won her attention. They seemed inseparable for the last hour. He'd pull her in close for a few seconds of seductive dancing and then pull away, as if teasing her with his sexual competence. Amy enjoyed the attention of the handsome man. With Amy and Penny almost certainly securing their overnight company, Mel and Desi danced with each other. Neither seemed to need the attention of the flirtatious men. They were having fun on their own.

As if on cue, that all changed in an instant. Vance mysteriously appeared alongside them and joined both women in their dance. His smile captivated both, indicated by their stares and helpless grins. As he danced close and seductive with them, they were suddenly competing for his attention with dueling dance moves. There seemed to be enough of Vance to go around for both women, although they probably wouldn't cherish the suggestion.

Chapter Eight

$\mathcal{I}$t was nearly two o'clock in the morning. Hailey and Skyler walked through the ankle deep surf in their bare feet at a leisurely pace. The gentle waves washed across their feet and gently tugged on their ankles as it pulled back out again. Hailey had to admit, the night was peaceful and serene. She could easily get used to beach life. To her surprise, she'd been in Skyler's company nearly six hours, and she wasn't even tired of him. He shared his life stories with her, and she shared hers with him. It was possibly the most she'd ever shared with anyone about her life.

"My uncle died when I was six," Hailey gently remarked. "I never knew my parents. I barely even knew my uncle."

"Sometimes I wish I never knew my parents," he informed her. "They thought I was a freak like everyone else. I didn't exactly have a great childhood." Skyler hesitated and appeared reluctant to continue. He drew a deep breath and avoided looking at her. "When I was seventeen, I took a bottle of anti-anxiety pills and washed them down with a fifth of vodka."

She suddenly stopped him in the surf and looked at him with surprise. "Skyler!"

He managed a soft laugh even though it wasn't the least bit funny. Apparently, it was to him.

"It put me into a coma. They said I was clinically dead," he announced then stared at nothing. "It was then that I had a vision of a beautiful angel in a brilliant white light. She said I had a purpose, and that my destiny had been predetermined. She told me that I was chosen; that I would receive a gift and to use it wisely." He smiled proudly while off in some fantasy world then cast a glance at Hailey. "And when I came out of the coma--" His smile vanished. "Nothing changed."

Hailey stared at him with surprise. She was sort of expecting to hear some epiphany he'd had while clinically dead. Skyler's life had been one bad beat after another, and she felt sorry for what he'd gone through. He apparently noticed her sympathetic look and attempted to cover.

"It wasn't all for nothing," he quickly added. "Despite nothing having changed, I was left with the feeling that I'm here for a reason. I believe there was an angel, and she spoke the truth. I know one day, it'll all have been worth it."

Hailey couldn't help but feel bad for Skyler. Although he was optimistic, his life leaned toward tragedy. He was that poor, awkward shelter puppy left unwanted and unloved alone in his cage. She desperately wanted to take him in and give him a good home, one he deserved, but she was barely scraping by herself. If Lucinda fired her, she'd be worse off than Skyler. Both thoughts would be enough to keep her from sleeping tonight, which wasn't a terrible loss, since she couldn't stop the endless parade of nightmares that recently seemed to plague her.

†

It was a little after three o'clock in the morning, and the lounge party had mostly dissipated once the bar closed. Penny finally selected a worthy young man as her overnight entertainment while Desi and Mel battled over Vance's attention into the early hours. Unfortunately, he seemed to disappear before they could declare a winner, leaving both disappointed. Amy and Daniel drunkenly walked barefoot along the surf in the romantic moonlight, having the entire beach to themselves. The night seemed perfect for the pair as they talked and laughed, enjoying one another's company. Daniel pulled her against him and stole a firm, quick kiss. Amy returned the kiss then playfully pulled away. She seemed almost innocent now that they were alone together.

"It's late," Amy finally said with a look of regret in her eyes. "I should be getting back to my room."

"You could always come back to my room," he announced while pulling her into his arms and again kissed her.

She pulled away and attempted to keep their interaction casual. "I told you, I'm not ready for that," Amy announced. "We've just met."

He grinned slyly and again pulled her into his arms with increased determination. "So you'll get to know me." Daniel kissed her more aggressively.

Something about his aggressive kiss caused alarm in the young woman, and she harshly pushed him away.

"Stop it!"

The look he gave her was more than disappointment; it was hostility. "I knew I should have gone after your friend," he snapped. "You wasted my entire evening."

Amy stared at him with a look of disbelief as he stormed back to the hotel.

"Prick," she scoffed.

The only comfort to the situation was that the dance party was winding down and there would be little hope of the bastard finding worthy company anymore tonight. She stood near the surf for several minutes with the annoyance clearly on her face. Amy wasn't a prude; but she also wasn't a one-night-stand. Another afternoon together or even brunch would have been enough to seal the deal, but there were too many young men who required instant gratification. Anything more than a few hours spent on any woman was considered a waste of their time. Amy finally staggered along the sand toward the hotel. Her fun evening ended in disappointment. That and the late hour showed on her weary face. As she looked toward the hotel, she saw someone standing within the shadows of the cabana bar near the pool area. Amy paused and squinted. She couldn't make out who it was, but it looked like a man.

"Who's there?" she asked with concern in her voice.

Being drunk and alone on a dimly lit beach wasn't exactly smart, though being alone hadn't been part of the plan. The dark figure hiding in the shadows of the cabana took a few steps toward her. His approach didn't put her at ease. Amy held back her gasp and took several steps back toward the gently crashing waves. There was a snarl near the large rock only a few feet away from her. Amy quickly turned toward the rock and the frightening sound coming from it. Her eyes widened and her shrill scream followed.

†

Skyler slept restlessly beneath the covers in his simple bedroom in the staff wing of the hotel. He suddenly gasped and flew up in bed while clutching his head. He still wore his work dress shirt and pants, despite having gone to bed. His white shirt was nearly wrinkled beyond repair. Skyler breathed heavily while staring blankly across the dimly lit room. His dream had clearly shaken him. He allowed his fingers to run through his mussed hair then groaned softly as he collapsed to the bed. He stared at the ceiling and attempted to control his heavy breathing.

"You're not a freak," he whispered softly to the ceiling. "You have a purpose. Your destiny has been predetermined." His eyes rolled shut as his arm draped across his eyes. "Who are you kidding? You're a fucking freak, Skyler."

Chapter Nine

*T*he following morning brought another perfect day to the beaches of Smuggler's Bay. The sun was shining and beckoned sun worshipers to take to the sand for another glorious day in paradise. Guests obliged and flooded the beach, securing lounge beds and lounge chairs in the best locations. Hailey and Mel had been fortunate enough to secure one of the round lounge beds for their brief visit in the sun. Both were dressed for another fun filled morning of work and hostility from the barracuda. They sipped their orange juice and attempted to make the best of what little free time they had before their morning began, which was basically whenever Lucinda decided to get out of bed. Despite looking a little disheveled, Mel wasn't in too sad of shape after spending most of the night in party mode. Hailey knew her friend was feeling worse than she looked, since she hadn't recapped her entire evening at the lounge turned dance club.

Mel cast a look above her sunglasses at Hailey. "Remember, you promised we'd lay out after your brunch with boss lady and the stud she wishes to breed you with."

Hailey glared at her friend. "I'm regretting telling you about that," she remarked then looked back to the insanely gorgeous view from their lounge bed. It was the same lounge bed she and Skyler had spent half the night upon while talking. "I haven't forgotten about our afternoon together." Hailey cast a look at Mel. "I'm surprised you have the energy to tackle a day of sun, sand, and surf. I'm sure you were dancing the night away."

"With a god among men," she announced with a dramatic sigh and sank back on the lounge bed. When her best Scarlet impersonation garnered no applause, she glanced at Hailey and offered a teasing look. "I guess you won't be pursuing that handsome warrior you were so sweet on in the lobby."

Hailey's cheeks immediately reddened, although she wasn't sure why. "Rafe?" she announced his name so gruffly it almost sounded like the bark of a dog. "That fantasy died the moment he opened his mouth."

"I can't tell you how many times I've been there," Mel teased. "Usually dumb as rocks and twice as thick."

"More like arrogant and rude," Hailey replied.

Mel stared past Hailey, lowered her sunglasses, and suddenly gasped as she shot up straight on the lounge bed. "That's him!" Her hands started flying around uncontrollably, alternating between fixing her hair and adjusting her shirt to reveal maximum cleavage. "Act casual."

Before Hailey even knew what had her friend behaving so dramatically, Mel was already posing seductively on the lounging bed. When she glanced in the direction Mel had been staring, Hailey saw Vance approaching. He was dressed casually smart with his pants legs rolled up to his knees, barefooted, and his expensive jacket slung over his shoulder by one finger. Hailey marveled at the way his every action and move resembled that of a man in a cologne commercial. He sat on the edge of their oversized lounge bed by Mel's legs and faced her. His best playboy grin was generously plastered on his face, revealing excessively white teeth. Despite the slight breeze, he didn't have a hair out of place, although the gentle wind caused it to flow as if on command. Mel immediately smiled while straightening and pretended she hadn't seen his approach.

"Well, good morning, Vance," Mel announced cheerfully in an attempt to act casual.

Vance took her hand and affectionately caressed it. If he kissed her hand, Hailey was certain she was going to vomit.

"Good morning, Melana," he replied in a suave tone. "I'm surprised you're up so early after we closed the lounge at three in the morning."

"It'll take more than a night of dancing to wear me out," she replied in a flirty tone. "What happened to you? You left before I had a chance to say goodnight."

45

"When you and your friend started arguing, I feared it may have had something to do with me, so I bowed out," he replied. "Did you two make up?"

"Oh, we're fine," Mel replied and attempted to hide that she was blushing. She casually indicated Hailey. "This is my friend, Hailey."

Vance glanced at Hailey with little acknowledgment then looked back at Mel. "Yes, we'd met yesterday in the lounge."

Hailey stared with disbelief at the handsome man, who again barely acknowledged her existence. She shifted and attempted to control her irritation.

"Yes, I remember," she hissed slightly while cleverly arching her brows. "You were quite cozy with our boss, Lucinda."

Her comment must have taken him by surprise, or at the very least, he hadn't realized Lucinda was Mel's boss as well. Vance shifted uncomfortably, cast a quick, disapproving glare at Hailey, and then looked back at Mel. His charming smile immediately returned as if on cue, but it was obvious he was on a quest to put some distance between himself and Hailey.

"Would you care to join me later for lunch, Melana?"

"I'd love to," she chirped a little too eagerly and apparently realized it. She fidgeted and attempted to regain her composure. "I mean, since I have the afternoon off anyway."

"Fantastic," he announced cheerfully and stood. "I'll meet you in the dining room at noon."

"I'm looking forward to it," Mel replied with the returning style and grace she had earlier attempted.

Vance gave her his best charming smile then glanced at Hailey and managed a tiny, impolite nod. He left them almost as quickly as he'd appeared. Mel stared after him while lowering her sunglasses. She almost whimpered while watching him then shot an annoyed look at Hailey.

"You were rude," Mel boldly announced. "What's gotten into you?"

"Please!" Hailey announced loudly while rolling her eyes for effect. "He's a playboy and a gold digger, Mel. You have to know that."

"I know he's a smooth talking Don Juan, but I'm entitled to one fling," Mel remarked sternly.

Hailey waved off her friend. "If you want to share the same man as your boss, you go right ahead. Personally, I couldn't imagine allowing a man to touch me after he'd had his hands on Lucinda's assets."

Mel was set back by the bold comment and clearly offended. "That was a low blow," she snorted then stood with disgust.

Mel then frowned after debating the reality of what her friend had said. Hailey's comment had obviously hit a little too close for comfort, and she lost enthusiasm to fight the argument.

"I'd better remind boss lady of the time."

Hailey waved dramatically at her friend. "Go! Dress your boss lady!"

Mel finally relaxed then laughed at the comment and hurried across the beach toward the hotel. Hailey reluctantly stood from the comfortable lounge bed and walked along the surf while carrying her dress shoes. She wished she had time to enjoy the morning, but she knew she had to deal with Lucinda and Brody. She couldn't pretend her conversation with Lucinda didn't bother her still. She looked across the beach and saw Amy standing on the path just within the woods. Amy, still dressed in her slinky dress, stared strangely at Hailey then turned and disappeared into the woods. Hailey was suddenly curious and slightly concerned by the woman's behavior and her choice of morning beach attire. Hailey approached the path and uncertainly looked around. The thick woods appeared peaceful without a trace of the young woman. As she scanned the woods, Hailey saw Amy just ahead on the path, although she would have sworn she wasn't there a minute ago. Closer inspection revealed bloodstains on Amy's slightly tattered dress. Amy turned and walked along the path away from her and deeper into the woods. Hailey saw scrapes and bleeding scratches along her exposed arms and legs, which alarmed her.

"Amy?"

She didn't respond or even look back but continued walking along the path in bare feet. Hailey hurried along the path after her, scanning her injuries and torn dress from a distance. She didn't like what she saw and concern rushed over her. Amy entered a clearing up ahead and momentarily vanished from Hailey's sight. Hailey reached the clearing. Amy was gone! Hailey looked around but didn't see any sign of the injured woman. There were several paths beyond the woods, but she didn't know how Amy could have reached any of them so quickly and unnoticed. She'd only been behind her by a few yards. Hailey heard a low snarl and rustling at the woods' edge not far from her. Hailey nervously looked around and backed up, hoping she was moving away from the sound and not mistakenly toward it. She heard the snap of a branch directly behind her. Hailey cried out, turned around with horror, and collided with Rafe. She bounced off his firm body and nearly lost her balance. She caught herself but couldn't stop from breathing heavily. Hailey nervously placed her hand to her forehead and quickly scanned the area for traces of the growling sound.

"What are you doing out here?" he almost demanded, as if it were any of his concern what she did.

"Freaking out," Hailey gasped, wishing she could stop from panting. She suddenly glared at him with surprise. "Were you following me?"

"Yes," he announced while casually placing his hands in his pockets without a care. "Brody sent me to find you for pre-brunch coffee."

Hailey stared at him a moment as if he were speaking some foreign language. Why hadn't she seen him following her? He couldn't have been more than a few seconds behind her. Rafe was the least of her concerns at the moment. She wanted to know what the hell was going on and what happened to Amy. She then considered the strange snarling sound she'd heard just seconds before she literally ran into Rafe. She looked back toward the clearing just behind her and scanned the area with increasing concern. Rafe looked past her toward the clearing as well.

"You see something?" he asked as if attempting to locate what she'd seen.

Hailey looked back at him and saw the way he stared past her. She was convinced he'd hoped she had seen something so he'd have an opportunity to inflict bodily harm on someone or something. She finally collected her emotions and straightened proudly.

"I'm pretty sure you scared it away," she remarked and maintained enough decency not to add more to the comment.

He seemed to indicate with a look that he knew she wanted to follow-up the comment with an insult. Without thinking about her actions, Hailey placed her hand on Rafe's shoulder and balanced herself while she slipped into her high heels. He gave her a strange look as she teetered while clinging to his shoulder, her heels sinking into the sandy ground, but didn't comment. Once she realized she'd actually touched him, she pulled away and gave him a scathing look. Despite her inability to balance in her heels on the soft terrain, she proudly walked past him. It didn't even matter that she nearly fell twice; she kept going.

†

$\mathcal{T}$he terrace beyond the dining room was serving a free buffet brunch for its late rising guests. Several men and women were already enjoying their morning meal beneath fancy, thatched umbrellas. Despite the casual atmosphere, expensive china plates and crystal glasses were used for an elegant touch. Fresh, tropical flowers added sophistication to the terrace atmosphere. Hailey had joined Nevin Brody at one of the small tables nearly thirty minutes earlier. She sipped tea from her china cup while casting glances across the terrace for signs of Lucinda. Considering how important she insisted their meeting was, she thought her boss would at least have the decency to show up on time. Rafe was seated at a separate table not far from them. He maintained his moderately intimidating look and scoffed secretly at the tiny, china cup containing his manly morning coffee. The waiter refilled his delicate cup each time he passed. Hailey now found herself looking from her watch to the dining room doors every few seconds. She didn't like that her boss abandoned her with Brody. It was possibly payback for last evening.

"I don't know what's keeping Lucinda," Hailey apologetically said to Brody. "It's not like her to be so late."

Brody casually waved off the comment while maintaining his grin. "She was in the middle of some crisis and sent her regrets," he announced without care. "I thought you knew that. She gave your briefcase to Rafe. It's in my suite whenever you're ready to go over the proposal."

Hailey's mouth fell open as she stared at Brody across the table from her. She was screaming inside, secretly cursing Lucinda. How could Lucinda do that to her? It took every ounce of strength Hailey had to keep from exploding. She shifted in her chair and attempted a polite response.

"We were supposed to discuss business over brunch," she informed him.

"I know, but I thought my suite would be more private," he replied while grinning slyly as he boldly placed his hand on Hailey's thigh.

Hailey smacked his hand, which possibly stung her own hand as much as it did his. The crack was heard by those at nearby tables. Hailey abruptly stood, nearly knocking the chair to the stone floor. If smacking his hand didn't get the attention of other guests, her shooting up from the table certainly did.

"I'm not part of the deal," she lashed out while feeling her cheeks become hot and red. Everyone was now staring at them. "We'll talk when you're ready to act professional."

Hailey turned away from the table and nearly collided with Rafe, who was now standing directly in her path. Hailey met his gaze with hostility. She wasn't in the mood and didn't mind making a scene with the handsome, hired goon. To her surprise, Rafe's lips curled in a strange, twisted sort of smile. He politely stepped out of her way. She swore his look almost praised her hostile outburst. Hailey tried not to smile, but she was secretly grateful for the tiny glimmer of encouragement he showed her. Maybe there was a human heart beating inside him after all. She stormed across the terrace without looking back.

Chapter Ten

*H*ailey spent a better part of the afternoon on the beach with Mel and two of her three new friends, Desi and Penny. Hailey was hoping to avoid her boss after her meeting with Brody. She knew the incident with Nevin Brody was a deal killer and possibly a career killer for her as well. It only seemed natural to enjoy what might be her last day at the tropical island resort. All four lie on their lounge chairs soaking up sun while sipping on strong, fruity drinks. Hailey, like Desi and Mel, wore a conservative bikini. Penny wore yet another 'barely there' bikini. Her ample breasts were attempting to break free from the tiny material barely containing them. Despite the perfect afternoon, Hailey just couldn't relax. Her mind continually strayed to her earlier altercation with Brody and the thought of losing her job because of it. She knew she was in the right, but it didn't ease the sting of potentially being unemployed.

Her mind occasionally strayed from her self-pity, allowing her eyes to shift to the path in the woods. She couldn't shake the image of Amy on the path. Her condition was alarming, yet it seemed inconceivable she'd disappeared so easily. Hailey wasn't above citing her overactive imagination for what she'd seen that morning. If Amy had truly been injured or in danger, she would have walked toward Hailey, not away from potential help.

"Where is Amy anyway?" Penny finally demanded while looking around.

Hailey felt uncomfortable by the question, but she wasn't about to admit to what she may or may not have seen, especially if it had been all her imagination.

Desi grinned and raised her brows with suggestion. "She was getting pretty hot and heavy with that cute guy from the club last night. I'm thinking they're sleeping in after a full night of extracurricular activity."

"Please!" Penny loudly protested. "Amy doesn't do that sort of thing."

"I don't know," Mel swiftly interjected. "She did just dump her boyfriend. Revenge sex is a powerful motivator."

"She had a lot to drink too," Desi informed her friend. "After that many drinks, morals take a backseat to a guy with a great ass. And that guy had a great ass."

Penny considered both comments, conveyed her defeat, and groaned softly. "Yeah, you're probably right."

"Maybe someone should check on her," Hailey suggested and shifted uncomfortably on her lounge chair.

If she knew Amy was in her room sleeping, she might be able to enjoy her afternoon a little more. Personally, Hailey didn't know Amy well enough to be knocking on her guestroom door. What if she was sleeping off a night of great sex? Hailey would feel quite foolish.

"And interrupt something kinky?" Desi remarked while casting a look at Hailey from over her sunglasses. It was almost as if she read Hailey's mind. "No, thanks!"

"She's your friend," Hailey remarked while shifting. "Someone should make sure she's okay."

"If she's still not around before dinner, I'll check on her," Penny announced. "She could be nursing the world's worst hangover. I know I've been there before."

Desi laughed softly. "Yeah, you've been there a lot since you started college."

Hailey felt a little better that Penny would check on her friend. It was getting close to dinnertime anyway. If Hailey didn't get something to eat soon, the alcohol would start hitting her harder than she'd like. She had no intention of getting drunk anywhere near

Lucinda. She didn't trust the barracuda not to sacrifice her drunken body to Nevin Brody.

✝

𝒯he lobby seemed fairly empty a little before dinnertime, as it usually was at that hour. Hailey stepped out of the elevator a little after five that evening now freshly showered and changed for a casual dinner. She knew she couldn't avoid Lucinda forever and would probably run into her around dinnertime. There were only so many places to eat at the resort. Guests could get bar food in the lounge and at the poolside cabana or have dinner in the dining room. Room service was an option, but Hailey didn't need to add additional expenses to her room, in case Lucinda decided to play hardball with her and make her pay for her tab. As she walked across the lobby, she was immediately greeted by Skyler, who was just getting off work. The look on his face and his spastic movements conveyed deep concern.

"Where have you been all afternoon?" Skyler suddenly asked while fidgeting more than usual.

He appeared unable to stand still, telling her something had gotten him worked up beyond his usual issues.

"I was on the beach with Mel and her friends cooling off in the hot, tropical sun," she informed him.

Skyler appeared baffled by her comment, causing him briefly to stand still. The moment was short lived. His baffled look almost humored her, causing her to hold back her own laugh.

"I'll tell you all about it later." She studied his expression and wondered what had him riled into a state of constant movement. "Is something wrong?"

"I saw a woman killed in my dream," he informed her in rushed speech, barely able to contain the news. "I know I'd seen her at the hotel."

Hailey stared at him as her mind reeled from his announcement. She didn't know why, but she was getting a strange image in her head, and it troubled her.

"A short, blonde girl around my age?"

"How did you know?" he suddenly asked as his eyes widened with alarm.

Something seemed strange about his premonition, which oddly coincided with what she'd seen earlier. She didn't like the thoughts going through her mind.

53

"I followed her into the woods this morning," Hailey announced as her heart rate increased at the thought that Skyler had a vision involving Amy. "She'd been injured. I tried to talk to her, but she kept walking and then disappeared."

"The woods?" Skyler suddenly gasped louder than anticipated and nearly jumped out of his skin. "That's where I saw the woman killed in my dream."

She shouldn't have believed him. Everything indicated their reasoning was insane, but she couldn't help feeling something was terribly wrong. What if Skyler had foreseen Amy's death after she'd wondered off into the woods? Hailey suddenly felt terrible for not pursuing the injured woman. If something unfortunate happened to Amy and she could have prevented it, she'd never be able to live with that guilt.

"We have to find her, Skyler," Hailey suddenly announced, feeling overwhelming concern. "I should have gone after her. I should have made sure she was okay."

"Show me where you last saw her."

Hailey hurried across the lobby toward the main entrance with Skyler on her heels.

†

Hailey and Skyler entered the clearing in the woods and looked around the knee-deep grass covering several acres, which was surrounded by more woods. It seemed almost impossible they'd find her beyond the thick grass and with so many adjoining trails. Hailey couldn't help wonder how she disappeared so quickly. Where did she go so fast? The better question almost seemed to be, why would the injured woman return to the woods rather than seek help? She'd seen Hailey, and she was sure she'd heard her calling to her. Why not let her help? Skyler touched a thick blade of the tall grass and stared at what was possibly dried blood. He appeared alarmed while looking around and released the blade of grass.

"That's blood," Skyler gasped with concern. He then indicated more blood on some grass a few feet away. "There's more this way."

Hailey scanned the area and saw some blood in the opposite direction. "It goes this way too," she announced.

Skyler gently parted the tall grass with a stick and followed the blood trail. Hailey walked in the opposite direction, following her own trail.

"She can't be dead, Skyler," Hailey insisted as they drifted further apart. "She was alive when I saw her, which was after your dream."

"My visions aren't an exact science," he announced without looking back at her. "In my dreams, dead could just mean injured or missing."

Hailey straightened and looked toward the nearby woods. Something darted into the shadows and growled at her. Hailey gasped while taking a quick step sideways, stumbled over a rock, and fell to the ground, landing in the thick grass. From where she lie, she stared at the decomposing body of a young woman only inches from her. The woman's eyes were open and there was a large amount of dried blood from several scratches along her shoulder to her chest, slicing her tattered dress. Her right arm was missing, having been seemingly ripped from her body. Hailey cried out and scrambled to her feet, unable to take her eyes off the butchered woman. To her surprise, it wasn't Amy, but she somehow looked familiar.

Skyler ran toward her, saw the body, and immediately clung to Hailey from his own fright. Hailey stared helplessly at the dead woman, and was suddenly aware that she was missing the lower half of her body as well as her arm. It looked as if something had been feeding on her decaying corpse. Skyler also stared at the body and alternated clutching Hailey's arm and pulling on her shoulder. She was almost certain he wanted to jump into her arms, so she'd carry him. There was more growling from the nearby woods, causing them to freeze in place and stare at the woods' edge.

"Did you, uh, hear something?" Skyler asked without taking his eyes off the woods.

It was possibly the first time he remained motionless for more than a second. Something large and black jumped from the dark shadows for them. Before either could get a good look at it or even react to the animal leaping for them, it was tackled into the tall grass by a black panther. Skyler grabbed Hailey's arm and pulled her to his side, possibly due to his own fright more than attempting to protect her. They could hear loud, vicious snarls as the panther and creature fought in a massive, black ball mostly hidden within the tall grass. Hailey had no idea what she'd just witnessed, but she was certain the creature wasn't any animal she'd ever seen before.

Both watched the grass sway beneath their fighting bodies. Hailey was almost unable to move, wanting to know what sort of creature had come close to attacking them and the fear of it chasing them if they ran. Skyler had ideas of his own. He grabbed Hailey's hand and nearly pulled her off her feet while hurrying her back for the path. She had little choice but run behind him with his hand nearly crushing hers. She found it difficult to keep up with his long, fast strides, but he wasn't about to release her hand. She could hear the vicious sounds from the fighting animals in the clearing growing faint the further they ran.

Chapter Eleven

The lounge was practically empty and void of life during the popular dinner hours as most guests were in the dining room. Logan played a soft ballet on the piano while keeping his attention focused on the small group, who had collected at the bar. Tam leaned on the bar, listening intently, with her mouth partially opened. She watched Hailey and Skyler, who sat across from her. They attempted to hold their drinks in trembling hands while they recounted what happened to them in the woods. Lucinda sat on the other side of Hailey and stared as well.

"What sort of wild animal was it?" Tam asked.

"It wasn't any wild animal I'd ever seen," Hailey insisted while glancing at the bartender. "It was hideous; some sort of beast." She shook her head defiantly, not believing her own words. "I didn't get a real good look at it, but it sounded nasty."

"All I saw was a black blur, but I heard it," Skyler quickly interjected, talking almost too fast to be understood. "Whatever it was, it was larger than that panther that attacked it."

"And you think either this creature or the panther killed the girl?" Tam asked.

"I don't know," Hailey replied while taking another swallow of the special cocktail Tam created for her. Despite its potency, she took large swallows. "She had slash marks across her chest. Something had been eating her body."

Tam and Lucinda stared with horror in their eyes then simultaneously made faces. Marcus, Delaney, and Talbert entered the lounge and approached them at the bar. Rafe followed in less of a hurry. Skyler saw them, appeared panic riddled, and jumped up from his bar stool. His eyes were so wide, they were about to bulge out of their sockets.

"Did you see it? What was it?" Skyler demanded.

"We didn't find anything," Marcus informed him in a low, firm tone while staring him down. "No creature, no panther, and no dead, half eaten girl."

Delaney and Talbert wore looks of annoyance on their faces and withheld comment. Hailey could tell they doubted her story of the creature killing that woman. Hailey jumped up from her seat to defend what she saw. Lucinda gently pulled her back down to her seat by her shoulder. Skyler was clearly wound enough for both of them.

"Did you look by the ravine?" Skyler demanded while throwing his hands around in frantic gesture.

"We searched the entire area including several paths and the ravine," Marcus informed him while folding his arms across his broad chest. His look was cold and disbelieving. "We didn't find anything."

"We didn't imagine this, Marcus," Hailey firmly insisted, despite Lucinda attempting to keep her from reacting.

Hailey hesitated briefly and considered her comment. She was almost positive they hadn't imagined it, but she knew how ridiculous they sounded. The strong drink was going to her head, and she was having a difficult time collecting her thoughts. Marcus turned his attention on Hailey and showed more compassion than he had for Skyler. She was grateful that he wasn't playing the tough guy act on her after what she'd been through that afternoon. Just another reason to like the hardened man.

"I'm sure you saw something, we're just not sure what," Marcus replied with a sympathetic look.

Lucinda glared her disapproval at the imposing head of security. It was the first she offered an opinion of the incident, and Hailey feared what that opinion might be.

"If there's something out there killing and *eating* my guests, you'd better damn well figure out what it is," Lucinda growled in a tone that surprised Hailey.

Marcus fidgeted slightly to her comment then held up his head proudly, not wanting to disappoint her. Despite Lucinda being his boss, Hailey was surprised he submitted to her. She expected a little more fight out of the tough man.

"It's too dark to see anything more tonight," he announced reassuringly, attempting to please the barracuda. "We'll go back out when it's light and have another look around. If there's something out there, we'll find it."

Lucinda remained displeased, but she accepted his assurances. Hailey was grateful Lucinda was at least willing to believe her story even if she had to berate Marcus to prove it. Marcus attempted to regain his tough guy act then turned and indicated for Delaney to follow him. Hailey watched them leave and could almost hear them mocking her on their way out of the lounge. Hailey couldn't believe they didn't find the woman's body. They couldn't have looked very hard. They had to have missed her somehow. The dead woman didn't get up and walk away, considering her legs had been eaten along with the rest of her lower body. Could the creature have dragged her body away to finish its meal?

She suddenly recalled her nightmare on the helicopter ride the day they arrived. Something pulled a woman back into the woods by her ankles. Hailey could almost hear the woman in her dream screaming. Images of the dead woman's face were burned into Hailey's mind. Could it have been the woman from her dream? Was that even possible? Was her nightmare actually a premonition? She was starting to think she'd been hanging around Skyler too long. As if reading her mind, Talbert glared at Skyler and shook his head with irritation.

"No more scenic tours, okay?" Talbert announced in a civil tone, although it was obvious he wanted to berate the man, but he was too professional to do it in front of guests.

Skyler reluctantly nodded while frowning. There wasn't much he could say in his defense. They already thought he was crazy. Talbert didn't even bother looking at Hailey. He'd already formed his opinion of her as well. He left the lounge almost as quickly as he'd entered. Lucinda gently patted Hailey on the shoulder then quickly stood and hurried after Talbert. Hailey saw Lucinda's stone pendant necklace on the floor by her stool. She picked it up and hurried after Lucinda.

"Lucinda," Hailey called after her.

Lucinda and Talbert turned and saw Hailey holding the necklace. Lucinda subconsciously touched her bare chest, groaned, and snatched the necklace from Hailey.

"Damn that Melana," she scoffed.

"Why don't you lock it in your room safe," Talbert announced. "No point in losing your jewelry over a broken clasp."

Lucinda handed the necklace to Talbert. "You still have a key to my suite, don't you?"

Talbert forced a smile and nodded while accepting the necklace. "I'll take care of that for you."

Hailey passed Rafe and returned to the bar in time to see Tam straighten and shake her head while sneering at Skyler. He wasn't winning any points with anyone today.

"Just another one of your delusional fantasies," Tam scoffed. "I should have known."

Tam walked away from them and began wiping the top of the bar. Hailey collapsed onto her bar stool and exchanged looks with Skyler. Both appeared defeated. Rafe approached them without a word and placed a gold earring on the bar in front of Hailey. She eyed the earring then looked at Rafe with surprise.

"Where did you get this?" she suddenly demanded.

His expression never changed while staring at her. "Where you claimed you saw the girl's body."

Hailey felt her entire body twitch with her rising blood pressure as she stared at him with astonishment. "Why didn't you tell Marcus you'd found this there?"

"The former police sergeant turned hotel rent-a-cop would never listen to me," he replied. "I only went along to cover my ass and make sure I wasn't accused of anything."

They stared into each other's eyes only briefly. She actually understood his reasoning. He was probably used to being accused of things. Rafe walked away without further comment. Hailey and Skyler studied the earring she now held in her hand. The piano music abruptly stopped, although neither had noticed. Logan appeared alongside them at the bar, startling both. The look on his face was serious.

"Tell me about the panther," Logan suddenly demanded.

They stared at him with the same look of surprise on each of their faces. His question was odd, to say the least. Out of everything they told the others, why was he so curious about the panther?

"There's not much to tell. A black panther fought with the creature," Hailey informed him and thought back to what she had actually seen and heard. The more she thought about it, the less she'd actually seen, but she had definitely heard it, and so did Skyler. "By the sounds we'd heard, I'd say that panther may have met his match." She maintained her odd stare at Logan. "Why are you so interested? Have you seen a panther on the island before? You should tell Marcus, if you had."

"No, I've never seen a panther, and I've been all over this island. With all the tourists, someone would have reported seeing one by now," Logan insisted. "That's what makes it so strange. I know how this is going to sound, but this is starting to mimic my fable." He leaned on the bar near them and stared both in the eyes. Despite his farfetched comment, his look was serious. "The Protector takes on the form of various animals to protect the princess and can't be destroyed as long as she lives."

Hailey and Skyler stared at Logan. Hailey was amazed. Finally, someone sounded crazier than she sounded. Hailey's mouth fell open from his comment. She wanted to laugh, but his look was so serious, she found it difficult.

"You can't seriously think some mystical creature was protecting me," she announced.

"I know how it sounds," Logan protested firmly, "but I know what I wrote." He hesitated while staring at both. "And I know what I'd left out."

"What do you mean?" Hailey suddenly asked.

"My original manuscript was over four hundred pages and not meant for children," Logan informed them. "My publisher edited it down to a twenty page fable. In the original manuscript, there were large, black beasts with claws and fangs. The beasts were sort of like guard dogs for their evil master. The princess also had her Numinous to guide her."

"Numinous?" Skyler asked while tilting his head. "What's this Numinous?"

Logan's brows suddenly arched as he studied him. "Her *psychic* advisor."

Skyler appeared stunned. His mouth fell open in response, and he abruptly straightened. "What is this fable?"

Hailey held her head and groaned softly. She couldn't believe her day could get any worse, but she was wrong.

"Great," she scoffed, "now you've sucked him into your delusion."

Skyler quickly turned toward Hailey with a serious look and defiantly shook his head. "Something about this seems very familiar to me, Hailey."

"This entire conversation is insane," she retorted.

"I know it's insane, but I'm willing to take the evening off and discuss it," Logan replied firmly. "I'll dig out the original manuscript so we can look at it. If nothing else, we can have a good laugh in the morning."

Logan and Skyler stared at Hailey and waited for her response. She was feeling ganged upon but managed a dreary sigh and gave in to their insistence.

"Okay, but there had better be alcohol being served," Hailey informed them then held her head. "It's not as if I'm sleeping after this anyway, so I may as well get silly with you guys."

Chapter Twelve

Logan's tidy studio style guestroom was covered in plants from ceiling to floor, lending an almost jungle like atmosphere. His odd fascination with plant life was curious for a man who looked more like a linebacker than a gardener. Hailey sat on the older, flower-patterned sofa with a drink in her hand. She'd had one too many drinks already in the two hours they'd been looking over Logan's old manuscript. It was only a little after eight o'clock, but it felt later. Hailey was having a difficult time hiding her drunken condition in front of the men. Although she didn't know them very well, she felt she could trust them not to try anything. Skyler slouched in an overstuffed chair while reading the old, tattered manuscript. Logan sprayed his plants with great care. Hailey couldn't be certain, but she thought she heard him softly singing to the plants. Skyler suddenly straightened in his chair and vigorously tapped the page.

"That's the creature I saw in my dreams!"

Logan glanced at him and showed almost no reaction. "Freaky, isn't it?"

Skyler's expression immediately dropped. "I despise that term," he muttered then studied Logan and appeared curious. "Are you psychic too?"

"No, I'm not psychic," Logan replied. "That story just came to me." He grinned almost proudly. "I'm considered a 'one hit wonder'."

Skyler gave Hailey a serious look. "Fate brought you here."

Although she believed his tales when they'd first met, she was regretting encouraging him. He was starting to sound like a raving lunatic.

"Listen to yourself," Hailey announced firmly. "I'm *not* some magical princess. If you want to be some mystical Numinous--go right ahead."

Despite her negativity, he wasn't about to be shot down. "It says here that the princess can communicate with spirits," he informed her. "You said you saw Amy walking in the woods."

"We don't know that Amy is dead." Hailey took another sip of her drink and groaned. "I'm not drunk enough to have this conversation," she muttered while covering her eyes. She took a deep breath, leaned forward, and stared Skyler in the eyes. "Let's suppose, just for argument's sake, I am this magical princess and you're my Numinous. What do you suggest we do? Ride our magical unicorn off to gumdrop city?"

"According to the story, you're supposed to choose your council," Skyler replied with enthusiasm and didn't seem at all bothered by her sarcasm.

She wasn't sure she wanted to encourage him, especially since he was completely sober and wanted desperately to believe the story. He was obviously getting caught up in something that allowed him to escape the life he hated. Of course, with all the alcohol Hailey had consumed, she found the situation a little more humorous than she had earlier.

"Okay, just for the sake of playing along," she announced, a little more giddy than usual. "That would leave Balance, Charmer, and the Guardian."

"Logan is Balance," Skyler interjected. "Artistically talented, musically inclined, and has a natural gift with plant life." He indicated the plants around the room while gesturing with his hands. "Need I say more?"

He wasn't completely wrong with his assumption, and she admired his enthusiasm.

"So that just leaves Charmer and the Guardian," Skyler continued.

Hailey sank into thought while leaning back on the sofa and smiled mockingly. "Who to pick?" She gave Logan a curious look. "Would Charmer be someone I find charming, or someone who just thinks he's charming?"

"Don't look at me," Logan announced while holding up his spray bottle defensively then nodded to Skyler. "Get your Numinous to translate it. That's his job."

"Well, Talbert certainly thinks he's charming, not that I think he's anything special," she muttered.

"I think we can all agree that Marcus would have to be the Guardian," Skyler announced and glanced at both for approval. "He was on the police force, and he's in charge of security. Seems only natural."

Hailey attempted to hold back her drunken giggle. "Okay, my council is in place. So what's next, Numinous?"

"We have a mystery to solve," Skyler informed her excitedly while nearly bounding out of his chair.

Hailey could no longer control her instincts to laugh at the entire situation. "Okay, Velma. You find Scooby and Shaggy. Fred and I will gas up the Mystery Machine."

Logan chuckled despite his attempt to contain it. Skyler muttered something under his breath. He obviously wasn't as humored as his friends were. Hailey finished her drink and stood with some unsteadiness.

"I'd love to stay and debate this all night, but her wicked, royal highness needs her beauty sleep," Hailey announced proudly and nearly tripped over the coffee table. "I have a dragon to slay in the morning, and her name is Lucinda."

Skyler groaned and reluctantly stood. "I'll see the royal lush to her suite."

†

Hailey and Skyler appeared from the staff wing and walked across the lobby toward the elevator. Hailey was clinging to Skyler's arm more for support than anything else. She was finding it difficult to contain her giddiness in her drunken state. They saw Cass, who was working the evening shift, standing behind the front desk while talking with Delaney. Delaney cast a strange look at Skyler and Hailey as they passed. Hailey was clearly drunk but transformed into a sober appearance for Delaney's benefit. She was painfully aware of what the security guard thought about them after their story about the dead woman. The way Delaney stared at them made her uncomfortable.

"I guess we gave them something to gossip about," Hailey muttered to her friend.

"I'm used to being stared at in *that* way," Skyler replied with little emotion.

Hailey then realized what Skyler went through every day of his life, and she suddenly felt bad for her earlier behavior. She gently squeezed his arm with hers.

"I'm sorry for mocking you earlier," she said softly. "It's been a weird sort of day."

"Every day is a weird sort of day for me," Skyler remarked while grinning.

They exchanged looks and laughed softly. Lucinda hurried along the corridor from the lounge and approached them, clearly with a mission. Hailey saw her and groaned softly. She didn't need to deal with the barracuda yet tonight. Lucinda had already seen her, so it was too late to make a hasty exit. Lucinda nearly cut them off on their approach to the elevator. Hailey was concerned about the upcoming conversation, because in her condition, she was likely to say just about anything to her boss. She then saw the strange smile on Lucinda's face.

"I don't know what you said to Nevin, but he wants the contract," Lucinda announced and could barely contain her enthusiasm.

Hailey stared at her with surprise. "Nothing very flattering, I assure you," she muttered.

Lucinda affectionately touched her arm. "Well, whatever you said, it worked," she remarked with an odd giddiness Hailey found slightly disturbing. "Would you be a dear and fetch the contract from my suite? I'd left it on my bedside table." She gestured down the corridor. "I'll keep him occupied in the lounge. Don't be long."

Lucinda handed her the keycard to her penthouse suite then hurried back the way she came. Both watched her with shared looks of surprise. Hailey had never seen Lucinda move that fast before. She glanced at Skyler and uncertainly shook her head.

"Huh? I guess I'm still employed," she remarked then laughed softly. "I'd better get that contract before Brody changes his mind. I'll talk to you tomorrow."

"Are you sure you don't want me to come along?" he asked with a look of concern on his face. "I wouldn't want you to get turned around in your condition."

"I'm fine," Hailey replied, although she appreciated his concern. "Seeing Lucinda scared me sober."

Skyler chuckled. "Then I'll be heading back to my room," he replied. "You know where to find me if you need me."

"Goodnight, Skyler."

"Night, Hailey."

Hailey hurried to the elevator and pressed the button. She glanced back at the front desk and saw Delaney and Cass still casting looks at her. Hailey desperately wanted to gesture like an enraged truck driver but thought better of it.

Chapter Thirteen

$\mathcal{H}$ailey entered the living room of Lucinda's penthouse suite from the secured twentieth floor corridor. The twentieth floor was home to only Lucinda's penthouse suite and the rarely used presidential suite. The penthouse suite had a large living room with a marble fireplace. The small kitchen was separated from the living room by a marble breakfast bar with a formal dining room to the right of the kitchen. The back wall of the suite was floor to ceiling glass windows with doors leading to the large balcony. To the left of the balcony doors was a sunken hot tub with enough room for eight people. Near the hot tub was a small but elegant wet bar. The penthouse suite contained two bedrooms, both with private baths, and there was a half bath off the living room. Hailey crossed the living room and entered the mostly dark master bedroom. She didn't need to turn the light on, since she could see the contract lying on the nightstand next to the bed only a few feet into the room. As she crossed the bedroom, she noticed the open balcony door swaying slightly from a gentle breeze. Hailey paused near the bedside table and was about to pick up the contract when she again looked at the partially open balcony door.

There was always a breeze off the ocean that affected the higher floors, so she didn't know why Lucinda had left the balcony door open. As Hailey approached the door to close it, she saw an intruder partially hidden within the corner just behind the curtains. Hailey gasped with surprise and ran toward the bed for the security button on the nightstand. She nearly made it to the button when she was tackled face first onto the elegant bed with the intruder landing on top of her. He skillfully flipped her over, rendered her motionless with his body, and held her wrists to the bed near her head. Between being startled by the man in Lucinda's room and the amount of alcohol in her system, she was frozen by the assault. Her head was spinning slightly, moderately disorienting her.

"I'm not going to hurt you," the man whispered close to her face.

She stared helplessly at the man on top of her in the near darkness. Her mind raced. She wasn't sure if she should scream, fight to free herself, or head butt him in the nose. She couldn't seem to convince her body to do any of those things. He had caught her off guard, leaving her completely paralyzed with fear. With his gloved hand, he snatched the sash from the bed curtain behind her head. Hailey gasped and suddenly fought against him. Fear that he was going to kill her, or attempt any number of other heinous acts, kick started her defenses. He easily rendered her immobile and again placed his face within inches of hers. Although she couldn't see his eyes in the darkened room, she could feel him staring at her.

"Which part of 'I won't hurt you' didn't you understand?" he whispered more firmly. "You're not on my 'to do' list."

She couldn't be sure, but she was convinced he was smiling at her.

"Relax," he said softly. "I just need a five minute head start before you call security."

She wasn't sure why, but she believed him. She cursed her body for relaxing as he had instructed, but in her moderately drunken condition, it wasn't as if she had a lot of options. As her head continued to spin, she feared she might pass out. He skillfully tied her right wrist to a brass headboard with the sash while keeping her immobile with his body. She could feel his neck brush against her face as he tied her right wrist. For a brief moment, she considered sinking her teeth into his neck. Her cannibalistic thoughts were short-lived as she inhaled the faint traces of his cologne. It was a familiar scent, but she couldn't place it. Just about every man at the resort wore expensive cologne. She wasn't sure why the scent relaxed her. Perhaps because it was familiar, lulling her into a false sense of security. For a moment, she thought maybe she even knew him. As he straightened over her, his lips brushed past hers. She was uncertain if it was by accident or intentional.

"That should keep you busy for a few minutes," he whispered in an almost mocking tone.

She stared at him through the darkness even though she couldn't make out any of his features. Hailey knew he was staring back at her, although she was positive he couldn't know she was staring at him. There was an awkward moment where neither moved. She could feel his heart pounding against her chest, and he seemed to stop breathing. She then felt the all too familiar feeling of male arousal against her hip. Hailey tensed to the sensation but, oddly enough, wasn't frightened by what was obviously going through his head. She felt his gloved hand gently touch her face. She trembled from the sensation of the soft leather touching her cheek, but she still wasn't afraid he would hurt her. He groaned softly and kissed her passionately on the mouth. She had to force herself not to return the kiss even though her body screamed for her to do it. She could taste the expensive alcohol on his lips and tongue. He broke off the kiss as quickly as he'd indulged in it and jumped off her with amazing reflexes. Although she couldn't see it, she knew he was smiling at her.

The intruder darted toward the open balcony door and disappeared through it. Hailey remained motionless a moment, still feeling the sensation of his hard body against hers. She finally came to her senses and frantically struggled to untie the rope on her right wrist with her left hand. She looked at the knot through the near darkness, frowned, and pulled the loose end, releasing the slipknot. He was an intruder with a sense of humor--and one hell of a great kisser. Hailey jumped from the bed and immediately regretted the sudden movement. She clutched her head until the dizziness passed. She then ran to the balcony and looked out, but he was gone.

t

*O*nly ten minutes had passed before Marcus and Delaney stormed the penthouse suite. Lucinda arrived only moments after her two security officers. The master bedroom light brightened the entire room to reveal its grandeur and expensive furniture. The wall safe, once hidden behind a painting, now stood open. Hailey sat on the large bed and subconsciously ran her fingers through her hair. She couldn't get the last few minutes out of her head, and it wasn't because she was thrown to a bed and tied up by a strange man. It was his kiss she couldn't shake. It had to be because she was drunk. She'd gone too long without male company, and being drunk didn't help her reaction to the intruder's charm. Lucinda frantically paced before the open wall safe while wrenching her fingers together. It appeared unclear if she was frightened or angry. Marcus returned to the bedroom from the balcony and shook his head with disgust. Lucinda turned toward him with a wild look. She wasn't frightened; she was angry and hateful.

"You said no one could break into the penthouse," Lucinda launched at Marcus, her eyes digging into him like daggers. "You said no one could crack that safe! Poor Hailey was nearly killed tonight! What are you going to do about it?"

"I wasn't nearly killed," Hailey replied softly, although she wasn't sure why she felt the need to say anything as she subconsciously touched her lips. She swore she still felt his mouth on hers.

Delaney hastily made his getaway, possibly to avoid the wrath of the barracuda. Hailey glanced at the safe in the wall not far from the bed, which contained many jewelry boxes and several bundles of cash. She found it odd that he left all the valuables behind. What surprised her more was what he actually did take.

"He left all that cash," Hailey marveled aloud then glanced at Lucinda. "Why did he only steal that old, emerald necklace of yours?"

Lucinda spun on her heels and looked at Hailey with rage on her face. "Because he obviously knew his jewelry," she exploded then turned to Marcus with equal hostility toward him. "Find my necklace! I don't care if you have to tear apart every room in the hotel!"

Lucinda snatched the contract from the nightstand and stormed from the room. The penthouse door was heard slamming as she left. Marcus and Hailey exchanged puzzled looks. She somehow knew he was thinking the same thing she was.

"That went surprisingly well," he announced then closed the safe and gave the dial a quick spin. Marcus looked back at Hailey, who still hadn't moved from the bed. He revealed the same sympathetic look she'd seen in the lounge then sat on the bed alongside her. As he stared into her eyes, she saw a genuine kindness he probably shared with few. "Are you sure there isn't anything else you can tell me about him?"

"No, it was too dark," she replied and gently rubbed her hands over her arms, feeling a slight chill.

Marcus stared at her a moment longer, making her slightly uncomfortable. She certainly wasn't going to tell him that the intruder kissed her or that she sort of enjoyed it. As he stared at her, she could smell faint traces of his cologne. Hailey suddenly felt compelled to lean closer and investigate the scent. She was almost afraid to learn the truth, so she maintained her distance. She shifted uncomfortably and looked away to avoid him possibly reading her eyes.

"If we're done, I'd really like to go to my room," she announced gently.

Marcus smiled gently and nodded while standing. "Yes, of course," he announced and extended his hand to her. "I'll escort you to your room."

She stared at his hand a moment and hesitantly accepted it while wondering what it was about him that peaked her curiosity. She brushed those feelings aside as he helped her to her feet.

"I'd appreciate that."

He offered a polite smile and guided her toward the bedroom door. "It's my job to protect you."

Hailey gave him a strange look as they walked out the door. She couldn't believe Skyler's story was actually getting to her!

†

Hailey soaked beneath the hot stream of water in the large, elegant standing shower encased in stone and frosted glass doors. She'd considered soaking in the jetted tub after her ordeal, but she was exhausted and feared falling asleep, drowning herself. Her thoughts were scattered, yet they kept returning to the scene in Lucinda's bedroom. She could still feel the intruder's mouth on hers and could almost taste the expensive alcohol. The man broke into her boss's safe, tied her to a bed, and practically assaulted her, yet she couldn't get his kiss off her mind. It concerned her that she wasn't scared. She should have been frightened to death, especially with his untold arousal against her hip. There was something familiar about the man, but she couldn't quite grasp what it was. She wasn't going to rest until she smelled every man at the resort. She desperately wanted to know who he was, and it had nothing to do with getting Lucinda's necklace back.

Through the frosted doors, she saw a dark object move across the bathroom. A clunk followed. Hailey strained to look through the shower doors and saw the dark mass beyond the glass standing at waist level. Hailey gasped with horror, snatched her towel from over the shower door, and wrapped it around her. The dark mass moved, indicating whatever it was, it was alive. She quickly opened the shower door. A large black cat sat on the sink playing with her toothbrush. Hailey groaned, stepped out of the shower, and petted the cat. It seemed friendly enough.

"Where did you come from, little kitty?" she asked then laughed at her earlier overreaction. "Did Skyler put you up to this?"

The cat purred as she stroked its fur and then turned serious as it pounced on her toothbrush in the sink. The little kitty was determined to save the world one toothbrush at a time. She laughed at the playful kitty.

"Okay, you can stay; but just for tonight."

Chapter Fourteen

*W*ell-dressed men and women danced to the pulsating club music in the dim lighting within the lounge. It was a little after one o'clock in the morning and the dance floor was again crowded to maximum capacity. Mel and Desi danced with several young men, although it seemed as if Vance was mysteriously absent. Judging by the way both women scanned the crowded dance floor, each was secretly hoping he'd show up. Penny was sitting at the bar and appeared disinterested in the fun time being had by others. Tam refilled her drink and studied her mood.

"Don't you know you're supposed to be having fun," Tam informed her.

"How can I?" Penny asked while returning the look. "No one's seen Amy since she left with that guy last night."

Tam easily shrugged it off. "It wouldn't be the first time a girl ran off with some stud for a weekend in the sack," she announced. "Another girl took off just a few days ago. I'd heard she'd called her friends from some rich guy's yacht." Tam groaned lustfully while sinking into her own fantasies. "Lucky girl. Why is it I never meet the rich studs?"

"I'm sure that sort of thing happens a lot around here, but it's not like Amy," Penny insisted. "She wouldn't even have gone back to his room with him let alone run away with some guy she barely knows. She doesn't do that sort of thing, and she certainly wouldn't run off without telling us where she was going."

"They always turn up," Tam announced while attempting to remain cheerful.

Penny sharply eyed the bartender. "I'd heard rumor someone found a body in the woods," she remarked. "Did you hear anything about that?"

Tam gave a disinterested wave. "That was just a cry for attention from a desperate guy with too much time on his hands," she remarked. "It wouldn't be the first time we'd heard wild rantings from that one."

"That's a relief," Penny said with a sigh.

Penny looked into the mirror behind Tam and saw Daniel making his way through the crowd. She turned on her stool and saw the familiar man leaving the lounge. Penny's expression dropped as she sprang to her feet.

"My God, that's him. I have to go," Penny cried out and weaved through the crowd after the man.

Penny hurried from the lounge and into the main hallway. Daniel walked along the nearly empty corridor toward the lobby and paused before the elevators. Oddly enough, he pressed the down button. Penny maintained her distance and watched him enter the elevator. Once the doors closed, she hurried to the elevators, noted it went down, and pressed the down button as well. It seemed odd that he'd be going down, since it only went to the basement. When the doors opened, Penny stepped inside and pressed the down button. She looked around the elevator and seemed to consider her actions with insecurity. She rubbed her arms and waited for the doors to open.

The basement corridor was well-lit with a massive laundry room just ahead and the maintenance department off to the right. The basement was nearly as large as the hotel itself. Daniel walked along the basement corridor with purpose. It seemed unusual that one of the guests would be familiar with the hotel's basement. Penny followed from a safe distance and appeared curious to his actions. She turned a corner, and he was gone. The door to the laundry room was locked. Not far from the laundry room was an old freight elevator. She paused before the old elevator and studied it while considering her next move. It was possible he entered the elevator, since it seemed improbable that he had a key to the laundry room door. There was a down button, indicating there was a floor beneath the basement. She hesitated only a moment before pressing the down button.

The elevator arrived and the old, creaking doors slid open. Penny nervously stepped into the elevator, stared at the button labeled 'one' below the basement button, and anxiously pressed it. The old elevator jolted with a strange grinding sound and headed down to the floor below. Penny clung to the side of the elevator with concern to her ride. If the elevator would become stuck, it would be hours or longer before anyone ever found her trapped inside the dank dirty monstrosity. The elevator finally jolted to a stop. Nothing happened. For a moment, she appeared to panic. The door finally opened with a hideous grinding sound. As the door slid open, Penny stared at the dingy and dimly lit sub-basement corridor. She slowly stepped out of the old elevator and looked both directions. Both were equally creepy and lined with cobwebs. She walked several feet along the dingy hallway.

There were odd archways leading into dark rooms scattered randomly along the corridor. At the far end of the main corridor, the hallway continued both right and left with even less light. It was a chilling, dismal area that left a lot to be desired. Penny stared down the corridor a moment, conveyed her fright, and shook her head.

"I don't think so."

She quickly turned and hurried back toward the elevator. She was nearly to the open elevator when she heard a low snarl behind her. Penny abruptly stopped, looked behind her, and saw glowing eyes in one of the rooms off to the side. She now hurried for the open elevator and looked back while passing another darkened archway. Penny was suddenly knocked off her feet. She barely had time to scream as she was dragged into the dark room. Her startled scream trailed off into the darkness.

†

*H*ailey slept restlessly in her short, satin nightgown beneath the sheets on her massive, king-sized bed. The little black cat remained curled at her feet despite her random thrashing. In her dreams, she ran through a dimly lit tunnel in a tattered nightgown. She could feel the cold, damp stone floor beneath her bare feet. Old lights exploded as she ran past them, leaving complete darkness behind her. She heard a strange sound and immediately stopped. She listened to the sound then felt something brushing along her feet. She looked down and saw hundreds of snakes surrounding her. They slithered across her feet and wrapped around her ankles. Hailey thrashed in her sleep, screamed aloud, and shot up in bed. One of the glass balcony doors shattered, terrifying both her and the cat. The cat jumped straight up from a dead sleep, puffed twice its size, hissed, and leaped from the bed.

"Skyler!"

After her panic-filled scream, the room was completely silent. Hailey's heart pounded so hard, she had a difficult time catching her breath. She placed a trembling hand to her head then looked at the broken glass door. There was an urgent pounding from the main suite door, startling her. Hailey leaped from her bed, hurried across the suite, and approached the living room door. She opened the door without even looking through the peek hole. Rafe stood before the door wearing only a pair of shorts and clutched a 26" rattan escrima stick used for self-defense in martial arts. He quickly scanned the room.

"I heard a scream."

As she stared at Rafe in her doorway, she couldn't believe her nightmare was still continuing. She fumbled for something to say and conceal her body beneath her thin nightgown.

"It's nothing," she announced, finally catching her breath from the shock of her nightmare. "I just had a bad dream."

Rafe bolted past her, apparently not caring what she said, and stormed across the room. He entered the darkened bedroom with a mission. She placed her hand to her head and groaned softly, wanting to crawl into a hole right about then. Rafe was obviously itching to kill something and was hoping he'd find it in her bedroom. Hailey often wondered what it was about testosterone that possessed men to run blindly into darkened rooms.

"It was just a nightmare, Rafe," she called after him while looking for something with which to cover herself. Before she could reach the nearby throw blanket, he was already returning from the bedroom.

Rafe stood in the bedroom doorway with an odd look on his face while indicating her room. "The glass on the balcony door is broken."

He wasn't telling her anything she didn't already know, and she was quickly losing patience.

"Yeah, I guess a bird must have hit it." At least she hoped that was all it was.

"It's broken from the inside," he remarked firmly.

She stared at him with a strange look and squinted to the comment. "What?"

That didn't make any sense. How could the glass be broken leading outside to the balcony? Had someone been in her room and broke the door while attempting to flee? She couldn't help think about the man who broke into Lucinda's suite. Thundering footfalls were heard in the hallway, interrupting her thoughts and startling her. Hailey turned as Skyler appeared in the doorway in a pair of satin pajamas and clearly out of breath.

"Are you okay?" Skyler gasped. He then saw Rafe with his rattan stick and jumped in front of Hailey with his arms stretched out. "Run, Hailey!"

Rafe rolled his eyes then groaned and muttered, "Give me a break."

Hailey turned Skyler around to face her and attempted to keep him calm. "I appreciate you becoming a human shield to protect me, but Rafe just got here."

"What are you doing here?" Rafe demanded while scanning the satin pajamas he wore.

"Hailey called for me," he replied while panting heavily.

Hailey cast a strange look at Skyler. She knew she didn't call him. She would have remembered that. Was he hanging outside her room in his pajamas? If that were the case, it would be taking stalking to a new level. Rafe groaned with annoyance, walked past them, and headed from the room.

"Why am I always next to the crazies?" he muttered as he entered the hall and disappeared.

Hailey looked back at Skyler and slowly shook her head while folding her arms across her chest. "I never called you, Skyler."

"You did. I was in my room reading Logan's manuscript when I heard you call me," he insisted. "I thought you were in trouble, so I ran up here as fast as I could."

His words almost made no sense to her.

"As in telepathy?" she suddenly asked with surprise then another more concerning thought occurred to her. "Did you say you were in your room?" Her arms fell to her sides. "Are you telling me you actually ran from the employee's wing to the nineteenth floor in less than a minute?"

Skyler casually shrugged with little forethought. "I got picked on a lot when I was a kid. I learned to run fast," he replied. "So what happened?"

Hailey inhaled deeply while running her fingers through her hair then sighed.

"The usual--snakes and tidal waves."

Chapter Fifteen

It was late the following morning and yet another sunny, warm day in paradise. They were all pretty much the same, but that was what the guests were hoping for on their expensive vacation. Rather than enjoying the sun, surf, and beach like a normal guest, Hailey stood with Skyler on the path just inside the woods by the clearing. Both watched as Logan wandered through the tall grass where the beast and panther had gotten into their altercation close to where she had seen the dead woman's body. Hailey hated to admit that she didn't want to explore the clearing after what they'd witnessed yesterday, but she was quite rattled just thinking about it. Thankfully, Skyler was less inclined to hide his feelings about venturing into the clearing, giving her just cause not to join Logan in his search. Logan finally straightened, looked back at them, and shook his head.

"I don't see any remains of the panther or your beast," Logan announced. "I'm seeing some blood, but not enough to indicate anything was killed."

"You believe us though, right?" she asked, feeling almost defeated.

"Why would you lie?" Logan countered.

Hailey stared at the path not far from Logan and indicated it with a general nod. She hated to ask, fearing the thought of exploring deeper into the woods.

"Where does that path lead?" she reluctantly questioned.

Logan looked behind him then met her gaze from several feet away. "To the ravine," he replied. "It has one of those old-fashioned rope and board bridges, but it's been out of operation for years. If Amy attempted to cross that bridge, she'd certainly be on the bottom."

Hailey couldn't believe the words coming from her mouth, although it did take some courage to say them. "I think we should have a look."

Skyler's body twitched in response. He was apprehensive about their secretive journey and didn't mind letting it be known. Hailey reluctantly joined Logan, giving Skyler little choice but obediently follow. They walked along a well-worn path in the woods for several minutes, passing a less traveled trail leading downhill. They finally reached another, larger clearing containing the ravine. The deep ravine had an old rope and board style bridge crossing the fifty-yard opening. All three stood near the edge and looked to the bottom of the one hundred yard drop. The bottom was a bed of large and small boulders. Anyone falling from the bridge would meet with a very painful death on the field of rocks below. If Amy had fallen, her body would be clearly visible on the rocks. Skyler made a face and took a step back from the edge.

"Man, I hate heights," Skyler muttered.

Hailey stared into the ravine a moment longer. She hated to admit that Marcus had been right. Neither Amy nor the dead woman were at the bottom of the ravine, which was evident. Whether or not she had actually seen Amy walking in the woods was one thing, but she had definitely seen a half-eaten woman in the field. Something dragged her away, but to where? She groaned softly with defeat then looked back at Logan, who continued to stare into the deadly drop.

"Where did that other path lead?" Hailey asked while pointing back the way they'd came.

"Downhill to the stream," Logan replied. "It's rarely traveled. A real bitch to climb back up. An old mineshaft collapsed beneath it years ago."

Hailey and Skyler suddenly looked at Logan with shared concerned.

"Mineshaft?" Hailey asked softly and felt something inside her body twitch.

"Just like the cave in Hailey's nightmares--" Skyler gasped as his entire body appeared to tense.

"There are tunnels beneath this entire area," Logan casually informed them. "A catacomb of condominiums for the native island bats."

"Bats?" Skyler said faintly, his eyes wide with alarm, unable to look away from the big man.

"Yeah," Logan replied casually and made a gesture of size with his hands. "Real huge mothers the size of cats."

"I'll pass."

"Is there an entrance to the mine shaft around here?" Hailey asked despite her apprehension.

"Yeah, part way down that steep path," Logan replied, "but I don't think you want to go that way."

"If something dragged that woman's body away, that mine would be the perfect place to stash it," Hailey informed him as her concerns increased. "And that still leaves Amy. I swear I saw her. What if she's injured somewhere around here? We need to look for her. She could be in that mine."

"If that beast dragged either of them into that mine, it also means that thing lives in the mine," Logan boldly announced. "You don't follow a wild creature into its home."

"We need to make sure she's not in there," Hailey replied and pleaded with their sensitive sides. "If Amy is still alive, we can't just leave her there."

Skyler chewed on his finger while shifting glances between the two but offered no comment. Logan groaned softly while throwing his head back with defeat.

"I know I'm going to regret listening to you," Logan muttered under his breath.

†

*M*el walked alongside Vance on the worn path in the woods. He held her hand reassuringly while practically pulling her to keep up with him. Mel had a look of apprehension on her face as she looked around the moderately creepy, nearly silent woods. For late morning, it seemed odd that there was no sounds in the wooded setting. If there were birds, they appeared unwilling to sing. Even the usual small woodland creatures were absent. She resisted his firm, guiding hand and attempted to slow her gait even more.

"I think we've gone far enough from the resort, Vance," Mel informed the handsome man, who continued to pull her along by her hand.

Vance had a smile permanently chiseled on his face while glancing back at her. "That's sort of the idea," he announced while raising his brows suggestively.

Mel remained unconvinced and continued to look around the secluded area while clinging to his hand. "Hailey said she saw a dead woman in the woods yesterday. It may not be safe out here like this."

"No offense to your friend," Vance remarked, "but she's been spending a little too much time with that crazy guy from the front desk."

"What do you mean crazy?"

"I've heard things around the hotel," he replied. "Cass at the front desk said he claims to be psychic or some bullshit. She thinks he's batty. Tam, the bartender, says he's insane. One of the maids thinks he's some sort of psychopath."

"For a guy who's only been here a couple of days, you've certainly gotten your share of gossip," Mel announced and appeared to consider his remark. She then muttered under her breath, "Ironically, from a lot of women." She again looked around with apprehension. "So where is it you're taking me?"

"There's a secluded, romantic spot not far from here," he announced. "You're going to love it."

"I thought we were coming out here for a scenic romantic walk," she announced. "I didn't realize that meant sex in the woods."

Vance suddenly stopped and looked at her. It was hard to tell if he was more disappointed or offended by her comment. He offered a gentle, reassuring smile.

"I'm more of a 'spontaneous, let the chips fall as they may' sort of guy," he announced. "When a man puts too much emphasis on whether or not he's getting laid, it just creates anxiety and disappointment. When you let go of those thoughts, it's easier to enjoy yourself. I'd much rather enjoy the here and now, wouldn't you? I expect nothing from life yet anticipate everything." He grinned proudly. "I didn't bring you out here to seduce you. I brought you out here to appreciate this wonderful life we're living. Life is good, Mel. You just need to relax and enjoy it."

Mel stared at the boyish grin across his handsome face. She seemed dumbfounded for a moment then threw her arms around his neck and kissed him passionately. Vance eagerly returned the aggressive, passionate kiss.

Chapter Sixteen

The crude opening to the mineshaft was framed with old, dried wood carved into the rocky hillside. It appeared sturdy despite its age. Hailey glanced at the dark shaft beyond the crude opening. She had to admit, the thought of entering the mine was frightening, but she needed to know what happened to Amy. She needed to know she wasn't crazy. Logan and Skyler watched her as she stared into the dark opening. They shared the same expression. Hailey was crazy!

"I know you're not thinking about going in there," Skyler announced firmly.

"Certainly not without a flashlight," Hailey muttered without looking at either.

"Did you forget the part about the cat-sized bats?" Skyler interjected, his rising anxiety indicated by the increased twitching of his body.

Hailey looked at the ground just outside the mine, approached the opening, and picked up a flashlight. Logan and Skyler stared at the flashlight in her hand with their mouths hanging open. The fact that it was there was concerning. Hailey flipped the switch. It still worked! All three suddenly looked around with combined panic to the only rational explanation.

"Someone's been out here recently," Hailey remarked.

"Marcus?" Skyler asked. "He said they'd come back out and look around more today."

"So where are they?" Logan asked, sharing his friends' concern as he looked around for the search party.

All three looked at the mineshaft opening and came to the same conclusion.

"Damn," Logan softly gasped while throwing his head back with concern. "Do you think they went in there and something happened to them?"

"There's only one way to find out," Hailey announced almost too softly for them to hear. Unfortunately, they did hear the comment.

Neither man appeared enthused. All three now stared at one another as if silently deciding their next move. What sounded like a low growl echoed from within the tunnel. All three tensed and slowly looked at the mineshaft behind them. Something large with glowing red eyes moved within the dark tunnel. All three slowly backed away, uncertain whether to run or remain still. A large, black beast the size of a bear leaped out of the opening, landed before them, and snarled with long, sharp teeth exposed. Although coated in black fur, it definitely wasn't a bear. It was a never before seen 'it' with a broad chest and sloping back to muscular haunches. It had sharp claws protruding from long toes on its large paws, a broad lion-like nose, and piercing red eyes.

As it stood before them snarling with bloodstained, cat-like teeth, they were frozen with fear. As it leaned back on its haunches, they saw it's long tail swish, indicating it was preparing to launch forward. All three came to the same conclusion and screamed simultaneously. The black panther suddenly appeared and tackled the creature to the ground. Both rolled, snarled, and bit each other. The beast was more than double the size of the panther, although not nearly as agile. Two more beasts of similar size and shape appeared from the cave. Hailey and the two men bolted into the woods and away from the snarling beasts. Hailey and Skyler ran down the steep ravine path toward the stream, while Logan ran up the less treacherous path with one of the creatures chasing him. The second beast ran after Hailey and Skyler.

Logan ran up the short path with surprising speed and took off along the path in the woods to the right. He appeared from the woods and stopped at the edge of the ravine. He'd made a wrong turn! He caught his balance and watched the rocks beneath his feet propel downward to the drop below. The snarling beast appeared in the woods behind him, stopping, as if knowing it had the large man trapped. Logan barely looked back before running along the edge of the ravine and heading for the old rope bridge. He grabbed onto both sides of the thick rope railing, ignored the posted warning sign, and tiptoed across the weak, rotted planks. They cracked and splintered beneath his weight. It was possibly another bad idea, but he had limited choices. He stopped ten feet across the bridge and looked back. The large, black creature stood before the bridge and snarled while staring at him. Its sheer size was frightening enough without the added sharpness of its teeth and claws. Logan contained his fear and stood proudly while clinging to the rope railing on both sides of the bridge.

"That's right, mother! You want me?" he cried out. "Come and get me!"

The beast placed a clawed paw on the first plank. It creaked under the creature's weight. The planks weren't sturdy enough to hold Logan let alone a three-hundred pound beast.

"That's it," he baited the creature. "Bring your fat ass out here!"

Rather than step onto the bridge, the beast pushed on the plank. The rope bridge bounced and swayed, slowly at first but soon increased in momentum. Logan gasped and clutched the rope railing on either side as the bridge creaked and swayed from the creature jolting it, tossing him from side to side. One of the rotted rope railings snapped. Logan released the rope, cried out, and clutched the only remaining rope. He attempted to stand on the slanted, rotted board as the beast continued to rock the bridge. The beast was somehow smart enough to know it could knock Logan off the bridge. Logan looked down to the ravine below. It was a long drop with a very unpleasant stop at the rocky bottom. He assessed the area surrounding him while clinging to the remaining rope railing. A vine dangled five feet from him. He reached for the vine, but it was too far to reach without releasing the rope.

The beast stood on its hind legs and pulled on the last rope, attempting to shake Logan from the bridge. Logan bounced up and down harshly while clinging to the rope and crying out. He again reached for the vine. The vine slowly stretched toward his hand. The bottom rope holding the plank snapped, and Logan's feet fell out from beneath him. He clung to the rope railing with both arms as his feet dangled freely. He looked past his dangling feet to the ravine below. The beast gave one final pull on the remaining rope to which Logan clung. It snapped. Logan screamed, clung to the rope, and shut his eyes while awaiting the fall. The rope didn't drop. The beast's loud, shrill yelp forced Logan to open his eyes. He looked at the rope he held. Several vines were tangled around the rope five feet away and held it in place, keeping him from falling to his death. The rope strained against the vines. Logan looked at the creature on the edge of the ravine. It gnawed at several vines now tangled around its head and paws. There was no time to speculate what had happened. Logan pulled himself up onto the rope, placing his feet beneath him, and teetered on what was now viewed as a medieval tightrope. A much *rotted* medieval tightrope!

"Holy shit--"

Logan attempted to maintain his balance on the rotted tightrope and looked at the vine just a few yards away. The rope strained under him and the weight of the bridge. He had seconds to make his move. Logan took a deep breath and ran across the rope, screaming the entire way. He leaped for the dangling vine, caught it with both hands, and swung from the bridge to the safety of the ledge. The vines holding the bridge snapped and it collapsed with a thunderous crash. Logan released the vine and fell harshly onto his backside not far from the snarling, ensnared beast. The creature fought the vines tangled around its body and couldn't be bothered with Logan. Logan stared at the struggling creature, marveled at its sheer size, then scrambled to his feet, and darted into the woods.

Chapter Seventeen

*H*ailey and Skyler slid down the steep, rocky path half on their backsides while avoiding the creature sliding down just behind them. They reached the bottom, nearly losing their balance. Hailey fell onto her backside. Skyler grabbed her hand and pulled her to her feet as the creature lost its balance and tumbled out of control past them. As the creature unsteadily stood, Skyler forced Hailey to run across the stream with him. Neither looked back in fear of the creature being directly behind them. They ran up the bank on the other side and nearly collided with Vance and Mel, who were coming down the slope. Hailey and Skyler screamed in response to the unexpected collision. Vance and Mel were startled more by their screams than their unexpected appearance and stared at the terrified pair.

"What's all the screaming about?" Vance demanded while hastily tucking in his shirt and attempting to catch his breath.

Hailey and Skyler pointed toward the stream, unable to get the words out. The beast was gone. Mel and Vance exchanged looks and almost certainly thought they were insane. Hailey and Skyler stared a moment longer then attempted to relax. Whatever caused the beast to retreat was a welcomed relief. Both were equally shaken but they had concerns that were more important.

"We need to find Logan," Hailey gasped and headed for the stream.

Skyler reluctantly followed. Mel and Vance again exchanged looks then hurried after them. Climbing back up the steep trail was a challenge. Skyler led the way; seeming better equipped for the challenge, and practically pulled Hailey the entire way. Mel and Vance struggled to follow them while attempting to avoid the rocks tumbling at them from the couple in front. They finally reached the area before the mineshaft and looked around. There was no sign of Logan. Skyler kept watch on the dark mineshaft opening while Hailey searched the area.

"Logan," Hailey called out.

There was no response. Vance approached the tunnel entrance near Skyler and picked up the discarded flashlight.

"What were you guys doing out here?" Vance asked while fiddling with the flashlight.

Mel rubbed her arms and looked around with concern. "Let's just find Logan and get out of here," she announced. "This place gives me the creeps."

"Logan," Hailey again called out.

All four heard movement from the woods and turned. Despite having no clue what had Hailey so rattled, Mel was possibly more frightened than the others. Skyler grabbed a thick branch and held it above his head, prepared to pummel anything that moved. Logan suddenly appeared from the woods. He was slightly winded but oddly enthusiastic.

"Man, I'm glad to see you guys," Logan announced while half doubling over. He shook his head and attempted to catch his breath. "You'll never believe what happened to me."

"Can we get out of here before something does happen?" Mel nervously announced.

They heard the faint, echoing sound of a woman screaming from deep within the mine. All five looked at the dark opening, and for a moment, none moved.

"That sounded like a woman," Vance announced with surprise while attempting to look inside the mineshaft.

"Amy--" Hailey gasped with alarm and darted into the dark tunnel.

Skyler appeared alarmed, grabbed the flashlight from Vance, and hurried after her. "Hailey! Come back here!"

"My God, she's insane," Logan gasped, still unable to catch his breath.

The woman's faint scream was heard again. Vance and Logan looked at each other in silent question. Logan shook his head with disgust and hurried into the tunnel after Skyler. Vance looked back at Mel. Her eyes widened in horror.

"No way!" Mel cried out.

Within the mineshaft, light from Skyler's flashlight glistened off the dark tunnel walls. Hailey walked alongside him with Logan bringing up the rear. They heard movement from behind them. Logan turned and nearly collided with Vance.

"Shit," Logan cried out while clutching his chest. "Don't do that!"

"Mel went to get Marcus," Vance informed them.

The scream was louder now. It sounded like Penny. Skyler tore down thick webs from across the tunnel and shook them from his hand with disgust.

"I hate spiders," he grumbled.

Logan looked toward the ceiling with concern. "I'm more worried about the bats," he muttered.

Skyler gasped and shined the light at the ceiling. Thankfully, there weren't any bats. They continued along the tunnel for several feet when a strange sound caught their attention, causing all four to stop. It sounded like air leaking, but the sound was loud and almost deafening.

"What is that?" Skyler asked slowly with fear in his voice.

Everyone remained still and listened. Hailey felt a chill run down her spine as a thought occurred to her. She slowly pushed the flashlight in Skyler's hand downward. Snakes slithered along the ground before them. Skyler screamed and jumped away from them. There was a cobra near Hailey's leg. Hailey stared at the cobra and stood frozen. She wanted to scream and run, but she knew it would sink its teeth into her leg before she even flinched. It was almost like her dream!

"Any suggestions?" she gasped softly.

"Don't move," Logan announced excitedly and wiped the sweat from his bald head. "I'll find a stick."

Logan quickly searched the area surrounding him. Another snake slithered up Hailey's bare ankle. She was paralyzed from the sensation of the creature's body wrapping around her leg and making its way upward. She knew she couldn't move, but the urge to freak out was strong.

"Guys, I could really use some help," she whimpered while attempting to remain still.

Skyler shined the light around the tunnel surrounding Hailey and beyond her. There were hundreds of snakes in the tunnel moving toward them.

"I found a stick!" Logan announced with enthusiasm from several feet away and picked it up. He saw the snake he held in his hand, cried out, and cast it aside. "Shit! Wasn't a stick!"

Vance slowly approached Hailey and lowered himself near her legs. The cobra hissed and turned toward him. Vance held his hand up to the snake and stared at it in silence. The snake relaxed and slithered away. He casually removed the non-poisonous snake from Hailey's leg. She exhaled with relief. The snakes slowly slithered away from them and disappeared deeper into the tunnel. All three stared at Vance as he released the snake he held. It slithered after its buddies. They all stared at him with disbelief.

"What are you? Some sort of snake charmer?" Logan questioned with surprise.

Skyler stared at Vance with wide eyes and gasped softly, "Charmer--"

Hailey and Logan looked at Skyler to his realization. Vance took the flashlight from Skyler and slowly walked through the now-cleared tunnel.

"I suppose you could say that," Vance replied casually. "I've always had a way with animals."

Skyler nudged Hailey and raised his brows while feverishly pointing at Vance. If he gestured any faster, he'd almost certainly injure himself. Hailey rolled her eyes and ignored him. Vance walked along the tunnel with the others following directly on his heels in case more snakes appeared. Vance stopped and shined the light at the unusual carvings etched on the walls.

"What do you make of this?" Vance asked.

Skyler ran his hands along the strange carvings. They appeared to be human faces and bodies carved in the stone. They were amazingly detailed and lifelike.

"Like ancient hieroglyphics, perhaps?" Skyler replied while shaking his head.

Vance followed the wall with the flashlight. Skyler and Logan studied the strange carvings on the wall while following him. Hailey ran her hand over the human outline on the wall before her. She felt a strange chill running up and down her spine as if someone placed ice down her back. Torches on the walls suddenly erupted into flames and lit the entire tunnel, startling the three men. As they looked around with concern, Hailey continued to stare at the walls. She was almost oblivious to the torches lighting themselves. With the light from the torches, they could see the entire tunnel was covered with the human-like carvings. It was beyond chilling. Hailey studied one of the female carvings and ran her hand along a rose on the woman's breast. Her hand trembled slightly while touching the familiar rose. As Hailey stared at the carving directly before her, she witnessed ghostly men and woman emerging from the wall. Vance, Skyler, and Logan continued to look around and appeared completely unaware of what Hailey was witnessing.

"I'm feeling a lot of energy," Skyler announced with concern as he looked around.

"What lit the torches?" Vance asked.

Hailey no longer heard their conversation. She stared at the ghosts stepping out of the human carvings, and it was suddenly obvious to her what the carvings represented. The ghostly men and women stared helplessly at her and reached out their hands for her help. She'd never seen ghosts before, but according to Skyler, they've been drawn to her from the moment she arrived on the island. The men's conversation sounded almost distant to her as she witnessed the strangest event she'd ever seen.

"Do you suppose this was some ancient burial site?" Skyler asked.

"Impossible," Logan replied. "People didn't populate this island until the late eighteen hundreds."

"Maybe this is a lost civilization," Vance suggested and added a sly grin.

"Yeah, maybe some volcano destroyed their village and they were mummified to the walls from the lava," Skyler remarked. "I'm getting a really strange feeling from these images."

Hailey continued to stare at the ghostly images before her. Amy's frightened spirit stood before Hailey. As she stared into the woman's eyes, she felt her entire body tremble. She knew now it had been Amy's ghost she saw on the path. She was already long dead when she'd followed her into the woods, explaining her ability to disappear so fast. Skyler *had* foreseen her death.

"It is a burial chamber, but these people didn't die years ago," Hailey softly informed them while attempting to contain her emotions.

All three suddenly looked at her.

"How do you know that?" Vance asked with surprise as he cast glances at her then looked back at the walls.

"Because," she gasped softly while staring into Amy's ghostly eyes, "their ghosts are staring at me."

Skyler looked at Hailey for the first time, studied the area around her, and appeared surprised. "My God, I see specks of light surrounding you. There are too many to count."

"It was Amy's ghost I saw in the woods," she informed him softly. "They've been mummified into stone."

Amy's spirit pointed down the tunnel. Hailey stared in the direction Amy's ghost pointed.

"Amy wants us to continue," Hailey said softly.

†

The large, darkened room was dimly lit by candles surrounding the crude, stone altar upon which Penny lie. Her wrists and ankles were attached to the altar by old, metal shackles, which she fought in vain. Tears streaked her face as she held back her sobs. She was covered in scrapes and her dress was slightly tattered from whatever had pulled her from the corridor. The snarling sound of unseen creatures within the darkness added to the fear of the unknown fate awaiting her. Someone or something could be heard moving around the dark corners of the room, indicating the room was fairly large. The snarling continued but didn't appear to get any closer. The soft, faint groan of someone echoed through the darkened chamber. Penny held back her sobs and looked around while fighting her shackles.

"Who's there?" she cried out softly. "Please, help me!"

There was no response. The groan came again, this time louder. It almost sounded pleased by her torment. Someone was heard moving closer toward the altar and the bound woman.

†

The four continued to examine the etchings in the wall of the mineshaft as they walked more slowly. Hailey stared helplessly at several ghosts surrounding her as she walked. Amy remained several feet ahead and was the only recognizable spirit Hailey could clearly make out. Penny's sharp, shrill scream suddenly broke the silence, causing all four to stop with alarm. The scream stopped abruptly and unnaturally. All four ran along the tunnel in the direction of the scream and stopped when they reached a dead end.

94

"It doesn't go any further," Vance remarked and pounded on the wall.

"Maybe a concealed lever," Hailey suggested.

They could hear something large moving within the tunnel. The sound was closing in behind them. All four looked around and came to the same conclusion to what they were hearing.

"We need to get the hell out of here," Vance quickly announced.

"What about the woman?" Skyler suddenly asked.

"Wake up, man," Logan cried out with conviction. "She's dead!"

"He's right, Skyler," Hailey informed him and clutched his arm. "We have to go--now."

They turned and hurried along the torch lit tunnel, revealing tunnels branching off in many directions. They could hear snarling and movement from all around them. All four ran in the direction of the opening. As Hailey looked behind them, she saw a beast running for them. It was going to reach them before they found the exit. The beast suddenly stopped and slowly backed away while snarling. Marcus appeared in the tunnel near the entrance, startling them. All four cried out then stared at the head of security. He stared back at them with surprise and possible anger.

"You shouldn't be in here," Marcus informed them. "The mineshafts are dangerous."

Skyler cast looks from Logan to Hailey. She saw Skyler raise his brows in suggestion to Marcus' sudden appearance just when they needed him. Hailey avoided looking at Skyler. She no longer wanted to entertain his fantasies; she just wanted to get as far away from the mineshaft and whatever caused the woman to scream.

Chapter Eighteen

Hailey and Skyler sat on the sofa in the living room of her suite with drinks in their hands. Logan leaned against the portable bar and refilled his own glass. There was an unusual silence among the three as they watched Vance pace before the balcony door. He repeatedly shook his head and looked at them as if they were crazy. Hailey wondered how long it would be until he actually spoke after Skyler told his nearly unbelievable retelling of Logan's fairy tale.

"Do you know how insane you sound?" Vance demanded, finally breaking the silence. "I can't believe I'm still standing here listening to the three of you."

"I walked on a rope one hundred yards above a ravine," Logan announced, astonished by his own words. "No, scratch that. I *ran* across a rope above the ravine."

"So you have good balance," Vance replied and cocked his head while grinning mockingly. "That doesn't make you a mystical warrior."

"You may not be willing to accept the fact that you're a part of this team," Logan informed him, "but you have to admit, what happened today was some pretty serious shit. You can't explain it, so you don't want to believe it."

"I don't want to believe it, because I'm not insane," Vance launched back. He indicated Hailey without looking at her and raised a brow. "Your magical princess isn't saying much. She thinks you're insane too."

Hailey knew she'd been unusually silent throughout the entire Vance initiation. The events of the day had her very confused. She wasn't ruling out the entire thing being just another one of her nightmares.

"I don't know what to think," Hailey replied softly. "Two women are dead, and I'm convinced we may have heard the fate of another. I'm just overwhelmed by all this."

"We need to talk to Marcus," Logan firmly informed the others. "He's vital to our mission."

"Our mission?" Hailey suddenly demanded. "Do we even have a mission?"

"See," Vance scoffed. "I told you she didn't believe you either."

Skyler looked at Logan while completely ignoring Hailey and Vance. "Yeah, and say what?" he demanded while flapping his arms around wildly and nearly spilling his drink. He then tilted his head and widened his eyes dramatically. "By the way, Marcus, you're the chosen Guardian of a magical princess."

"Well," Vance snorted with a humored look, "at least you know how you sound to me."

"So we'll just have to prove it," Logan replied and ignored Vance's comment.

"News flash, piano man; unless you've got some cute parlor tricks, I'm not buying it either," Vance launched back. "Are either of you even listening to yourselves? She's not a magical princess, you're not the Jolly Green Giant, although, you do look a little like Mr. Clean." He then looked at Skyler and waved him off. "And you're just a freak."

Skyler sneered at him and appeared offended. "I don't like that term," he muttered.

"Explain what happened," Logan fired back at Vance. "Explain those creatures."

"Hey," Vance snapped defensively, "I didn't see any creatures. I only heard something in the shadows. For all I know, it could have been a dog. And as far as what happened--*nothing happened!*" He wildly gestured with his drink. "We may or may not have heard a woman being killed." Vance stared at Logan with a serious look and pointed accusingly. "That's what happened."

Hailey groaned softly, stood, and approached Logan at the bar. She set her glass down and allowed him to refill it. He glanced at her several times, as if waiting for her to respond. When she didn't, his disappointment showed.

"Come on, Hailey," Logan announced firmly. "You have to believe this is real. You saw the creatures. You saw actual ghosts. Talk some sense into him."

"I'm not the one who thinks he's some mystic warrior," Vance snapped back at Logan.

Logan frowned and stared at Hailey with a demanding look. "Talk some sense into your Charmer before I charm my foot up his ass."

Hailey wished she knew what to believe. She finally glanced at Vance, still uncertain what she should say regarding what had happened over the last two days. Vance immediately looked away and continued pacing the room. She was suddenly curious. She studied him for a long moment and watched as he cast glances at her but never really looked at her. His behavior had struck her as odd from the beginning, but she had just assumed it was because he had no interest in her. The playing field had changed and any romantic illusions were thrown by the wayside. Why did he still refuse to look at her? She set down her drink and approached him with a curious look on her face. He cast a look, saw her approach, and turned away from her. His actions seemed so natural, yet so unnatural. What was hiding in his eyes that he didn't want her to see?

"Vance, look me in the eyes," she said simply.

"Why?" he scoffed while remaining turned. "What's that going to prove?"

Logan's expression dropped as he stared at them. He suddenly turned arrogant, leaned on the bar, and tilted his head. "What's the big deal, man? Just look at her."

Skyler slowly sat forward and watched intently as if finally understanding. Vance groaned with disgust then turned to face Hailey and attempted to look into her eyes. She saw something strange in his eyes, as if his world shattered. He immediately looked away and ran his trembling fingers vigorously through his hair. All three stared at him with the same look of astonishment.

"Why can't you look me in the eyes?" Hailey asked, clearly surprised by the reaction.

Vance immediately fidgeted and cast a glance back at her. "I don't know. I get this really messed up feeling." He turned oddly defensive. "Not in a sexual sort of way." He shifted uncomfortably and again ran his fingers through his hair, nearly pulling some out. "It's a strange feeling like in that dream I had."

"Dream? What sort of dream?" Skyler suddenly gasped and jumped from his seat.

Vance appeared reluctant to respond and continued his pacing. Skyler crossed the room, joining them near the balcony. Vance was unusually silent a moment then exhaled softly.

"Nine years ago, I was supposed to marry an heiress. I was going to have everything I'd ever wanted, and all I had to do was say 'I do'. I didn't love her, but I wanted to be someone." He hesitated and avoided looking at any of them. "You know; someone important."

Skyler nodded with complete understanding but didn't interrupt him.

"I felt trapped in my own private hell that I'd created," Vance announced. "A few days before the wedding, I had this dream that I had beautiful women crawling all over me. It was the most erotic dream I'd ever had. Then I saw a woman with a brilliant light surrounding her. The light was so bright; I couldn't even look at her. She told me if I went with her, I'd have everything I ever wanted." His voice trailed off with his thoughts. "She pulled me into the light with her--"

There was an odd silence as Vance drifted off into another world. Logan and Skyler stared at him with lusty anticipation to the rest of the story.

"Well?" Logan finally bellowed out breaking the silence. "What happened?"

Vance shrugged. "I woke up."

Logan and Skyler groaned with disappointment. Hailey hid her smile and shook her head at their reactions. She found their boyish fascination humorous.

"I know it sounds crazy, but something happened to me in that dream," he insisted almost defensively. "I woke up feeling *different*." His enthusiasm quickly returned along with his charming smile. "I broke off my engagement, fell into my own fortune, and enjoyed every moment since."

Skyler glared at Hailey and placed a hand on his hip while pointing demandingly at Vance. "He gets hot women and wealth? Feeling a little ripped off here, Hailey."

"Wait," Logan suddenly announced then looked at Hailey as well. "If that dream was your first encounter with Vance, then that means this was predetermined nine years ago."

"No, I met Hailey twelve years ago," Skyler insisted.

"That can't be," Logan said while shaking his head in disbelief. "That would mean I wrote "The Gift" after you'd met her."

Hailey stared at Logan and felt something she hadn't before. It was as if thoughts were coming to her from her subconscious, feeding her stories she wasn't sure she could believe.

"I must have given you the story," she remarked, astonished by her own admission.

Skyler threw his hands in the air excitedly and grinned his pleasure. "Finally! She's a confirmed believer!"

"I don't remember any of it, but there's no other explanation," Hailey informed Skyler then looked back at Logan. "Did your life change at some point?"

Logan leaned on the bar and considered the question only briefly before speaking. "When I was in college, before I wrote the fable, my father was pushing me to become a doctor, but I wanted to be a musician. I remember waking up out of a dead sleep, sitting at the piano, and playing every symphony I'd ever heard. That's when I changed my major." He stared at her and shook his head uncertainly. "But why give me the story to publish?"

Hailey shook her head and shrugged without a clue. She felt like everything was just speculation and couldn't really prove any of it. It again seemed more like a dream than reality, and the words she was speaking weren't even her own. She wondered if she overreacted by encouraging them but somehow couldn't help herself.

"She never knew her destiny," Skyler announced as if picking up some divine inspiration. "Her uncle died unexpectedly when she was young, so everything had to happen while she slept. I was her only link to the rest of you." He looked at Logan. "She chose you to write the story, so you could awaken her subconscious, which you obviously have."

"That means our meeting wasn't accidental at all," Logan suddenly announced.

"It was destined from the beginning. I knew it! We have to talk to Marcus," Skyler insisted with renewed enthusiasm. "Maybe we could combine our powers and communicate with him through our minds or some shit."

Logan glared at him while folding his arms across his chest. "Now I know you aren't suggesting something as pathetic as holding hands in a circle."

"We have to trust our instincts," Hailey replied then extended her hand to them.

Skyler was quick to take her hand. Logan groaned with defeat, joined them, and took her hand. He cast a stern glare at Vance as if commanding him to join in and look stupid with them. Vance rolled his eyes and reluctantly joined hands with them.

"I hope no one walks in and sees this," Vance muttered with disgust.

They shut their eyes and concentrated for only a few minutes, but it seemed like a lifetime. Nothing happened. Logan opened one eye and looked around.

"This is ridiculous," Logan scoffed. "Nothing happened and we look stupid."

Hailey gripped Logan's hand, silencing him. He again shut his eyes. The room suddenly rattled and objects bounced on tables. All four opened their eyes with surprise but didn't release the others' hand. The balcony doors flew open and a gust of wind blew into the room. The fireplace erupted into flames along with every candle, starling all four. Smaller objects levitated from nearby tables. Ivy and vines grew and stretched through the open balcony doors, filling the room. Parrots and cockatoos flew into the suite, circling them and dive-bombing the cat on the nearby chair. The black cat chased after them and leaped at them from its position on the floor, attempting to catch them. Hundreds of butterflies fluttered into the room and landed on all four. It was a strange realization that somehow they were able to create this. All four were overjoyed by what they were doing. The cat danced around on its hind legs and attempted to catch the butterflies.

A colorful parrot landed on Vance's shoulder and flapped its wings. The vines blossomed beautiful flowers and continued to travel the room. Before their eyes, the black cat stretched and transformed into the panther, startling everyone. It was true. Every word of it was true! There was a knock on the door. All four were startled and jumped apart. The levitating objects crashed to the tables, the birds flew out the open balcony doors, and the plant life shriveled and rolled outside. The balcony doors slammed shut with a gust of wind. The panther jumped onto one of the chairs, immediately changing back into the little black cat. They exchanged odd stares. Before anyone could speak, there was a louder more urgent pounding on the door. Hailey hurried to the door and opened it to reveal Marcus. He stood in the doorway with a serious look on his face. Hailey appeared surprised then almost humored to see him. Had they actually succeeded in summoning the Guardian to them?

"Marcus, what brings you here?" she asked while concealing her knowing smile.

"More bad news, I'm afraid," he announced then appeared curious and looked past her. "Did I hear a crash?"

"Yeah, I dropped something," Hailey replied. "I'm a little out of sorts today. What bad news?"

"Another girl has been reported missing."

Hailey felt her heart sink. It was the woman they'd heard screaming in the tunnel. She knew what they heard was Penny meeting her demise.

"I was afraid of that," she replied gently and fought the sick feeling in her stomach. "So you believe me?"

"I never said I didn't."

As she stared at him, she resisted the urge to blurt out everything she knew. With the way Vance had handled the news, she knew they had to proceed more cautiously, especially with someone as serious as Marcus was. She somehow didn't think he'd handle the news very well. She also hated to admit that she found him somewhat intimidating, but she couldn't let that stand in her way. She needed to tell him everything she knew, which included telling him who he really was.

"We need to talk, Marcus," she gently informed him while searching for a way to tell him his destiny.

"I really can't right now," he replied. "Time with this sort of thing is critical. How about this evening? I can meet you in the lounge around seven."

Hailey reluctantly nodded, knowing she couldn't rush the conversation. She would need time to convince him, and he wasn't willing to give her more than a few seconds right now.

"Yeah, that'll be fine," she replied.

They watched Marcus leave the suite. The three men stared at her with surprise that she allowed him to leave without attempting to explain everything.

"You should have been more persistent," Skyler announced firmly. "The fate of this world could be in our hands. This could be the single most important moment in our lives."

The grandfather clock chimed three.

Skyler looked at the clock, appeared horrified, and gasped. "Oh, hell! I'm late for work!"

Skyler bolted for the door, surprising everyone. All three turned and watched him.

"What happened to all that fate of the world bullshit?" Logan demanded.

He looked back at them as he reached the door. "I'm minutes away from being fired," Skyler announced. "We'll save the world at eleven."

Skyler darted from the room.

Vance snorted a soft laugh and tilted his head. "I guess this council meeting has officially been adjourned."

Chapter Nineteen

$\mathcal{I}$t was nearing four o'clock that afternoon. Several guests were enjoying the large pool, hot tub, and outside cabana bar. The younger crowd enjoyed the pool area since the bar was readily available and usually there were one or two waitresses working during the middle of the day. Hailey approached the cabana bar, sat on one of several empty bar stools, and ordered a fruity drink. The guys had managed to wipe out the entire minibar in her suite. She hoped Lucinda wasn't keeping a tab on her in-room bar. As her drink arrived, she caught a glimpse of Brody crossing the terrace and heading in her direction with Rafe in tow. She hoped he wasn't looking for her, although, she did admire how well he'd trained Rafe to follow him around on command. She'd always wanted a dog.

"I've been looking for you, Hailey," Brody announced cheerfully and joined her at the bar. He signaled the bartender for a drink. Apparently, the bartender knew his usual.

"I've been busy," Hailey replied with disinterest and avoided looking at him. She'd had a rough day and wasn't about to take any of Brody's sexual harassment.

"About the other afternoon," he announced. "I'm sorry if I offended you."

She cast a glance at him with some surprise. *If* he had offended her? She was certain he was old enough to know it was offensive to solicit sex during business transactions. Perhaps he was too used to getting his own way. Hailey decided to be the bigger person and make nice.

"If you're truly sorry, I can forgive you," she replied but still couldn't force herself to look at him.

"I'm not usually so *forward*," he announced and fidgeted slightly, acting genuinely bothered by his behavior. "I guess with the way Lucinda was building you up as her 'attractive' assistant, I thought she was sending some coded message." He smiled timidly and straightened. "When you're as rich as I am, you get used to ambitious women handing themselves to you. I don't like that I've become accustomed to doing business that way." Brody raised his drink to her. "And in our future dealings together, you have my permission to tell me when I'm being an ass."

Hailey looked at him with surprise then laughed softly and clinked her drink to his. "Deal."

"Hailey, Darling!" Lucinda cried out. "Here you are--"

Both looked across the terrace and saw Lucinda approach them in her flashy, revealing beach attire. She resembled a movie star from the forties, complete with big hat and sunglasses. She sat next to Hailey on the opposite side of Brody.

"Where have you been?" Lucinda questioned.

The bartender had a drink setting on the bar in front of Lucinda before she could even look at him. She gave the handsome, young bartender a quick once over and smiled her approval, but Hailey was certain she wasn't approving the drink.

"I took a walk," Hailey casually replied.

"You may want to stick close to the resort," Lucinda informed her sternly. "I don't know if you heard, but another girl disappeared. Young, attractive girls both of them." She shook her head then sipped her drink. "If you ask me, there's a pervert on the loose. I'll have Marcus' head if he doesn't find those girls and put an end to this insanity immediately."

"Have you seen Marcus?" Hailey suddenly asked, showing interest for the first time.

"No, but I'm sure he has his hands full with those missing girls," Lucinda replied firmly. "He'd better, if he knows what's good for him."

"I saw him talking to the staff," Brody informed Hailey. "One of the cleaning ladies saw a girl go into the basement. He was going to check it out."

"Now why the hell would a young woman be going into that dirty, disgusting basement?" Lucinda suddenly asked.

"Rumor has it some of the guests were secretly meeting in the laundry room to play poker," Brody remarked.

"I need to speak to Marcus," Hailey announced now preoccupied and stood, having barely touched her drink.

"In the basement?" Lucinda squawked then shook her head. "Absolutely not. It's dark, cluttered, and creepy down there. I won't allow you to risk it, especially with a pervert on the loose."

"Take Rafe with you," Brody announced without hesitation. "He needs to be kept busy or his sunny disposition turns questionable."

Lucinda gave Brody a disapproving glare. "I wish you wouldn't encourage her, Nevin."

Brody chuckled playfully at her comment then looked at Rafe and signaled him. He immediately approached.

"Stay with Ms. Aramis," Brody announced firmly. "Make sure nothing happens to her."

Rafe nodded without question or concern. Hailey was nearly stunned by what just happened. Did Brody just appoint Rafe as her baby-sitter?

"Thanks--" she said then muttered under her breath, "I think."

Hailey walked across the terrace and entered the lobby from the poolside entrance with Rafe following her. She glanced back at him several times. It felt creepy having him following her around in silence, as was his usual manner. She finally realized she no longer wanted a dog. Hailey wondered if he'd stop outside the ladies' restroom, or if he'd actually follow her inside. She considered testing the theory for her own amusement then saw Logan talking to Skyler at the front desk. Hailey abruptly stopped and turned to face Rafe behind her. He stopped almost in sync with her. She was impressed with how well he anticipated her movements. Although, it was somewhat creepy at the same time.

"Give me a minute, okay?"

Rafe obediently waited by the far end of the desk but kept an eye on her as she approached Skyler and Logan. She had to admit, he did take instructions well. If she didn't know better, she'd be a little turned on by how attentive he was. Logan and Skyler eyed Rafe suspiciously.

"What's with rent-a-killer?" Skyler asked.

Hailey held back her snicker. "Brody loaned him to me for my protection."

"Yeah? And who's going to protect you from him?" Logan muttered to her.

"Brody had heard Marcus went into the basement to check out a lead," Hailey informed them. "I thought if I could get him alone, he'd listen to me."

"I have an hour until my set," Logan informed her. "I'll go with you."

"I want to go too," Skyler whined.

"You have to work," Logan scolded.

"I get a dinner break," Skyler announced. "Merle will watch the desk for me." Skyler looked at the older bellman across the lobby. "Merle, I'm taking dinner."

Merle looked at his watch with bewilderment. It wasn't even four o'clock.

Hailey studied both men then casually shrugged. "I certainly don't need Rafe now," she remarked. "I'm sure he'll be happy to be off the hook."

She approached Rafe with Skyler and Logan in tow. Rafe casually leaned on the corner of the desk and eyed the trio approaching him.

"My friends are going with me to find Marcus," she announced. "You don't need to come along after all."

Rafe eyed Logan and Skyler, immediately making both uncomfortable. He looked back at Hailey with little emotion.

"I have my orders."

His reaction surprised her. She thought he'd be happy to go back to his regular gig. Hailey looked at Skyler and Logan and raised her brows. Neither man appeared pleased with the outcome. The three reluctantly walked toward the connecting corridor with Rafe bringing up the rear just a few feet behind them.

"Hmm," Logan muttered, "this is creepy. Usually when a suit is following a brother, someone's getting knifed."

"I don't know," Skyler teased. "I think he's like a little lost puppy following us home from school."

"That's one serious puppy," Hailey muttered just loud enough for them to hear. "Give me a few minutes to lose the hired goon then I'll meet you in the basement." As they approached the ladies' restroom, Hailey stopped. "I need to visit the girl's room," she announced to the guys. "I'll catch up with you."

Logan gave a half-hearted salute. Both men continued along the corridor. Hailey turned to Rafe and held up a warning finger.

"*You* wait out here," she announced firmly.

He cocked his head to the side and gave her a stern glare. She hated to admit it, but she was almost enjoying messing with him. Hailey entered the elegant ladies' restroom. It contained an outer sitting area with wicker and leather furniture and a long vanity with a wall-to-wall mirror for those who required extensive primping. There were baskets filled with amenities ranging from perfume to make-up and hairspray. She passed through the sitting area and entered the washroom area, which consisted of a long row of marble sinks and fancy little towels in a basket. Hailey was beginning to wonder if she'd ever reach the actual toilet area. She made a mental note to herself to have a peek inside the men's restroom. She didn't doubt they had a television and bar.

Hailey finally entered the elegant toilet area with at least ten stalls encased in tile. The private doors went down to the floor, completely enclosing each individual toilet. She approached the stained glass window along the back wall. Thankfully, it could be opened with plenty of room for her to squeeze through. Beyond the ladies' restroom window was an area restricted for maintenance, but it would only be a short walk to the back entrance of the spa, taking her close to one of the basement entrances.

†

*H*ailey, having made her great escape, hurried down the fire stairs to join the guys in the basement. It was almost fun eluding Rafe. She was certain he was going to be pissed, but being pissed was his usual state anyway. She finally reached the basement and looked around. She appeared to be by herself. Lucinda had been right; the basement was creepy.

"Skyler? Logan?"

There was no response. They wouldn't have gone far. It hadn't taken her that long to slip away from Rafe. Hailey approached the wine cellar just a couple feet away. She didn't know why, but she felt she was being followed. She was about to turn when a hand grabbed her shoulder. Hailey screamed and turned to see Vance behind her. He chuckled softly, having startled her, and then turned serious.

"Serves you right. What are you doing down here by yourself anyway?" Vance demanded.

Skyler and Logan darted out from the wine cellar and stared at Hailey with Vance. Both men relaxed.

Vance looked at the others then back at Hailey. "I must have missed the memo announcing this meeting."

"There's a subtle irony that we all gathered here for the occasion," Logan remarked.

Hailey looked at Logan, despite still holding her chest, and extended her hand. "Lead the way, Mr. Tour Director."

Chapter Twenty

Several large storage rooms were cluttered with tall rows of shelves filled with boxes. Each holding area looked similar to the next. Most of the storage rooms also contained old furniture and various unwanted or damaged items from guestrooms. The basement was a holding tank for every piece of junk from around the resort. Most should have been discarded, but someone seemed to have a tough time letting go of clutter. Garbage removal, particularly larger items, was a little more difficult on the island. Hailey didn't doubt that somewhere toward the island's interior there was a dump for larger appliances and mattresses. Lucinda's money troubles were beginning to show. Hailey and the three men looked around the cluttered room in which they stood. Their frustration was clearly showing on their faces. They were no closer to finding Marcus than they were forty minutes ago.

"A person could hide for weeks down here," Vance remarked as he ran his finger over a chair covered in a layer of dust.

"We're running out of basement, and my lunch break is nearly over," Skyler informed them.

"Maybe we missed him," Logan announced. "Maybe he was never down here to begin with."

"Let's go back to the laundry room," Hailey suggested. "If we don't find him there, then we'll call it an afternoon."

All four turned toward the door and nearly collided with Marcus, who had mysteriously appeared seemingly out of nowhere. He stared at the four, surprised to see them in an area clearly off limits to hotel guests.

"What are you doing down here?" Marcus suddenly demanded with irritation in his voice.

All four exchanged looks. The three men then stared at Hailey and encouraged her to speak to the head of security. Hailey suddenly felt uncomfortable with what she needed to say. With the way Vance had reacted, she didn't see Marcus just accepting his destiny without some convincing. His intimidating look wasn't helping release her tensions any either.

"There's something important we have to tell you," Hailey announced then held her breath a moment. "I know you're not going to believe any of it, but you need to hear us out."

Hailey recapped everything that had happened between the four of them since their arrival. Marcus listened in near silence and just stared with his mouth hanging open. His lack of comment was concerning, but it was possible he was just being polite. When Hailey had finally finished her story, which included him as the chosen Guardian, Marcus stared at them and appeared at a loss for words. All four watched him and awaited some reaction. After his uncomfortable stare, any reaction would do.

"I think you're all out of your minds," Marcus finally bellowed out then glared at Skyler. "Did you infect them with your wild tales?"

"Actually, they were Logan's wild tales," Vance announced and offered a cheap grin.

"We can prove it, Marcus," Hailey informed him.

"Really? How?"

Hailey looked at the guys, took a deep breath, and extended her hands to them. They reluctantly clasped hands and concentrated while Marcus watched with apparent doubt to their sanity. The lights flickered and the room vibrated. Several rats scurried past Marcus' feet, startling him. Skyler's expression turned serious, despite his eyes being shut.

Skyler's voice shouted in Hailey's mind. *"Hailey, I sense something evil nearby!"*

Hailey gasped with surprise and pulled away. His voice echoing in her mind startled her. The others broke concentration and looked at her, awaiting an explanation. Hailey and Skyler stared at each other. She couldn't believe she'd heard his thoughts. Judging by his reaction, he was amazed she'd heard him as well.

"Okay, *that* was strange," Marcus announced and now seemed open to the notion that they weren't insane. "Not saying I believe a word that you've told me, but what exactly is the role of this Guardian?"

"The Guardian is Hailey's protector," Logan replied then appeared slightly embarrassed. "We're all kind of learning as we go."

"Skyler sensed something," Hailey informed them with concern. "There's still a chance Penny's alive. We need to find her. She was down here."

"How do you know that?" Marcus asked.

"I just do," Hailey informed him. "You have to trust me, there isn't much time."

Hailey left the storage room with the three men following her. Marcus gave in and hurried after them. The five walked in silence along the basement corridor. Skyler stopped in the corridor and stared at the old elevator several yards away, where he witnessed a tiny, glowing light.

"There's a spirit by the elevator," Skyler informed them.

Hailey looked at the elevator and saw Penny's spirit staring back at her. Her heart sank. It was too late for Penny, as she had already feared. As Hailey approached, Penny stepped into the elevator through the closed doors. Hailey stopped and stared at the elevator a moment. She looked back at the others.

"Penny took that elevator," Hailey announced.

Marcus appeared surprised. "How--?"

When the elevator doors opened, Hailey hurried inside without waiting for Marcus to finish his question. The others followed with some apprehension. They rode the rickety, old elevator down to the sub-basement. The five stepped out of the elevator and walked through the dimly lit, sub-basement corridor. Penny's spirit floated ahead of them in the distance, guiding Hailey. They followed her for a few minutes along several corridors.

"I never knew this existed," Logan remarked.

"I'd actually forgotten it was here," Marcus informed them. "I hadn't been down here since I first started working here. Some of

112

the old security guards felt it best to pretend the entire area didn't exist. For a long time, it had been sealed. I wonder who unsealed it."

"Well, I hope you know how to get out of here," Vance informed them. "We've made at least six turns already and all these corridors look the same to me."

"I'm more worried about where we're going than how to get back," Marcus announced then looked at Hailey. "Are you sure your ghost is reliable?"

Hailey glared at Marcus. He seemed puzzled by her look. They approached an intersection, which led both to the right and to the left. Hailey suddenly stopped and looked around. Penny's ghost had vanished.

"She's gone," Hailey announced with surprise.

A low snarl echoed through the dark corridors, starling all five. They looked around for any indication of where the sound had originated.

"Uh, which direction did that come from?" Logan nervously asked.

"Is that one of your beasts?" Marcus suddenly asked.

"Sure sounds like it," Hailey muttered.

Glowing eyes approached them from behind. They were immediately alerted to the creature as they stared at the red eyes moving closer. The five then turned to the connecting corridor. There were more glowing eyes approaching from the opposite direction.

"Okay, Marcus, you're up, brother," Logan announced and stepped behind him.

Marcus appeared stunned by Logan's comment. He removed his gun and nervously looked around. There was more snarling and more glowing eyes from the right and left corridor. The five slowly moved closer together with their backs to one another. They were trapped in the corridor hub by approaching creatures from all directions.

"Now's as good a time as any to see what we can do," Hailey announced.

They grasped one another's hands behind them. Marcus eyed them, replaced his gun to his holster, and then joined them. They attempted to concentrate. Several lights brightened and momentarily revealed the approaching beasts then the lights exploded, returning the corridors to near darkness.

"The hell with this--" Marcus released their hands, removed his gun, and fired into the darkness at the glowing eyes.

One of the beasts leaped for them. The black panther leaped out of the darkness, tackled the beast to the floor, and fought with it. Whether it had been part of its plan, the panther had cleared an escape route for them.

"This way!" Hailey cried out.

They ran down the only safe corridor and away from the creatures. Marcus fired shots at the beasts until he ran out of bullets then ran after the others. Another set of glowing eyes appeared before them. All five stopped and looked back. More glowing eyes approached them from behind. Marcus looked to a door alongside them and violently kicked it several times. Vance slowly lowered himself to the floor and stared at the glowing eyes. The creature came out of the darkness then stopped and snarled at him. Hailey heard the faint sound of parting air, which grew louder. A swarm of bats suddenly appeared. Everyone except Vance cried out. The bats swarmed the beasts. Marcus finally managed to kick open the door. Vance cast Hailey and Skyler into the dark room. One of the beasts leaped for Vance. Logan dove onto Vance and tackled him to the floor. The creature was already in mid-leap and collided with the first creature. A third creature appeared.

"Run!" Marcus shouted.

Vance and Logan ran down the corridor with Marcus behind them and the creature on his heels. Two creatures bolted into the dark room after Hailey and Skyler. Hailey and Skyler fumbled across the room and collided with objects scattered about in the darkness. The glowing eyes grew closer, frightening both. Candles within the room suddenly erupted into flames and brightened the entire area. The room was filled with furniture from the forties. Skyler grabbed an old umbrella, turned toward the two creatures, and took a fighting stance.

"Run, Hailey! I'll hold them off!"

Hailey eyed the umbrella that he held like a sword and frowned at him. "Don't be stupid."

The creatures snarled and closed in. Hailey looked around the room while Skyler gripped his umbrella. The room suddenly vibrated causing both to look around.

"What are you doing?" Skyler cried out.

"I'm not doing that!"

An entire shelf creaked, crashed down, and narrowly missed the first creature. Hailey ran across the room for an antique sword in a decorative box. The second beast bolted after her. She grabbed the sword. It was bolted inside the box! Hailey cried out with surprise and alarm. The creature lunged for her. She ran for the door to escape it. As the first creature leaped for Skyler, he shut his eyes and thrust forward with the umbrella. It caught the beast in the mouth, causing it to leap back with surprise and pain. Skyler opened his eyes and saw the beast swatting at its mouth. Hailey ran for the doorway, stumbled over an old trunk in the darkness, and fell to the floor near the doorway. She flipped onto her back, knowing the creature had been right behind her. She screamed as she helplessly watched the creature leap for her. A hand caught the large beast by the throat and stopped it mid-air. The three hundred pound creature thrashed against the grip on its throat. Hailey rolled into a crouched position and saw Rafe standing behind her while holding the beast in the air by its thick throat. That Rafe didn't appear strained by the weight of the thrashing creature was startling.

The beast slashed its claws at him, nearly scratching his arm. Rafe coiled back and projected the creature across the room with amazing force, causing it to strike the shelves near Skyler. Skyler ducked and opened his umbrella to shield him. A third creature leaped through the doorway behind Rafe. Rafe didn't even look behind him. He spun into a high, roundhouse kick and struck it in the head, dropping it. The creature near Skyler charged for Rafe. Rafe moved into a series of kicks and repeatedly struck it. The creature within the broken shelves recovered and leaped for him as he fought the third creature. As the charging creature attempted to pounce on him, he flipped and kicked the beast in the underbelly. The first creature recovered and came back at him. Rafe remained in a crouched position with one hand to the floor and stared at the approaching beast. It snarled and stared into his eyes. Rafe's expression never changed. The creature slowly backed out of the room. The remaining two beasts scrambled to their feet, shook off, and ran after the first creature. Rafe straightened and stared at the doorway. He seemed annoyed more than anything else. Hailey and Skyler appeared stunned while staring at him.

"It's him--" Hailey gasped softly.

"It can't be him," Skyler muttered to her and defiantly shook his head. "I never would've allowed that."

Rafe turned toward them and glared at Hailey with a look of annoyance. "You ditched me."

Hailey was stunned by the comment as she stared at him. "That's all you have to say?"

Rafe reconsidered his comment while maintaining his annoyance and demandingly raised his brows. "Don't *ever* do that again."

"We were nearly killed by three snarling beasts," Skyler exploded. "Don't you find that even a little disturbing?"

"Maybe you'll remember that the next time you consider ditching me."

Rafe turned back toward the doorway, showing little emotion toward what had just happened, while Hailey and Skyler exchanged stunned looks. Logan, Vance, and Marcus ran into the room and stopped when they saw Hailey and Skyler with Rafe. All three men were out of breath.

"Is everyone okay?" Marcus asked.

Skyler and Hailey slowly nodded, although neither could take their eyes off Rafe, who casually brushed some dirt from his expensive jacket. He put his finger through a small tear on his sleeve and groaned with disgust.

"That's great," Rafe muttered.

The three men eyed Rafe with distrust then looked back at Hailey and Skyler.

"They had us cornered then they just took off," Logan informed them while shaking his head. "I don't know why."

The black cat trotted into the room and ran for Hailey. She caught the cat as it leaped into her arms.

"Maybe we should regroup at the bar and have a couple of shots," Vance suggested.

"Seriously, let's get out of here before *they* regroup," Logan cried out.

Chapter Twenty-one

The patio and pool area was abandoned during the late dinner hour. The only people remaining on the patio were the six sitting at the cabana. Hailey was having a difficult time dealing with the realization that Penny was dead, and their venture into the basement only proved they had no clue what they were doing or if there even was a mission. The creatures were clearly too much for them to destroy on their own. The resort didn't need warriors; it needed exterminators. The bartender filled shot glasses for everyone, including Marcus. Marcus drank the entire contents of his shot glass and waited until the bartender was preoccupied with other duties before speaking.

"I'm going to seal off the entire sub-basement and see if we can stop these things from making their way into the hotel," Marcus informed them. "When I get back, someone had better tell me what's really going on at my hotel." His look was stern. "I don't want anyone breathing a word of this until I figure out what's going on here."

Everyone except Rafe nodded in unison then watched Marcus return to the hotel lobby through the less traveled side door. He was having a difficult time dealing with what he'd witnessed. They all were. Hailey, Skyler, Vance, and Logan waited until Marcus was gone then exchanged looks while casting glances at Rafe, who stood near the far end of the cabana bar, keeping to himself. Rafe glared at them in response.

"Maybe I should speak to Rafe alone," Hailey gently suggested to the others.

The three men were more than happy to grab their drinks and leave her alone with Rafe. Hailey waited for the three to disappear inside before approaching Rafe at the far end of the bar. As she sat alongside him, he cast a glare at her. He sipped his expensive brandy and set the glass on the bar. She knew he was going to be difficult no matter what she said. Hailey pondered their situation for a moment then eyed his glass of brandy. She picked it up and took a sip from it, catching his attention. She made a face and returned the glass to the bar. He gave her a puzzled look then shook his head and ignored her.

"How long have you been able to fight like that?" she asked.

"Why do you ask?"

He really wasn't going to make it easy on her, and she wasn't sure there was a good way to approach the subject, especially with him. She saw only one way to deal with the delicate conversation. Head on.

"You were given a gift when you were chosen as the Guardian," Hailey finally blurted it out.

"I don't remember accepting that particular position, and no one's ever given me anything," Rafe informed her as he cast a glare at her. "My abilities and talents are my own."

Hailey stared at him with surprise. What he said almost didn't make any sense.

"You mean you've fought like that before?"

"Of course I have," he scoffed. "But as far as being some chosen member for that pathetic team of misfits; that's not happening."

"It's your destiny."

He didn't bother looking at her. "Not if I don't choose it to be." Rafe casually stood, finished his drink, and finally met her gaze. "Do yourself a favor. Don't play superhero. You'll only get hurt."

She knew he wanted to walk away, but for some reason, he didn't. He seemed compelled to stare at her as if waiting for her to stop him. She didn't disappoint.

"I know you stole Lucinda's necklace."

He showed no reaction, although he didn't deny it. "Is that what you intend to tell Marcus?"

"I don't intend to tell Marcus anything," she replied. "For whatever reason, fate brought us together. We can't do this without you."

He suddenly snorted a laugh. "You may need me, but I certainly don't need any of you."

Rafe walked away from Hailey and headed onto the beach, disappearing into the sunset. She found it difficult to believe she still wanted him, but his raw sex appeal just kept drawing her in.

✝

*T*he beach was quiet and abandoned as the sun was setting. The sunset glistened off the ocean, lending a romantic overtone. It was another breathtaking evening in paradise. In another hour, guests would return from dinner for romantic, moonlit strolls. Rafe sat casually reclined on the large rock not far from the surf. Hailey approached and stared out to the ocean in silence. She didn't bother looking at him. He'd proven she couldn't say anything that would change his view about her, the guys, or their unique situation. He cast a casual glance at her, although he didn't make an effort to move.

"If you've come out here to change my mind, you're wasting your time."

Hailey still didn't look at him. "I know that," she informed him. "No point wasting my breath."

"Never stopped any woman before," he muttered.

She continued to stare out to the ocean rather than remark on his sexist comment. Her lack of interest seemed to peak Rafe's curiosity. Hailey slowly lifted her hand and extended it toward the ocean. She shut her eyes and drew a deep breath. The waves gently crashed to shore then rolled back out again. They continued to roll out further and further from shore without returning. The sound of the rolling ocean was loud and unusual. Hailey's hand trembled as she gasped softly while concentrating. Rafe slowly sat up and watched the water retreat with a bewildered look. A large wave nearly ten feet high formed beyond the horizon. Hailey lowered her hand and exhaled as if she'd been punched in the stomach. The large wave hurled to shore and crashed harshly past her and the rock upon which Rafe sat. The water ran past her as high as her knees then rolled back out again at its normal rate. Hailey drew a deep, shaken breath. It had taken a lot out of her, and she was almost surprised by what she was able to do. She glanced at Rafe with little expression.

"Maybe I don't need you after all," she remarked then turned and walked back to the hotel.

She couldn't admit that her legs were weak and her lungs hurt. Her arms felt as if she'd lifted a thousand pounds, but she'd made her point. She just hoped her point made some impression on the hardened man.

†

*T*he lobby was moderately busy for early evening as a flux of guests were finishing dinner and either returning to their rooms or heading outside to take nightly strolls on the beach. Cass was tending the front desk, appearing mostly bored. She attempted to hide her steamy romance novel beneath the desk as guests passed. Desi approached the desk in her finest, formfitting red dress and signature high heels. Despite having dressed for a fun evening, her look conveyed deep concern. Cass quickly hid her book and offered a cheerful smile to the approaching woman.

"Good evening," Cass announced, enthusiastic for something to do.

"Is Marcus around?" Desi asked without returning the cheerful greeting.

Cass noted the expression on Desi's face and immediately turned concerned. "Is everything okay?"

"I think I should talk to Marcus about the disappearance of my friends," Desi replied.

"Have they found them?" Cass asked with great interest. "I was sure they'd turn up--"

"No, they didn't," she responded curtly and grew more impatient. "I heard some rumors about guests sneaking into the laundry room to play poker. I think Penny may have followed Amy's guy into the basement. I think I should report it to Marcus."

"Of course," Cass announced and picked up the phone without hesitation. "I'll get someone from security right away."

Desi paced the area before the front desk while Cass spoke with security on the phone. Less than five minutes had passed before Delaney crossed the lobby and approached Desi at the desk.

"It's Desi, right?" Delaney announced politely although he was obviously concerned by Cass's call. "Cass tells me you may have some information on your friends' disappearance."

"The bartender told me Penny saw the man Amy left with the other night, and that she took off after him," Desi informed him. "I ran into a guy who said he was playing poker in the laundry room. He said he saw a girl matching Penny's description heading into that old elevator in the basement." She wrenched her fingers together and shifted uncomfortably. "I'm concerned Penny confronted this man about Amy, and he did something to her. Those guys playing poker in the laundry room may know something."

"Did you get the name of Amy's date?"

"No, but I can give you a description," she announced. "We were around him a couple of hours that night."

"I have a better idea," Delaney announced with enthusiasm. "Why don't we review some security tapes around the time your friend left the lounge last night? Maybe you'll recognize Amy's date and can point him out. Once we have a face, we'll be able to come up with a name."

"That would be great," Desi replied while releasing a deep sigh of relief.

Delaney offered a gentle smile and extended his hand across the lobby toward the staff wing. Cass watched them leave together then shook her head while frowning.

"Drama queen," she scoffed under her breath then returned to her book.

Chapter Twenty-two

*H*ailey slept peacefully beneath the covers on her bed as moonlight was cast upon her through the crudely fixed balcony doors. The black cat slept curled by her feet. A dark figure hovered over her, casting a shadow across her. Her eyes opened as if she felt the presence of someone. Lucinda's necklace dangled before her face. Hailey slowly sat up and looked at Rafe holding the necklace from where he stood alongside her bed. She was puzzled by his actions. It wasn't as if she had any real proof he took the hideous thing, so why admit his guilt?

"Why are you returning Lucinda's necklace?" she asked while squinting at his outline through the moonlight.

"To put things straight. I don't want to return to that life," he casually replied then appeared curious. "How did you know it was me?"

She hid her smile and laughed softly at his question. "Seriously? As close as you were, you didn't think I'd smell your cologne?" She continued to stare at him. "I'll admit it did take me a while to figure out where I'd smelled that scent. I wasn't positive it was you until I tasted your brandy. That's when I knew. It was the same alcohol on your breath that night."

He stared at her and showed little reaction to the comment. "I knew I should have stayed retired," he muttered. "I'm getting sloppy." Rafe appeared curious. "If you suspected, why didn't you tell Marcus?"

"I almost did, but something troubled me," she informed him. "I couldn't stop wondering, why would you steal one worthless, old necklace?"

Rafe casually sat on the edge of the bed while staring at her. She watched him closely. His presence on her bed made her heart pound, but she wasn't sure why. She knew she was over him. Now if she could only convince the aching in her body--

"I don't really know. I've seen Lucinda wearing this worthless piece of junk a dozen times. It's not like it's worth anything," he announced. "For some odd reason, at dinner the other night, I just felt the need to take it. Honestly, I wanted to take it and smash it, you know, just to be a prick."

"You really don't know why you risked getting caught to steal that thing?"

"Maybe I was just scratching an itch," he replied without care. "I couldn't get police work after my discharge from the Marines. There were too many questions, so I became a cat burglar and jewel thief instead. The pay was good, but the hours sucked, so I gave it up a few years ago."

"I can't accept that you were just scratching an itch. I have to believe there's more to it than that," she informed him. "You need to hide that necklace for now."

"I didn't come here to be part of your team."

"And you didn't come here to return the necklace," she countered while raising her brows.

Rafe placed the necklace in his pocket and stared at her a moment in silence. His look intrigued her because she couldn't read it.

"I did, but amuse me with your version," he replied.

Hailey hugged her knees to her chest over the covers and studied him. "When did you first notice your unique abilities?"

Rafe appeared tense for the first time and seemed reluctant to share his story with her. He took a deep breath while staring at her and finally spoke.

"My commander sent my unit on a suicide mission. I was shot while trying to save my buddy," he replied. "I was convinced I'd died. I saw a bright light. A voice called me into it and everything. When I woke, enemy soldiers were standing around me. I don't know what happened, but I displayed combat techniques I never knew existed." There was a long pause. "When the rest of my unit finally found me, I'd taken out six enemy soldiers and had been shot and stabbed several times. The doctors didn't know how I managed to survive." He drew a deep breath and drifted out a moment. "It wouldn't be the first time I cheated death."

She stared at him a moment in silence and was curious about what he'd left out. The thoughts racing through her mind were little more than faint dreams from a long time ago, and she wasn't even sure if she'd actually dreamt them. Hailey decided to leave it to chance and play her hand, even though she didn't know what cards she held.

"What about the woman in the light?"

He tensed while staring at her, almost showing his surprise to the comment, and then immediately covered his reaction with his usual arrogance.

"I never said there was a woman in the light."

His reaction almost confirmed she hadn't dreamt it. She was remembering experiences, possibly out of body experiences. Her dreams weren't just dreams after all. The thought made her slightly tense, but she needed to press.

"She kissed you, didn't she?"

Rafe's expression dropped and, for a moment, he was unable to speak. He couldn't control his startled reaction, which told her everything she needed to know.

"How could you possibly know that?"

"Because that's how it happened in my dream eight years ago," Hailey informed him. "Most of it is fuzzy, but it's slowly coming back to me. It took years to find the perfect man to be the Guardian." She shifted slightly at the thoughts racing through her mind. "Skyler considered you to be 'tainted and corruptible', but I knew you were the one."

Rafe stared at her a moment, not knowing how to respond. His harsh expression returned as if on cue.

"If all of this is true, then you've misjudged me," he boldly announced. "That pitiful team you've assembled will undoubtedly abandon you at the first sniff of danger."

"You're wrong."

"You need to stop playing games before you get one of those idiots killed," he boldly announced.

"Could it be you actually care about those idiots?" Hailey remarked.

He immediately turned defensive. "I don't care about anyone," Rafe informed her. "I've lost everyone I've ever given a damn about. That tends to sour a man."

"What happened on that mission wasn't your fault," she replied. "You have to know that."

"You want to psychoanalyze me?" he demanded. "After my high school graduation, I crashed my car killing four of my closest friends. Despite what little I remember about the accident, killing your friends isn't something easily forgotten. That's why I joined the Marines. I had to escape what I'd done. Then I lost nearly half my platoon in a senseless battle." His glare was stern. "That's what happens when you care about others. When you get those guys killed, I doubt you'll be able to live with the guilt."

"Which is why you're here," she casually replied.

Rafe leaned over her while uncomfortably close. His closeness caused her heart to pound with anticipation.

"You want to know why I came here tonight?" he demanded while staring into her eyes and placed his mouth close to hers. "I came here to con my way into your bed. That's the man I am."

Rafe pulled back just far enough to stare into her eyes but maintained his closeness. As she stared back into his eyes, the comment about seducing her sent shockwaves through her body and caused her heart to race. She tightened her grip on her knees just to keep from reacting. Hailey wanted desperately to throw her arms around him and feel his body against hers. She shamed herself for secretly wishing he actually had come to seduce her, but it wasn't his intention, and she knew it. Thankfully, he couldn't see the redness in her cheeks or read the lust in her eyes. She had to hide her true feelings from him.

"If you came here to seduce me, what's stopping you?" she asked while pulling off a casual lack of reaction, despite how she really felt. "You obviously have the upper hand."

Rafe tensed to the come-hither comment while staring into her eyes. His gaze briefly strayed to her mouth. She could almost hear his heart pounding in his chest along with his rapid breathing. For a moment, she was uncertain of his reaction as her body ached for what would certainly be a wild night of passion. She still wanted him, and she didn't care if it was just a brief fling. Everyone was entitled to one fling in his or her life. To her disappointment but not surprisingly, he pulled away from her and composed himself.

His look turned unnaturally hostile. "I don't screw mentally unstable women," he scoffed, although his voice lacked the necessary conviction.

Rafe sprang up from the bed and headed for the balcony doors in a little more of a hurry than usual. She had successfully called his bluff, and he knew it. She watched as he effortlessly jumped onto the half wall to the balcony and leaped to his own balcony next door. Although disappointed that she wouldn't feel his body against hers, Hailey smiled nonetheless.

"Welcome aboard," she announced softly.

Chapter Twenty-three

The faint glow of candles surrounding the altar partially brightened the large, eerie chamber. Desi lie on the altar in her lacy, red bra and matching panties. Blood streaked the side of her head from a scalp laceration. She slowly woke, realized she was shackled by her wrists and ankles to the stone slab, and immediately fought her restraints. Faint snarling was heard in the darkness not far from the altar. She gasped with alarm and looked around. A soft female groan followed by a giggle was heard. Desi again yanked on the shackles while attempting to see beyond the faint candlelight.

"What are you doing?" she demanded, although her tone was frightened. "This isn't funny. Let me go!"

"I believe she's awake," came the soft, female murmur.

Desi strained to follow the voice in the darkness. The woman was heard pacing the back of the room.

"Who are you?" Desi cried out.

Cass stepped into the dim glow surrounding the altar and smiled sweetly at Desi.

"You?" Desi suddenly gasped with a look of surprise on her face. "But the last thing I remember--"

Delaney appeared behind Cass and shared her devious grin. "I don't think she remembers being hit after she entered the security office," he informed Cass while gently cocking his head.

"I'm just glad you didn't accidentally kill her like you did that other girl," Cass boldly remarked without looking back at him. She mocked Desi with her smile. "Don't need to leave more leftovers for the snappers."

Desi stared at them, not understanding the comment, but she didn't appear exactly curious at the moment either.

"I don't think she's met a snapper yet," he remarked then gave a general nod into the darkness.

One of the large, black creatures stepped into the light from the candles. It snarled then licked its sharp, fanged teeth. Desi cried out and pulled sharply against her shackles. Cass placed her hand on Desi's forehead and shushed her softly, as if attempting to comfort her.

"Shh, it's okay," Cass cooed softly. "I won't let that nasty snapper eat you."

"Please, let me go," Desi gasped while not only struggling against her restraints but also the hand touching her head.

Delaney moved against Cass from behind and ran his hands firmly along her hips and thighs. His hands pulled her skirt slow and seductively upward. Cass caressed Desi's shoulder and sensually ran her hand along her arm to her shackled wrist. Desi stared in horror and silence as Delaney bent Cass over the altar in a compromising position. Cass pressed her face against Desi's bra clad chest and ran her lips down her arm to the restrained wrist that she caressed. Delaney grinded slow and firmly against Cass, causing her to cry out softly in ecstasy. Desi stared with her mouth hanging open in disbelief and horror to what she was witnessing.

Cass groaned her pleasure and lifted her head slightly to meet Desi's stunned gaze. Cass smiled, revealing sharp fangs. Desi saw the fangs and screamed with horror. Cass's fangs punctured Desi's inner arm just above the shackles, tearing through her flesh and ripping into her veins. Desi screamed to the sharp, sudden pain. Cass groaned her pleasure while slurping the rapidly spilling blood from the screaming woman's arm. There was nothing refined about lapping up the warm, sticky blood as it pulsated from her vein. The blood covered Cass's entire lower face and ran down her chin. Cass slurped and groaned her intense pleasure as Delaney continued with his duties.

The snapper paced the area near the altar, licking its fangs, and listening intently to the gruesome slurping sound. Desi's screams became dull in comparison to Cass's groans of delight. The snapper waited patiently while watching the scene on the altar. Desi let out a shrill, weak cry, gasped, and fell silent. The snapper sprang to attention. A blood-soaked heart was tossed from the altar. The snapper caught the pulsating organ and gnawed on it with its powerful jaws. It was tough to chew, but the snapper devoured it in only a few seconds. The creature waited patiently for more treats to come its way.

Delaney released Cass and moved alongside Desi's lifeless, blood-soaked body on the altar. Her chest was crudely torn open, revealing a large opening where her heart was once located. Delaney revealed his own fangs and punctured the dead woman's upper inner thigh. He lapped the blood as it more slowly ran from her vein. Cass dove for Desi's neck and tore into her jugular, sucking as much blood as she could. Both were nearly drenched in blood from their chins to their chests. They paused only a moment to lock eyes over the dead, bloodied woman. They smiled lustfully at each other through bloodstained teeth then resumed their feast.

†

After her encounter with Rafe, Hailey found it difficult to go back to sleep. His story, combined with his actions from the other night, invaded her every thought. She hated that he'd successfully turned her on. Hailey walked onto the moonlit beach a little after midnight and attempted to clear her head of Rafe. There appeared to be no one around, and she was enjoying the solitude despite the loud dance music from the lounge. The details of her *first* encounter with Rafe were fuzzy at best. She briefly remembered him. She remembered a dying soldier consumed with anger and hostility after a failed attempt to save his comrade. He was left for dead. He wasn't the first. There were others. She remembered what seemed like dreams of other men who had been near death and were possible candidates for the Guardian. She had to leave them. It was impossible to save them. Only one could be saved, and against Skyler's better judgment, she chose Rafe. Someone approached her from behind while she remained deep in thought. She was suddenly grabbed. Hailey cried out and turned in the sand.

Mel laughed drunkenly while holding her shoes in her hand. "Scared you."

"No shit!"

"You shouldn't be out here alone," Mel announced and remained giddy. "Two women are already missing."

"Yes, Penny and Amy," Hailey informed her while folding her arms across her chest. "Doesn't that bother you?"

"They're not missing," Mel replied and offered a lustful grin. "Tam thinks they met up with some horny, young men. She says it happens all the time."

Hailey wasn't going to argue with Mel in her current, drunken condition. It's not as if it'd do any good anyway. She wouldn't even remember their conversation by morning.

"You're certainly in no condition to be anyone's chaperone," Hailey remarked, "and you have no business being out here alone either."

"Shows what you know," she teased. "I followed you. Sneaked right up behind you. What are you doing?"

"I was hoping to find Skyler," Hailey replied while looking around. "He wasn't in his room, and he sometimes walks the beach when he can't sleep."

"That creepy desk guy?"

Hailey glared at her friend with disapproval. "He's not creepy," she muttered.

"Please! He's the definition of creepy!"

Both heard a low snarl and looked around. Hailey knew exactly what the sound meant. Although neither saw anything, even Mel knew the sound wasn't good.

"What was that?" Mel asked nervously.

"Our cue to move."

Hailey grabbed her arm and hurried her toward the hotel. A beast suddenly cut off their path. Mel screamed and turned toward the ocean. Another beast leaped down from the rocks as a third approached from the woods. With the loud music playing in the lounge, no one would ever hear their screams.

"Skyler, now would be a good time," Hailey called out even though no one was there to hear them.

Hailey grabbed Mel's arm and pulled her toward the cabana. Another beast leaped down from the cabana, stopping the women from reaching the poolside. Mel again screamed. The four beasts closed in.

"What are they?" Mel cried out while staring at the creatures. "What's happening?"

"When you see the signal, run for the hotel and don't look back."

"What signal?"

The panther appeared seemingly out of nowhere and leaped for one of the beasts. Mel screamed as the panther and creature collided, rolling fiercely around the sand.

"Go!"

Mel and Hailey ran for the hotel. The three remaining beasts ran after them. Mel was tackled to the sand by one of the large creatures. Hailey threw herself to the sand and narrowly avoided a second pouncing beast. The first beast grabbed Mel's dress near the back of her neck and dragged her along the sand at top speed. She thrashed and screamed frantically while being dragged toward the woods. Hailey scrambled to her hands and knees and stared helplessly as Mel was pulled onto the path and out of sight. One of the creatures tackled Hailey to the sand, knocking the wind from her from its weight. She finally managed to scream as she held it back, attempting to keep it from tearing into her throat. With most of their weight in their upper bodies, the beasts had to rely on their fangs versus their claws during an attack. It was possibly the only thing keeping the creature from tearing her apart, although she wouldn't be able to hold it back much longer.

"Hailey!" Skyler cried out from across the beach.

Skyler treaded sand at top speed toward her and leaped onto the creature's back. He had jumped on the creature with such force and speed that they both toppled off Hailey and rolled across the sand. The beast recovered a second before Skyler and found the perfect opportunity to use its claws to slash him across the chest, throwing him across the sand. Hailey moved into a crouched position and stared at Skyler where he lie motionless and bleeding. She heard a loud, sharp roar of pain. She looked to her right. The black panther lie in a bloody heap on the sand and no longer moved. All three beasts slowly circled Hailey. One snarled and made its move. There was the faint sound of shattering glass. Hailey looked back at the hotel. Rafe leaped through the air from the nineteenth floor, landed in a crouched position twenty feet from the hotel doors, and charged for them.

Two of the beasts ran for him while the third leaped for Hailey. Hailey rolled out of the creature's path. It struck the sand harshly then spun with a snarl. Without slowing his momentum, Rafe spun through the air into a roundhouse kick and struck one of the creatures in the head. Rafe rolled across the sand as the creature was catapulted backwards several feet. The second beast lunged for Rafe. He kicked the large creature in the side and flipped it across the sand. The first beast recovered from the hard kick and charged him. Rafe caught the creature by the throat and kicked it in the underbelly, causing it to whine painfully. Hailey outmaneuvered the beast chasing her and rolled across the sand not far from the pile of panther. The black mass suddenly twitched, catching her attention. She jumped back with surprise and watched as a white tiger clawed its way out of the pile of black fur.

The beast chasing her stopped in its tracks and stared at the fully emerged white tiger. The remaining black fur turned to dust. The tiger roared viciously. The beast turned and ran. The white tiger chased it into the woods. Rafe punched one of the last two beasts in the nose. It lunged back for him and sank its sharpened teeth into his shoulder. Rafe cried out with pain and then countered by biting the beast's paw. The beast yelped and pulled away. Rafe crouched down and bared his own bloody teeth. The beast slowly backed up, turned, and then ran for the woods. The remaining beast turned for Hailey. She placed her hand on the ground. The sand rippled and sank. The beast leaped backward, nearly sucked into the sand. It whimpered and ran for the woods. Rafe sneered, spit out the creature's blood, and straightened. Hailey ran to Skyler's fallen side. Skyler moved slightly with a low, painful groan. There were deep scratches across his chest. Rafe approached while examining the bleeding bite wound on his own shoulder.

"Skyler, can you hear me?"

Skyler moaned softly and barely opened his eyes to look at her. "Am I dead?"

Hailey felt her entire body sag with relief. She had been certain he was dead. Judging by the severity of his wounds, they'd need to find the helicopter pilot and fly him to a mainland hospital immediately.

"I don't know whether you're incredibly brave or extremely stupid."

"The answer would only disappoint you," he muttered.

As she applied pressure to the wounds on his chest, Logan and Vance appeared from the hotel and ran for them. Rafe glared at them while clutching his bleeding shoulder.

"Excellent timing," he scoffed.

Hailey looked at Skyler's cuts beneath her hand. The wounds vanished before her eyes. Logan and Vance approached just in time to see the last of the wounds rapidly healing. Skyler slowly sat up and felt his chest with surprise. Hailey looked at her blood-covered hand. The blood appeared to evaporate on her skin. Logan and Vance backed away from her. Hailey looked at Rafe. He stared with a concerned look and took a step back as well.

"I think I'll call it a night," Rafe hesitantly announced and turned to leave.

Hailey stood and caught him by his injured shoulder. He gasped with agony and turned to face her.

"They took Mel," she announced with fear in her eyes. "They'll kill her!"

"Will you let me bleed in peace?" Rafe demanded as he pulled away from her.

Hailey looked at the deep, bleeding bite wound then met his gaze with concern for his injuries. She reached for his wounded shoulder. Rafe moved back a step, defensively clutched his bleeding shoulder, and glared at her.

"Keep your hands off my wounds, witchy woman."

Hailey stared into his eyes and again moved her hand to his wounded shoulder. Rafe slowly lowered his hand, almost helpless to her power of persuasion.

"She's my friend," Hailey gently informed him while clinging to his bleeding shoulder. Her look was stern. "I'm going after her with or without you."

Hailey removed her hand from his now healed shoulder. Rafe stared at his shoulder beyond his torn shirt and uncertainly touched it with disbelief.

"If they took her to the cave in the woods, we'll never reach her in time," Skyler informed her.

"That tunnel led to the hotel basement," Logan announced. "We can take the back route and meet them there. I know where we can find some weapons along the way."

"Rescue the damsel in distress?" Vance asked while cocking his head slightly. "That's right up my alley."

"You're all crazy," Rafe scoffed while fixated on his now healed shoulder.

"You know you'll just show up anyway," Hailey replied.

He suddenly frowned while rubbing his shoulder. "Yeah, I'm an idiot. Don't remind me."

Chapter Twenty-four

*R*afe stood by the storage room doorway within the basement and watched the corridor while Logan routed through several old boxes to secure weapons. Skyler practiced swinging the baseball bat he held while standing alongside Hailey, who insecurely studied the ax in her hand. She would have preferred the baseball bat. The thought of using an ax on anyone or anything made her nauseous. She didn't understand why she had been given such a messy weapon. Vance gleamed over a nine-iron golf club he'd secured as his weapon and practiced his imaginary golf swing. He had great form, obviously having played often.

"What is all this stuff?" Vance finally asked while glancing back at Logan.

Logan routed through an old chest without looking up. "We had a very strange man on staff a few years back. He took off one day, leaving behind everything in his room. Since his family didn't claim his belongings, we put all his stuff in storage. It's been here ever since."

Logan appeared to find what he was looking for and removed a pair of samurai swords. He grinned his pleasure and tossed one to Rafe. Rafe removed the sheath and touched the blade. A twisted smile crossed his face, indicating the sword was to his liking. Logan kept the other for himself. Rafe skillfully twirled the sword, took a frightening fighting stance, and smirked.

"This works," he announced.

The nervous tension among the other men as they watched Rafe's sick pleasure to the weapon conveyed their concerns. He was a dangerous man, and now he was armed. Hailey, on the other hand, tried hard to keep from being turned on by his skill with the sword. She brushed the image from her mind and looked at Logan holding his own sword.

"What's in the rest of the boxes?" Hailey asked Logan as she glanced at the room filled with similar boxes.

He casually shrugged. "Employees sometimes quit and leave their belongings behind," Logan replied. "Seems to happen a lot. It's mostly junk."

Skyler glanced at Logan and appeared concerned by the comment. "Define *a lot.*"

"I don't know," he responded. "A few employees here and there."

Hailey wasn't convinced with the response. There was a pattern among random guest disappearances and employees mysteriously quitting. What if there was more to it? Despite her concerns for Mel, the circumstances surrounding those patterns had gotten the better of her.

"Tam said a lot of guests take off for romantic interludes," she remarked and looked at the three men who'd spent more than their share of time at the hotel. "She insists they always show up. Do they *always* show up?"

Logan and Skyler exchanged curious looks as if never really considering the question before now. Rafe looked back at them with a similar expression. A few thoughts on the subject were obviously going through his mind, but no one expected him to share those thoughts.

"I don't know that I've ever heard anything either way," Logan replied, now looking concerned.

"Yeah, I mean, no one has ever said anything," Skyler announced.

"Women disappearing for 'flings' seems common around here," Rafe added, surprising everyone with the offering of information. He then considered his own comment. "It always sounded plausible, but maybe there's more to it than what we're told."

"Is there any way to figure out how many people have disappeared over the years?" Logan asked.

"I could do some digging," Skyler informed them. "Might be something in the computer. I mean, there would have been investigations if someone's son or daughter never returned home after a trip."

"You're overthinking it," Vance insisted. "If tourists start vanishing from the island, it would eventually become suspicious, and we would have heard about it by now."

"We'll worry about that later," Hailey informed them, her curiosity now replaced with concern for her friend. "We need to find Mel before those creatures do something to her."

All four nodded in agreement and prepared to head out of the storage area. Although no one else heard anything, Rafe suddenly turned toward the doorway with his samurai sword skillfully wielded. Marcus saw Rafe with the sword clutched in deadly fashion and jumped with surprise. Rafe lowered the sword and frowned. Either he didn't care to see Marcus, or he was disappointed he didn't get to use the sword.

"What's going on here?" Marcus demanded, eyeing all five with a look that conveyed his concern.

"We don't really have time to explain right now," Hailey informed him with growing concern. "Mel's been taken, and we're positive she's down here somewhere."

She attempted to move past him to leave the storage room. Marcus stopped her and firmly indicated the weapons they carried with a nod.

"I can't allow you to gallivant around the hotel armed to the teeth," he announced.

Rafe placed his hand on Marcus's chest and easily pushed him against the doorframe. His eyes remained locked on Marcus. The usually intimidating man stared back with surprise. What should have escalated into an altercation was quickly defused by Marcus' unwillingness to engage Rafe.

"We'd love to stay and chat, but you heard the lady," Rafe growled.

Hailey, Skyler, Vance, and Logan hurried from the storage room, glancing only briefly at the tense scene in the doorway. Rafe released Marcus, who immediately straightened and attempted to compose himself. Marcus seemed unprepared for a confrontation with Brody's guard dog and backed down.

"Fine, but I'm going with you," Marcus informed Rafe without taking his eyes off him. "I'm in charge of missing persons, and I'm in charge of security in this hotel."

"Suit yourself," Rafe replied without emotion then casually twirled his sword and left the room.

Marcus sneered his obvious distaste for the man and hurried after him.

Chapter Twenty-five

$\mathcal{R}$afe led the five through the basement and into the sub-basement along the dimly lit corridor with his samurai sword ready for action. Marcus brought up the rear with his gun in his hand. Rafe looked around and seemed moderately troubled by something, which concerned Hailey. He suddenly stopped at a junction in the corridor then looked right and left. He remained preoccupied by whatever he was unwilling to share.

"We need to split up," he suddenly announced while barely glancing at the others in his group.

"Split up?" Hailey gasped, sharing the same reaction as the others. Was he insane? What could possibly be gained by them splitting up?

"This is the right direction," Logan insisted, refusing to be bullied by the intimidating man. "My sense of direction is perfect. Straight will take us in the direction of the cave. We go this way *together*."

Logan shared Hailey's distrust of Rafe's authority and was the only one willing to call him on it. Rafe suddenly grabbed Logan by the shirt, startling the big man, and pulled him a couple of feet away. Despite Logan's size, he was too much of a teddy bear to be confrontational. Although she couldn't hear what Rafe said to him, Logan seemed concerned and defensive while nodding in agreement. As they returned to the group, Logan nodded Vance in the direction of the left corridor.

"We need to check this corridor," Logan informed him. "We'll catch up with the others."

Vance appeared skeptical but obediently left with Logan. The others looked at Rafe with surprise. Rafe ignored them and continued along the corridor heading straight. Hailey and Skyler exchanged concerned looks then reluctantly followed. They walked for several minutes before reaching a large section of stone wall broken away. Beyond the broken wall was the familiar mineshaft tunnel. They only walked ten yards before reaching an old, medieval looking door with extinguished torches on either side. Rafe attempted to open the heavy wood door by its wrought iron ring, but it wouldn't budge. He looked back at Marcus.

"Where does this door go?" Rafe asked.

Marcus stared at the door with disbelief and shook his head. "I don't know. I've never seen that door before. I've only been out this far once a few years ago. That stone wall back there had been intact. This tunnel must have been hidden."

Rafe frowned his disapproval to Marcus' answer then swiftly kicked the door inward. Despite the thickness of the door, it splintered and nearly broke off its old hinges from the hard hit. Everyone jumped with surprise. No average man would have been able to break down the door as Rafe had. Marcus stared at Rafe, almost certainly amazed by his superhuman strength. Rafe lit one of the torches on the wall, removed it from its base, and entered the dark room. The other three followed him with some apprehension. There were shadows in the short tunnel behind them, following them, but none seemed to notice. Rafe's torch barely lit the large room, giving little indication to what it contained. They only thing they knew for certain was that the room was very large.

"There must be other torches--" Hailey began but was interrupted by a chilling, familiar sound.

They heard a low snarl from nearby. All four stopped and looked around. They saw several sets of glowing red eyes within the room.

"We are so fucked," Skyler muttered.

Marcus turned back for the broken door and felt along the doorframe. A sword suddenly appeared before Marcus' face, immediately stopping him. Logan held the sword only inches from the hardened man's face. Vance maintained a frozen look of annoyance as he snatched the gun from Marcus' hand.

"What's wrong with you?" Marcus demanded with forced panic in his voice. "We need to get out of here! Those things are in here!"

The beasts continued to growl and the glowing eyes circled the room getting closer to them. Hailey watched the glowing eyes then gasped with alarm. Several torches erupted into flames and brightened the large, oval room. Mel could now be seen shackled to an ancient altar with duct tape over her mouth. She stared at them, attempted to scream, and fought the old, metal shackles. There were eight beasts within the room, watching and waiting to strike. Vance eyed the iron gate just inside the doorway, ready to fall at a moment's notice, and the crude button close to Marcus, which would release the gate, trapping them inside.

"You were right, Rafe," Vance announced. "The bastard set us up."

Skyler and Hailey stared at Marcus with surprise to the double-cross. Marcus suddenly sneered at them and didn't bother denying his role.

"You won't make it out," Marcus boldly announced. "The Emperor can't expect to stop us with a pathetic council put together by a little girl."

"Will someone shut him up?" Rafe groaned.

"You've got it," Vance announced while smirking.

Vance swung the large golf club for Marcus' head. Marcus ducked the flying club and rolled out the doorway. The club struck the nearby wall, hitting the button. The heavy gate fell from the ceiling with a loud clang, trapping them inside the chamber. Vance and Logan attempted to lift it, but it wasn't moving. The ancient pulley system had to be within the stone itself.

Marcus stood just outside the gate and mocked them with his grin. "That worked nicely," he announced cheerfully.

Logan rammed his sword through the opening in the iron bars, nearly stabbing him. Marcus jumped back with surprise then wagged his finger while chuckling.

"You're no match for me," he announced.

Vance removed the gun he'd taken from Marcus and fired several shots at him. Marcus gasped and bolted down the corridor, away from the gunshots. Vance turned with the gun still in his hand, appeared annoyed, and shot one of the beasts. The beast yelped from the gunshot wound then looked at Vance, snarled, and charged for him. Vance squeezed the trigger, but the gun clicked empty. The little black cat appeared through the bars, leaped into the air, and transformed into the white tiger, tackling the beast to the stone floor. The other beasts snarled and attacked simultaneously. Rafe swung his sword and decapitated the first beast, but a second beast tackled him to the floor, knocking the sword from his hand. He wrestled with the massive beast on top of him. Hailey leaped out of the path of the creature before her. It struck the altar, appearing momentarily dazed, then turned around and lunged for her. She cried out and swung the ax, striking it in the shoulder, but the blow didn't even slow it down. The creature easily took her to the floor. Skyler struck the creature on top of Hailey repeatedly with his baseball bat. Another creature tackled him against the altar. Mel muffled a scream. Stones from the ceiling suddenly crumbled above them. Skyler looked up with alarm, saw a large stone about to fall, and shielded Mel with his body. The large chunk of stone fell and crushed the creature as smaller stones pelted Skyler's back.

A creature lunged for Logan near the iron gate. Logan scaled the gate and held himself in midair with only a few finger clutching the bars, defying gravity. The beast ran headfirst into the bars. Logan thrust his sword downward with his free hand and impaled the creature in the head. Logan jumped off the gate and reclaimed his sword. Vance backed away from an approaching beast and swung the golf club for the creature's head. The creature was suddenly thrown upward and across the floor. The creature attempted to return to its feet. Vance leaped for the creature and repeatedly struck it with the golf club. Skyler straightened from his position over Mel and looked across the room to Hailey, who was still pinned beneath her beast and struggled to keep its teeth from tearing into her face. Skyler bolted across the chamber, jumped over the back of the beast that had Rafe on the floor, and reached Hailey. He pulled the ax from the creature's shoulder. The creature wailed, forgot about Hailey, and swiped its claws at Skyler.

Hailey rolled out from under the creature. Skyler leaped backward, narrowly avoiding the sharp claws, and swung the ax into the creature's head. The creature barely had time to wail from the ax penetrating its skull before collapsing to the floor. Rafe held back the beast on top of him by the throat and fumbled for his discarded sword not far from his head. He grabbed the baseball bat instead and thrust it in front of his face. The creature bit the baseball bat and attempted to pull it from Rafe's hands. Rafe placed his foot between him and the creature and catapulted it over him. The creature was thrown through the air with amazing force and harshly struck the iron gate just inches from where Logan stood. Logan appeared stunned as Rafe sprang to his feet.

"You nearly crushed me, Rafe!" Logan cried out.

"I'm working here," Rafe growled back.

Another creature leaped for Rafe. Rafe threw himself to the floor, grabbed his sword as he rolled into a sitting position, and swung at the lunging beast. His slit the creature's throat, spattering blood across him and the room. The beast wailed and struck the floor. Another creature charged for Rafe's back as he straightened. Without turning or even looking, he flipped the sword in his hand and impaled the creature behind him. He casually pulled the sword free, flipped it again, and then looked around the room as the creature behind him fell to the floor with a soft groan. All eight beasts lie dead. The little black cat sat on top of a dead creature and casually cleaned its bloody paws while purring.

As Rafe assessed the number of dead creatures, he snorted a laugh and appeared humored by the sight. "Not bad for a company of misfits."

Hailey hurried for Mel, removed the tape from her mouth, and stared down at her moderately battered friend. It pained her to see Mel scratched and bruised from having been dragged by the creature, although it obviously could have been a lot worse.

"Are you okay?"

"Never better," Mel gasped and violently pulled against the shackles. "Can we go home now?"

Rafe pulled the ax from the dead beast, approached Mel on the altar, and chopped through the chains binding her wrists and ankles. Mel sat up and hugged Hailey while the others reclaimed their weapons. Vance placed his severely bent golf club over his shoulder and looked around the chamber littered with dead beasts and strewn with blood. Logan marveled at the painstaking construction of the chamber.

"I never would have guessed the hotel came with its own sacrificial chamber," Logan remarked while shaking his head.

"We should get the hell out of here before Marcus returns with more friends," Skyler announced, seeming more anxious than usual. He could barely stand still.

"Where do we go?" Hailey asked.

"Marcus isn't stupid," Rafe casually informed them. "He won't risk anything in front of the guests. If we stick together, we'll be safe in Hailey's suite for tonight."

Vance casually indicated the iron gate across the doorway. "There's just one minor setback," he announced. "How do we get out of here?"

Rafe casually approached the iron gate and pulled it up with one thrust. The gate grinded as it ascended roughly back into the ceiling. He walked out of the chamber without a care. The others exchanged looks.

"You know," Logan announced while shaking his head, "I always found that man to be a little intimidating. I was wrong. He's beyond intimidating."

Skyler and Vance helped Mel from the altar and to her feet. She was still unsteady from an evening of excessive drinking and sore from being dragged away by a snarling beast. Hailey again had more questions than answers as she looked at her battered friend.

"After the creatures brought you here, who shackled you to the altar?" Hailey asked Mel, since she knew it wasn't the creatures who cuffed her.

"I don't know," Mel replied while shaking her head, appearing almost dizzy. "I passed out when that monster dragged me into the woods."

Hailey glanced over the scrapes and bruises along Mel's entire backside as they headed for the chamber doorway. She felt bad for her friend, but at least they saved her from whatever fate that awaited her on the altar. Hailey took one last look around as they left the blood-strewn chamber. She was sure it was the same room where Penny had been killed. If the creatures were killing guests for food, it would make sense, but that wasn't the case. What happened to those who died? How did they become fossilized into the mineshaft walls? It was almost too much to think about with Mel having come so close to learning the answer.

Chapter Twenty-six

*M*el sat on the sofa within Hailey's suite wearing one of the plush, signature hotel bathrobes. She had a drink in her hand and appeared moderately sedate, although being drunk was a possibility. Vance, Rafe, and Logan stood at the breakfast bar while studying a map of the hotel and attempted to pinpoint the location of the sacrificial chamber in relationship to the tunnels. Skyler was standing alone on the balcony and stared out to the ocean. He hadn't said a word since they'd returned to Hailey's suite from the sub-basement. Hailey sat in the overstuffed chair with the black cat nestled on her lap. The cat purred as if it didn't have a care in the world. Hailey stared intently at a lit candle on the coffee table and flicked her finger at it. Nothing happened. She was quickly becoming frustrated and glanced at the guys by the breakfast counter.

"What's the point of having powers if you can't control them?" she demanded.

"Join the club, Hailey," Logan replied while leaning on the counter near Rafe.

"The only one who seems to have control of his powers is your little protector there," Vance remarked and indicated the little cat on her lap.

Hailey lifted the black cat and looked into its eyes. "What's the secret?"

The cat appeared completely relaxed while dangling in her hands and purred. She returned the cat to her lap.

"Forget it, he's not talking," she remarked.

Too many unexplained things had happened that night, and she was growing tired of more questions than answers. The last few days had thrust upon them some bizarre notion that they were brought together for an unknown assignment against never before seen creatures. Now Marcus was thrown into the mix. Again, there were more questions than answers. She casually turned in her chair to watch the guys at the counter.

"What does Marcus know that we don't, Logan?" Hailey asked with a defeated sigh.

"He said you were sent by some emperor to stop him," Logan replied then shook his head with limited understanding. "I don't know anything about an emperor. Perhaps he's the ruler of the kingdom. I'm guessing whatever world you came from, Marcus was a part of it."

"I lived with my uncle as far back as I can remember," she bluntly informed him. "I was a little girl when he died. I may not remember much, but I can assure you we lived on this planet. I think I'd remember coming from an alien world. It doesn't make any sense."

"Your uncle had to be from that same world and brought you here when you were very young," Logan replied. "He may have been the one with all the answers, but he died before he could share them with you. Without your uncle, you would have been left to your own resources."

Hailey groaned and allowed her head to fall into her hand. "And I gave us away to Marcus," she scoffed then looked back at the men. "That's why those things attacked us on the beach. He sent them to destroy us. I'm so stupid."

"What did he intend to do with me?" Mel finally asked, seemingly coming to life on the sofa.

Hailey had almost forgotten her friend was still with them. She'd been unusually quiet since their return. Hailey wasn't sure she wanted to tell Mel about her suspicions. It would only cause her further stress. She seemed frightened enough from her ordeal and didn't need any added trauma. While Hailey thought of a tactful response, Vance felt compelled to answer her question.

"Judging by the condition of the victims in the tunnel, he somehow absorbs their fluids," Vance replied. "Maybe it's how they survive. A feeding process?"

Mel stared at him with her mouth hanging open. "You mean he wanted to suck my blood?" she suddenly cried out.

It would seem Hailey was the only one concerned for Mel's delicate emotions at the moment. She was about to scold Vance when Logan chimed in.

"It would explain the disappearances over the years," Logan remarked. "I'm guessing all those victims were abducted from the hotel at some point, drained of their fluids, and mummified into the cave wall." He shook his head. "Being sucked dry has to be an awful way to die."

Mel had a look of alarm clearly plastered on her face. Hailey groaned softly and moved onto the sofa alongside her terrified friend. She placed her arm around her shoulder and attempted to comfort her.

"Guys can be so insensitive," Hailey gently informed her while attempting to keep Mel from freaking out.

"I need another drink," Mel muttered and attempted to get up, but seemed unsteady on her feet.

Hailey gently pulled her back down onto the sofa. "Maybe you should try to get some rest."

"Are you kidding?" Mel gasped with alarm. "I'm never sleeping again!"

"There's more to the story than we know," Logan announced to the guys. "We need to find out what Marcus knows."

Rafe was becoming annoyed with the entire conversation. "How about we just eliminate Marcus and forget about the petty details?" he demanded.

Vance glared at Rafe and smirked with a hint of irritation. "I doubt he's simply going to roll over and play dead."

Rafe flashed an insincere grin at Vance. "I'll ask nicely."

"Marcus has had years to guard his game," Hailey informed them as she stood and joined them at the counter. She couldn't deny the tinge of envy she harbored. "He's ahead of us on the learning curve. I'd feel better if we knew half what he does."

"You're giving him far too much credit for intelligence, Hailey," Rafe announced.

"Are you serious?" Hailey demanded while staring at him with surprise. "He *knew* who I was. I don't even know who I am these days." She couldn't believe someone as smart as Rafe could be so naïve at times. He lacked any sense of curiosity and only concerned himself with the urge to swiftly and harshly deal with any threat. Of course, as the Guardian, being a warrior was his only job. "Where is he getting his information? How many of those creatures are there? How does he control them? We need a few more answers if we hope to survive another day in this nightmare."

"Don't overcomplicate things," Rafe announced boldly. "Who cares why? He controls the creatures, so we eliminate him. Problem solved."

"Run in guns blazing, huh?" Logan announced demandingly. "The problem with your solution, Rafe, is you don't know what you're running into. You see a cockroach, and you think stepping on it will solve the problem. What about the one million others hiding in the walls? You can't step on all of them."

Rafe placed his hands on the counter, leaned forward, and stared Logan in the eyes. "Oh, so now I'm supposed to take tactical military advice from the froo froo lounge player?"

"Did you just call me froo froo?" Logan suddenly demanded while throwing his shoulders back as he straightened, puffing his chest to its full size.

"Come on," Rafe snorted and appeared humored by Logan's intimidation attempt. "You're an overgrown Boston Terrier!"

Vance laughed but refrained from comment.

Logan glared at his playboy sidekick and appeared offended. "Oh, the pretty little Pomeranian finds that funny."

Hailey shut her eyes and groaned. So much for her mystic warriors.

Chapter Twenty-seven

Nearly an hour had passed and the scene within Hailey's suite was escalating. Overinflated egos were trumping common sense. Hailey had enough of her boys acting like less mature boys and finally joined Skyler on the balcony. She leaned on the half wall alongside him and enjoyed the solitude with him. His preference to remaining on the balcony by himself seemed to be something more than just recovering from being ambushed earlier that evening. Rafe and Vance's raised voices were heard snapping at each other through the open door. It was going to be a long night. Hailey studied Skyler a moment in silence.

"Are you okay?" she gently asked. "You haven't said much since we got back."

He finally straightened and glared at her with a look of annoyance he'd never displayed before.

"Let's see," he announced with a slight hiss in his voice. "Talbert fired me earlier this evening, oh, and I was nearly diced into quarters!" He collected himself and groaned lowly. "No, I'm not okay. I'm not okay with any of this. I'm just not cut out for this sort of thing."

She knew Skyler wasn't much of a fighter, and the events throughout the evening had finally taken their toll on him. It wasn't easy to accept. Even Hailey didn't care for the responsibility suddenly thrust upon her.

"None of us are cut out for this, Skyler," she gently informed him.

Rafe's raised voice was heard from inside. "Oh, come on, Vance," he lashed out. "It's not rocket science. It's not as if those beasts have any real tactical abilities. Am I the only one with any balls around here?"

Hailey held her breath and reconsidered her comment. "Okay, maybe one of us is."

She pulled the balcony door shut, eliminating most of the raised voices from inside. Skyler finally turned to face her with a strange, lost look on his face.

"You don't get it," he gently informed her. "I'm not like the others. I don't have special powers. I just don't have what it takes to be Numinous. I can't protect you."

There was an awkward silence as she stared at him. It wasn't about the attack or the danger he faced. He didn't fear for his life; he feared he didn't deserve his position. She gently placed her hand on his lower arm.

"It's not your job to protect me."

He again leaned over the half wall, stared off toward the ocean, and seemingly pouted. "I should have known Marcus was setting us up, but I didn't. Rafe somehow figured it out, but I couldn't sense the danger."

"You took out two of those creatures tonight," she proudly reminded him.

"One," he muttered insecurely. "The falling ceiling took out the other. That hardly counts."

She gently patted his arm and stared at him even though he didn't look at her.

"You have an amazing gift, Skyler," she informed him. "You can see the future and communicate with me through your mind. That is a very special power."

He snorted a soft laugh and looked at her. "Vance can command animals. Logan communicates with plant life," he boldly announced then gestured wildly as his words came out faster and louder. "Freakin' Rafe is a one-man commando unit. And you," he gave her a quick once over, "well, let's just hope no one ever pisses you off." He looked away from her and muttered, "Even the cat has more power than I do."

"Don't feel you have to compare yourself to the others--or the cat."

Skyler stared out to the ocean in the distance and leaned heavily on the half wall. There was a strange silence. He seemed beaten down by the world he'd been secretly wishing for his entire life.

"I just thought I finally fit in somewhere," he said gently. "I was supposed to be *someone*. When you came to me in my dream, you told me it was my destiny." His head hung down with despair. "I thought for the first time in my life that I was someone important. It was a lie. I'm still just me."

"You are important," she announced firmly. "You're my best friend and have been for a long time."

He was silent a moment then glanced at her and uncertainly straightened. "I'm sorry," he said gently and gave a slight wave. "It's been a traumatic day, you know--beasts and all."

Hailey smiled, placed her arms around him, and hugged him. Skyler appeared surprised then returned the embrace. She kissed him quickly on the cheek, pulled away just far enough to meet his gaze, and smiled.

"I need you."

Skyler hid his pleased grin as his cheeks reddened. "Well, as long as you need me--"

She clung to his arm as they turned toward the balcony doors. Through the closed glass doors, the others stared at them from inside, having seen the kiss and embrace. Their expressions were priceless. Skyler hid his tiny smile and cast a quick glance at her.

"Do you suppose we can give them a minute longer to get the wrong idea?"

Hailey smiled and laughed while hugging his arm.

✝

*F*aint laughter was heard within the laundry room just a little after three in the morning. A folding table and chairs were crudely set up in the center of the vast laundry room with its industrial sized washers and dryers. Six men played poker while another man and a woman stood nearby with drinks in their hands and watched the remaining players increase their bets, tossing cheap plastic chips onto the center of the table. There was no doubt the plastic chips represented actual cash. The remaining players were serious about their play, wanting to secure the sizable pot in the middle of the table. Cigar smoke had already filled the air, despite several machines designed to eliminate the smoke. The game was unauthorized and illegal. Daniel watched the man across from him lay his cards down to reveal three queens. There was a faint round of groans. Daniel silenced them with a grin and affectionately spread out his full house, tens over jacks. Those who had groaned now laughed at the losing man's expense. Daniel grinned and collected his sizable pot of plastic poker chips, pulling them toward him in a sweeping motion. He gloated a little more than socially acceptable.

There was a faint growling sound from across the room. Everyone heard the unusual sound and looked in unison toward the main door. The door was suddenly thrown open, and two massive creatures bolted into the room. Everyone screamed in response to the hideous, charging beasts. One attacked the standing man while the other leaped onto the poker table, knocking it and several people to the floor. It landed on top of another man and sank its teeth into his throat while slinging its large head, snapping the man's neck. Those who hadn't been knocked from their folding chairs sprang to their feet, the metal chairs crashing to the floor as they simultaneously stood. The first creature ripped out the man's throat and immediately turned for the others as they screamed in terror while bolting for the main door. Two more creatures lunged into the room and tackled the first few men. The creature already within the room leaped onto the fleeing woman's back and rode her to the floor. She was unable to scream from the hard impact with the floor. The beast grabbed the back of her neck in its mouth and violently slung her around like a ragdoll. She barely released a whimper before her neck snapped. As one of the employees ran into the open doorway, a fifth creature appeared from the corridor and mauled him, tearing into his flesh. The creature tearing apart the man in the doorway blocked the only exit.

Daniel and the two remaining guests were trapped within the room. As they turned, the four beasts had finished disabling their prey and charged the three men. There were more screams as the creatures leaped onto two of the men, tackling them to the floor. Two beasts tore into one man, while the third beast easily ripped out the throat of another guest. Daniel attempted to run for the industrial sized dryer and possible safety. The charging beast slashed his calf, leaving four large gashes. Daniel fell to the floor from the forceful strike and the enormous pain. Despite his torn leg, he attempted to pull himself for the dryer. The beast grabbed his arm and slung him around like an old chew toy. Daniel landed on his back in agony from both his arm and leg injury. He looked up as the beast hovered over him with blood dripping from its mouth. He attempted to scream but nothing came out.

The guests who were left wounded writhed in agony from their severe injuries. The beasts ignored those who were already dead and began devouring those still moving. The beasts savagely tore flesh from their live prey. Most were unable to scream as they bled out from their torn throats. Daniel watched helplessly as the beast hovering over him anchored his torn body down with its large front paw and ripped into his soft belly with sharp teeth dripping blood. There was little he could do but watch the beast ripping out his insides until the pain finally overtook him, allowing him to slip out of consciousness. The creatures feasted on the eight guests and staff at their leisure, leaving the laundry room floor strewn with blood and mutilated bodies.

Chapter Twenty-eight

It was a little after three in the morning, and the debate was still going strong within the living room of Hailey's suite. Mel had fallen asleep on the sofa despite Hailey and the guys sitting on the floor around the coffee table not far from her. They kept their voices down as the conversation turned more civilized. Skyler suddenly drifted out and seemed to be in another world. As Hailey stared at him, the guys fell silent with their own curious looks. Hailey gave him a gentle nudge, immediately bringing him out of his trance.

"Everything okay?" she asked.

Skyler slowly shook his head without appearing convinced. "I'm not sure. I just had a really strange feeling," he replied gently. "I think I'm still a little rattled from that creature carving me up like a Thanksgiving turkey on the beach. I had this horrible image of their claws and fangs." He shuttered from the thought then forced a smile and shrugged. "I'm sure it was nothing. The feeling has already passed."

Hailey gently patted his arm and added a sympathetic smile. The guys relaxed by his reassurance and continued with conspiracy theories, ancient history, and every subject in between. They'd gone over the events of the evening numerous times and seemed to be no closer to an answer just exhaustion. After another hour, Hailey wanted to block out their voices. Even Rafe's smooth, manly voice was starting to grate on what little nerves she had left. Someone had to end her torture soon.

"This isn't getting us anywhere," Vance finally announced while stretching his legs beneath the table. He rubbed his eyes and blinked several times in an attempt to keep them open. "I'm too tired to think straight anymore."

"It's late, and we've been hashing through this all night," Hailey finally announced, grateful for the save, and feeling exhausted herself. "Rafe's room is next door. Why don't we split up between the two rooms and get some sleep?"

"I'll go with Mel to Rafe's suite," Vance announced with enthusiasm, appearing to catch his second wind along with his rising hormones.

"Nice try, lover boy," Logan scoffed.

"Mel and I will take my bedroom," Hailey announced to the men. "We have the Protector. Skyler should go to Rafe's suite, because we can communicate telepathically. That means one of you should stay here with us and the other two can go with Skyler next door."

Vance grinned in response, raised his finger, and was about to make his own suggestion. Hailey suddenly shifted and cleared her throat.

"Let me rephrase that," she announced, having reconsidered her comment. "Rafe or Logan should stay here."

"Was I just insulted?" Vance suddenly asked with a boyish innocence.

Rafe tossed Vance his room key. Logan folded his arms across his broad chest, glared at Rafe, and appeared offended.

"Was that your subtle way of tossing me out?" Logan demanded in a cocky tone.

He shrugged without care. "The Guardian protects the princess," Rafe announced bluntly. "It's in my job description." He casually held up the manuscript. "It says so right here. See for yourself."

Logan's eyes narrowed conveying his disapproval. "Thanks, I've read it," he snorted.

The three men wearily stood and left Hailey's suite, shutting the door behind them. It made enough noise to startle Mel on the sofa. She abruptly woke, shot up on the sofa, and looked around in a state near panic.

"What's wrong?" she cried out.

"Nothing," Hailey replied gently. "You and I are sharing the bed. I'll be along shortly."

Mel stood with exhaustion, offered no protest, and shuffled into the bedroom. Hailey crossed the room and locked the balcony door even though Rafe would be the only one bold enough to enter her suite from the balcony. Rafe kicked off his shoes and collapsed onto the sofa, making himself comfortable with his ankles crossed and one arm beneath his head. His other arm draped across his eyes. Hailey glanced at him on the sofa and admired his relaxed yet somehow sexy pose. She considered ignoring her thoughts and pushing herself into the bedroom, but against her better judgement, she approached the sofa and sat on the coffee table before him.

"I'm grateful for what you did tonight," she announced softly, hoping he hadn't already fallen asleep.

He peeked at her from under his forearm. "I know what you're thinking, but it doesn't change anything," he informed her. "I'll see this through, but then you're on your own."

"I know there's part of you that cares what happens to this 'pitiful' group," she announced then hesitated before adding, "and maybe even me."

Rafe slowly sat up but didn't bother looking at her. He casually leaned against the back on the sofa. "Yeah, well, that's where you're wrong."

She wasn't wrong about him! She wasn't wrong when she chose him all those years ago, and she wasn't wrong today. He wasn't the bad man he pretended to be or he never would have given his life to save his friend.

"Stop it," she scolded. "Stop pretending. You're not that uncaring."

He finally looked at her and appeared annoyed by her tone, or maybe he was just tired. "Because you think you saved my life once, do you honestly believe that makes you an authority on my character?"

"Yes."

There was an awkward silence between them. Rafe shifted on the sofa, seeming uncomfortable with their conversation, and then studied her a moment.

"Let's say, for the sake of argument, I'm your chosen Guardian," he announced then stared at her and slowly shook his head. "What the *hell* were you thinking?"

She found his lighthearted comment almost amusing but held back her laugh. "Beats the hell out of me," she remarked. "I was only fifteen at the time. Best guess? You probably looked good in your uniform."

Rafe stared at her, surprised by the comment. Hailey flashed a teasing smile. Rafe shook his head and chuckled. He groaned softly while maintaining his humor to the situation.

"Great, we're the 'boy band' of mystic warriors."

Hailey moved onto the sofa alongside him. He eyed her closeness and seemed uncomfortable by it. She inhaled deeply and considered his question with more seriousness.

"There would have been many candidates over several years," she informed him. "Whatever my reason, you were carefully chosen. Somewhere along the way, you must have made a very good impression."

Rafe placed his hand on her bare leg with some apprehension, gently caressed it, and grinned almost lustfully. "I prefer the tweener crush scenario."

Hailey casually removed his hand from her leg, offered a tiny smile, and stood. Rafe appeared disappointed and leaned back on the sofa.

"It's been a long, weird day," she informed him. "We should get some sleep."

Rafe frowned, flopped down on the sofa, and grinned at her. "Just when we were having fun--"

Hailey approached the door and turned down the living room lights. She removed a blanket from one of the chairs and covered Rafe. Without warning, she joined him on the sofa beneath the blanket. Rafe appeared surprised as she nestled against him. He groaned and immediately pulled her into his arms.

"If this is a test, I'm going to fail," he warned.

"You need to trust your instincts," she informed him. "Whether you believe it or not, that's your most powerful gift."

"Your theory is flawed," Rafe teased while nuzzling her face with his. "My instincts are telling me to ravish you."

"Is that what they told you the other night in Lucinda's suite?" she cooed softly while attempting to look into his eyes through the dim lighting.

He let out a soft laugh and appeared almost embarrassed. "That was a lapse in judgment," Rafe remarked gently. "I've never behaved that way, and I felt terrible for taking advantage of you like that. I'm not sure what came over me that night."

Rafe stared at her through the darkness, shifted uncomfortably, and seemed compelled to speak.

"When I'm around you, I'm reminded of some of the most intense erotic dreams I've had." He suddenly hesitated. "I shouldn't have said that. I'm not sure why I did." His look turned more demanding. "Why do I feel the need to talk when I'm around you? It's like I can't control my mouth."

Hailey smiled and shrugged. She was actually enjoying his ramblings, particularly the intimate ones.

"Like in the restaurant," he announced. "I don't know why I said those things to you. I've been at dozens of business meetings where sexual favors go hand in hand for Brody's signature on some contract." He was again silent and seemed to consider his own remark. "It bothered me."

"What bothered you?"

"The thought of you sleeping with Brody." Rafe groaned with disgust. "It's that whole Guardian protector thing, isn't it? You're going to tell me I felt the need to protect you from Brody."

"Actually," Hailey remarked, "I think you wanted me for yourself."

He stared at her a moment in silence then grinned. "I may have had a few dirty thoughts." There was an awkward silence as they stared at each other through the darkness. "From the moment I met you, I felt as though we'd, you know, been *together*. That strange feeling of sexual tension I get when I run into an ex-girlfriend. I would swear that we'd been intimate." His look turned awkwardly serious. "Please tell me we didn't have sex in the light when you were just fifteen."

"I assure you, that wasn't the case," Hailey abruptly informed him. She fell silent, considered his comment, and attempted to stare into his eyes. "Skyler and I have been communicating with each other through our dreams since I was a little girl, but that's only possible because he's Numinous. I couldn't have given you that sort of gift."

"Then I guess I'm just an overly horny bastard," he announced while hiding his smile. "From the moment I saw you in the lobby, I remembered this amazing erotic dream I'd had a few years ago. Sort of struck me like a bolt of lightning."

"Want to tell me about it?"

He appeared surprised while staring at her. "You really want to hear it?"

She shrugged while grinning. "Sure, why not?"

"Aren't you the cool girlfriend," he remarked with humor. He gently brushed the hair from her face while recalling his dream with a look of boyish fascination. "There was this gorgeous, tropical waterfall flowing into a glacier blue pond--"

Hailey stared into his eyes and suddenly tensed.

Chapter Twenty-nine

It was a little after sunrise the following morning, but there wasn't any sun to be found. It was a dark, dreary morning on the beach with heavy storm clouds rapidly rolling in, promising to ruin everyone's fun-filled day in paradise. The winds were harsh and the surf was fierce, indicating the potential for a tropical storm was great. Several maintenance workers ran around outside the hotel stacking lounge chairs and moving them closer to the building to prevent damage to the chairs. Other than the staff preparing for the worst, the area surrounding the hotel was deserted. Even the early risers seemed to have little reason to be up and about on such a dreary morning.

With the curtains closed and little light outside breaking through, Hailey's suite was only dimly lit. The bedroom door opened to the quiet, nearly dark living room. Mel shuffled across the room and approached the kitchenette, briefly glancing at the sofa. Rafe and Hailey were nestled together beneath the blanket and appeared to be sleeping peacefully. Mel hid her humored grin to the cuddling, sleeping couple. She grabbed a bottle of water and quickly returned to the bedroom, making as little noise as possible. Once the door closed, Rafe groaned softly and moved against Hailey. She gasped, clung to him, and kissed his neck.

"That was close--" Rafe announced as he returned his mouth to hers and kissed her passionately and with aggression.

Hailey returned the aggressive kiss and pawed at his chest as he moved against her beneath the blanket.

†

*D*espite the early hour, Lucinda exited the elevator and crossed the lobby toward the front desk. She wore a stunning yet casual sundress with thin shoulder straps and matching wedge sandals. Lucinda slowed her approach, giving Cass a strange once over. Cass seemed surprised to see the boss that hour of the morning, since it wasn't her usual routine to rise so early.

"Good morning, Ms. Keenan," Cass announced cheerfully while hiding her surprise. "Is everything okay?"

"No," Lucinda replied abruptly and again studied the young woman behind the desk. "Weren't you working the evening shift last night?"

"Talbert fired Skyler," Cass timidly informed her. "The night clerk was supposed to relieve me at six this morning, but he never showed."

"Delaney was in charge last night, wasn't he?" Lucinda demanded.

"Well, yes," Cass replied and fidgeted, "but I haven't seen him since midnight."

Lucinda appeared impatient while strumming her manicured fingernails on the marble desktop. She was obviously deep in thought, which put Cass on edge. She looked into Cass's eyes with a stare that alarmed the young desk clerk.

"There's something funny going on in my hotel," Lucinda remarked lowly without taking her eyes off the girl. "I don't know what's going on, but I do know I'm going to get to the bottom of it. Tell Delaney I wish to see him in my suite at ten o'clock." She straightened proudly but didn't take her eyes off the clerk. Her look was intimidating and cold. "I'm sure you'll get the message to him-- seeing how close the two of you have become."

Cass's cheeks reddened as her lips parted with surprise, but Lucinda hadn't noticed, having already turned and stormed off across the lobby. Lucinda was heading for the elevator when Talbert appeared and nearly ran into the fuming woman. She jumped back a step in response and glared at him as if it had been his fault they nearly collided. Talbert managed a polite smile, although he was obviously surprised to see her up so early.

"Lucinda," he announced in a tone meant to sound cheerful. "What are you doing up so early? Is anything wrong?"

She collected her rising temper and groaned softly. "No, I don't think so," Lucinda replied then hesitated, stared at Talbert, and seemed to reconsider her response. "I heard some rumors that have me slightly disturbed."

"Oh?" Talbert questioned while studying her with a curious look. "What sort of rumors?"

"I heard some of the staff have been organizing illegal gambling in the basement," she announced and folded her arms across her chest. "Do you know anything about this?"

Talbert hesitated and appeared uncomfortable by her directness. "I'd heard some of the guests had been playing poker, but I just assumed it was in someone's suite and saw no harm. I assure you, if I knew of any staff involvement, I'd have shut it down and terminated the offending employees immediately." He appeared curious. "Have you brought this to Marcus' attention?"

She exhaled deeply, allowing her arms to fall to her sides with disgust. "No, not yet," Lucinda replied. "When I heard it mentioned yesterday, I just assumed it was Brody indulging in gossip. Then this morning, I was awake when the penthouse maid stopped in with my morning tea. I questioned her about it. She'd heard gossip from some of the other maids that someone in security helped organize the illegal gambling."

"Maids have been known to stretch the truth," Talbert reminded her. "Most of our maids are notorious gossips."

"Yes, I'm aware of the housekeeping grapevine," Lucinda interjected, "but I have reason to believe this goes beyond a friendly poker game happening within my hotel. If someone in security is behind it, I want to know about it." She looked around, casting a strange glare at the front desk. "I have some suspicions as to which security guard is behind this little gambling ring." She shot a look back at Talbert. "I need to have a look around the laundry room."

"Laundry staff hasn't reported yet," Talbert reminded her. "They're not in until eight."

"I know that," she snapped while casting an impatient glare at him. "I can't wait for Marcus. I'm going down there to see for myself."

"I don't think--"

Lucinda glared sharply at him, stopping him mid-sentence. He gently cleared his throat and offered a polite smile.

"If you insist on going downstairs to the laundry room, I'll accompany you."

She nodded and turned toward the elevator. Talbert frowned with annoyance while her back was turned. As the elevator doors opened, Lucinda bolted inside. Talbert obediently followed the barracuda.

$$\dagger$$

Lucinda and Talbert walked along the quiet basement corridor and approached the laundry room. The massive, double doors were closed, catching their attention.

"That's odd," Talbert remarked almost to himself. "Those doors are never closed."

"So it's true," Lucinda launched. "They're probably still in there gambling!"

"The laundry staff will be here in less than thirty minutes," Talbert reminded her. "If someone was doing something illegal down here, I doubt they'd cut it that close."

"I want to see for myself," she announced boldly. "I want to catch my employees in the act. Open the doors!"

Talbert opened both doors simultaneously, pushing them inward with added vigor to surprise anyone on the other side. Lucinda and Talbert stared into the laundry room with surprised looks on their faces. The large laundry room was empty without any indication anyone had been there since the staff left yesterday evening. Lucinda looked around the spotless room. The smell of disinfectant was almost overwhelming, although neither commented on it. Talbert inhaled deeply and glanced at his boss for her reaction.

Lucinda shook her head with disbelief. "I was positive we'd find something," she remarked and continued to look around for anything unusual.

"Well, if something happened here last night, we missed it," he informed her.

"This isn't over," Lucinda proclaimed. "I'm going to have Marcus install security cameras in every nook and cranny. I won't have my staff taking advantage of the guests and disregarding my rules."

†

*O*t was a little before eight o'clock that morning. Rafe stood in the kitchenette on the kitchen side of the breakfast counter and poured a cup of coffee. His condition suggested he got very little sleep last night, although the tiny smirk on his face conveyed he wasn't complaining about it. Mel appeared from the bedroom freshly showered and dressed in borrowed clothing from Hailey. Despite her refreshed appearance, she was stiff, sore, and moderately bruised along most of her body. Rafe glanced at her and raised the coffeepot as she approached.

"Coffee?"

She gave him a strange look, as if questioning the odd smile on his face. His smile immediately faded to keep her from reading his expression.

"I'll have to pass," Mel replied, shaking off his good mood. "Lucinda will have my head if I'm not on time. I don't know how I'm going to explain all the bruises." She gingerly rubbed the bruises on her wrists from the shackles. "Hailey's in the shower. Tell her I went to the penthouse--"

"Sorry, I can't let you do that," Rafe suddenly announced while glaring at her. "You're a target as well as bait."

Mel stared at him with surprise then became defensive. "You don't know Lucinda, I could lose my job."

"You could lose your life. Weigh it," he growled.

Mel was about to argue with him when there was a knock on the door. Mel sneered at him and headed for the door. Rafe stopped her with a warning finger as he passed her, looked through the peek hole, and then groaned.

"Speaking of the barracuda--" Rafe unbolted and opened the door to reveal Lucinda.

Lucinda stood in the doorway and looked at Rafe with some surprise and moderate concern. She looked back at the number on the doorframe then met Rafe's gaze.

"Do I have the right room?"

"Hailey's in the shower," he remarked, offering no other explanation.

"I'm sorry I'm late," Mel announced and groaned softly. "You won't believe what happened last night."

Lucinda eyed Rafe suspiciously then looked at Mel. "I'm not sure I want to know," she muttered then straightened proudly, dismissing whatever she was thinking. "We're leaving this afternoon. Brody signed the contract, and I want to get the hell out of here before anything else happens."

Mel glanced at Rafe, as if looking for approval. "I'll go with Lucinda, if that's okay?"

Rafe frowned his disapproval. "Fine, but wait for us in the penthouse."

Lucinda eyed both as if attempting to understand the connection between them. Mel joined Lucinda in the hallway, shutting the door behind them. Lucinda was heard commenting on Mel's bruises as they left. Hailey entered the living room from the bedroom. Her hair was still damp and slightly untamed. She saw Rafe as he returned to the counter for his coffee and hid her contented smile. As he turned and saw her, he looked away to hide his boyish grin. Hailey tried hard not to laugh. He was acting like a schoolboy after hearing his first curse word. She couldn't help think how adorable he looked.

"The shower's open," she announced.

"Considering you took your shower without me, I'll take one later," he remarked. "My paying boss called. He's uptight about the approaching storm. We need to stop in the dining room and see what he wants then meet the others in the penthouse."

Hailey was surprised by the comment. "You let Mel leave by herself?"

"Of course not. Your boss stopped by--"

She felt her cheeks redden as her mouth fell open. "Lucinda found you here?"

"Was I supposed to hide?" By the sneaky grin on his face, he took a little too much pleasure in letting Lucinda come to her own conclusions.

"I can hear it now," Hailey groaned, although it didn't bother her all that much. She could handle a little ribbing from her boss. "I should stay with them in the penthouse."

"Nice try," he remarked while sipping his coffee. "I'm not leaving you unprotected."

There was a knock on the door. Hailey turned for the door, but Rafe was already passing her to reach it first. He looked through the peek hole then unlocked and opened the door to reveal Skyler. Rafe immediately looked back at Hailey without acknowledging Skyler, although indicating him with a slight nod.

"You and Skyler can stay with Lucinda and Mel," Rafe informed her. "I'll see what Brody wants then meet you in the penthouse in twenty minutes." He brushed past Skyler without comment, leaving the room.

Skyler watched Rafe leave and smirked. "Good morning to you too." He shut the door behind him, looked at Hailey, and shook his head disapprovingly. "I don't know what you see in him," he scoffed. "All things considered, you'd think he'd be in a good mood this morning."

Hailey stared at Skyler and held back her startled gasp. "What do you mean?" she asked as her voice cracked.

He rolled his eyes and walked past her toward the coffeepot. "Come on, Hail, if the two of you glowed anymore, I'd need sunglasses just to look you in the eyes."

She felt her cheeks redden even more than they had from his first comment. She gently cleared her throat and turned away from him, hiding her embarrassment.

"I guess there's no keeping secrets from you."

"Not the big ones." He poured some coffee into a mug and glanced at her several times. "Something's on your mind."

She approached the counter and casually leaned on it. "Rafe and I met in a dream."

"I know," Skyler replied while sipping his coffee. He immediately grimaced and looked at the dark liquid. "Where did he learn to make coffee? This sucks."

"No, Skyler," Hailey announced firmly while straightening. "Rafe and I--" She hesitated. "I dreamt I had sex with a man in a pond by a tropical waterfall. That man was Rafe. He had the same dream. How is that possible?"

Skyler stared at her with surprise on his face. "It's not. Only your Numinous can visit you in your dreams. The only time you'd ever met the others was through me. I bridged your dreams."

"Could you have bridged the dream I had with Rafe?"

He frowned and vigorously shook his head. "I'd never do that. You knew how I felt about him. I certainly wouldn't arrange a hook-up between the two of you."

"I'm telling you, Skyler," she announced firmly and with some irritation. "It happened."

"Well, I disagree," he replied. "He'd have to be your Numinous, and that position has been filled."

She sank deep into thought and muttered, "Or someone else's Numinous."

"It's not as if there's a surplus of Numina, Hailey," he informed her and seemed irritated at the suggestion.

Hailey knew she had successfully offended him, but she couldn't resist teasing him over his last comment.

"Numina?" she questioned with a giggle.

"What?" he announced boldly. "It's a word."

Chapter Thirty

Only a few minutes had passed before Hailey and Skyler joined Mel and Lucinda in the penthouse suite. Having given her boss the shortened version of last night's events, Lucinda sat with Mel on the plush sofa and stared at Hailey and Skyler. She was obviously stunned by what her assistant was telling her about her trusted head of security. It was at that moment that Hailey realized how insane it sounded. She was glad she didn't mention the enormous creatures with claws and fangs terrorizing the resort. Lucinda was having a difficult enough time with the cute and fuzzy version. Her neatly crossed leg swung back and forth as if indicating her reaction to the revelation.

"Marcus? A killer?" Lucinda gasped and was unable to blink while staring at Hailey. "Are you sure?"

"He abducted Mel last night and tried to kill us," Hailey reminded her.

Mel nodded in agreement. Lucinda shook her head until she was finally able to blink after the shock. She fumbled a moment with her thoughts and had to force her leg to stop moving by placing her hand on her own knee. Once it sank in, her hostility erupted in true Lucinda fashion.

"I'll have Delaney detain him immediately," Lucinda announced and reached for the phone on the end table.

"He's extremely dangerous," Hailey offered before she could reach the phone, verbally stopping Lucinda. "We thought it best if Rafe took him down quietly."

Lucinda stared at her as if not even hearing the comment at first. She suddenly appeared enthusiastic and almost relieved by the suggestion.

"Oh, yes. Of course. Rafe," she chirped. "That's an excellent idea!" Lucinda finally seemed to relax after her shock and reverted back into 'boss mode'. She casually leaned back on the sofa and dramatically held her head. "Once this storm passes, we're leaving," she announced firmly then looked back at Hailey. "Hailey, would you get my briefcase in the bedroom? I don't want that contract out of my sight."

Hailey nodded and headed across the suite for the nearby bedroom. Skyler suddenly touched his temples as if in pain then looked at Hailey as she approached the open bedroom doorway. Skyler's eyes widened with alarm.

"Hailey!"

Hailey looked back at Skyler with surprise. Marcus appeared in the bedroom doorway and hit Hailey on the head with his gun, dropping her to the floor. Skyler lunged forward without a plan. Marcus turned toward him with his gun aimed. The white tiger leaped out of the bedroom and tackled Marcus. Marcus fired several rounds at the tiger as they fell to the floor together. The tiger took multiple shots, blood streaking its white coat, and fell limp on top of Marcus. He pushed the dead tiger off him. Skyler grabbed the fire poker and lunged for Marcus as he started to stand. Marcus sprang to his feet and aimed the gun at Skyler. Mel cried out and grabbed Marcus's arm as the gun fired and narrowly missed Skyler, who instinctively ducked. Marcus shoved Mel backwards and into Lucinda, who had been leaping to her feet. Marcus turned for Skyler as he swung the fire poker and caught it in his bare hand. He punched Skyler in the face and then kicked him in the chest. Skyler flew backwards, fell onto the coffee table, and smashed it beneath his weight. Two creatures suddenly leaped from the bedroom, stopped on cue, and snarled at the women. Lucinda clung to Mel as both women screamed.

Marcus shook his head with disgust, although he seemed humored by the situation. "I don't know why you people insist on fighting battles you can't win," he announced.

Skyler groaned as he slowly rolled onto his back alongside the broken coffee table. Marcus approached Hailey, who remained unconscious on the floor, and then casually eyed the frightened women.

"Fortunately for you two, I'm more interested in this one," he remarked.

Skyler slowly sat up while holding his bleeding temple and glared at Marcus several feet away. Skyler's fixated look was hateful despite his obvious pain.

"You stay away from her," he growled lowly as he weakly moved onto his knees.

"Don't worry about your little friend," Marcus announced and then flashed a devious smile. "I need her alive. You, on the other hand--"

Marcus motioned the creatures to attack Skyler. The beasts snarled and lunged for him. Mel and Lucinda screamed while clinging to each other. The room suddenly vibrated. Skyler cast his bloody hand toward the lunging beasts. Both creatures were violently hurled backwards and crashed through the glass balcony doors. All eyes were on Skyler. He slowly stood, transfixed on Marcus, as the room continued to vibrate with his rising anger.

"I *said* stay away from her!"

Marcus showed concern for the first time. His arrogance quickly returned as he aimed his gun at Skyler. The gun trembled in his hand, alarming the intimidating man. A vase suddenly shattered over Skyler's head, and he dropped to the floor. The room instantly became still. Mel screamed and looked at Lucinda, who casually tossed a small piece of the broken vase aside.

"Enough games, Marcus," Lucinda growled with a sneer on her face. "Deal with him!"

Marcus aimed his gun at Skyler on the floor. Mel screamed, lunged for Skyler, and shielded him as she clung to his head. She pinched her eyes shut as if anticipating the gunshot that was about to follow. Instead, there was pounding on the door, causing everyone to jump. Lucinda and Marcus looked at the door.

"Hailey! Skyler! Open up!" Logan yelled from outside the door.

"Rafe, hurry," Vance shouted. "We heard gunshots and no one's answering!"

"Shoot them now," Lucinda ordered in a harsh whisper. "We have to get out of here!"

The dead mass of white tiger twitched, concerning both, almost as if they knew what was about to follow.

"Get out of the way," Rafe was heard yelling just outside the door.

"We have what we need," Marcus informed her.

He swiftly picked up Hailey then hurried Lucinda to the bedroom. As the bedroom door slammed shut, the suite door was violently kicked open, cracking the frame. Rafe charged into the room with his samurai sword prepared to decapitate the first thing that moved. Logan and Vance entered behind him and saw Mel holding Skyler's head to her chest from her position on the floor. She frantically pointed to the bedroom.

"Marcus and Lucinda took Hailey!"

Vance and Logan ran for the closed bedroom door and attempted to bust through. Rafe ran for the balcony, scaled the half wall, and dropped over it. Mel cried out with horror while clinging to Skyler's head and stared at the dark skies beyond the balcony.

"My God! He jumped!"

Vance and Logan turned with surprise and hurried for the balcony beyond the shattered glass doors. Mounds of broken glass crunched beneath their feet as they hurried to the half wall. Both looked over the balcony for signs of Rafe. A mountain lion suddenly ran past them and gracefully leaped over the half wall. Vance and Logan were surprised as they watched the massive cat jump the wall. They hurried back inside. Both looked at the injured, unconscious man in Mel's arms.

"Is he okay?" Logan asked her.

"He's out cold, but he has a pulse, and he's still breathing," she announced while fighting her tears.

"Stay with him," Logan ordered.

Logan and Vance ran from the room as Talbert and Brody entered through the broken door. Both stared after the two men then looked at Mel with the unconscious Skyler alongside the broken coffee table.

"What happened?" Talbert gasped with concern.

"He needs a doctor," Mel quickly replied.

"The doctor is in the banquet hall with the others," Talbert announced as he hurried toward her. "We're using it as a storm shelter until the hurricane passes. The banquet hall is reinforced with shatterproof windows."

"Can we risk moving him?" Brody asked.

"He can't stay here," Talbert informed him. "With that hurricane coming, it's too dangerous."

The two men picked up Skyler, removing him from Mel's lap. As the men carried him toward the broken door, Mel looked around the room with concern while gently rubbing her shoulders. She groaned with frustration and hurried after them.

Chapter Thirty-one

*H*ailey couldn't understand why she felt so cold, almost damp. Her head was pounding in rhythm with the aching in her back. She kept hearing Skyler's voice talking over her, but his words made little sense. Hailey slowly opened her eyes and saw dozens of candles burning in the dim lighting of the sacrificial chamber. She then realized where she was. Although she still heard Skyler's voice, she knew he wasn't with her. He talked as if he were confused himself. She then realized that something had happened to him in Lucinda's suite, but she wasn't sure what became of him or Mel. Hailey thrashed against the newly replaced iron shackles that firmly held her wrists and ankles to the stone altar.

Candles lined the altar, surrounding her in some ritualistic fashion. Hailey was almost certain she was about to find out what happened to the men and women who had been mummified to the mineshaft walls. She then saw Lucinda standing alongside her. Lucinda leaned over her with a sympathetic smile and gently brushed the hair from her face.

"Are you okay, dear?" Lucinda softly asked.

Hailey again pulled on the shackles and felt panic sweeping through her cold, damp body.

"We have to get out of here!"

"The door is locked," Lucinda replied. "I checked already." She then looked around and appeared concerned. "What is this place? Are we still at the resort?"

"It's a long story," Hailey announced and attempted to look around. "You have to find the keys and unlock the shackles. We're in terrible danger."

Lucinda nodded, acknowledging the danger they were in, reassuringly patted Hailey's arm, and then searched the dimly lit room. As she searched the room with one of the candles in her hand, she cast a look back at Hailey.

"What's going on?" Lucinda asked. "There were these horrible creatures--"

The events of the morning were quickly returning to Hailey. She remembered seeing Marcus and realized he must have knocked her out. She glanced at Lucinda and felt an enormous amount of concern for her friends.

"Are Mel and Skyler okay?"

"I'm not sure," Lucinda replied from across the room. "Those things brought us here. I don't know what happened to Mel and Skyler."

Hailey looked around the large chamber while following Lucinda's voice and the tiny glow from her candle. Skyler was alive. He was still talking to her, but he didn't know where he was and seemed to ramble. She was almost certain he was unconscious. Several spirits materialized and floated near her with Amy, Penny, and Desi among them. She stared at the three familiar, ghostly faces. They whispered words that she couldn't understand and appeared frightened for her. Hailey glanced across the chamber to Lucinda's back. She had no signs of dirt or abrasions after claiming she was dragged by the creatures. Hailey looked back at the spirits hovering around her. They continued to whisper their concerns. She could still hear Skyler's voice as he spoke incoherently.

"You should have seen the teeth on those things," Lucinda dramatically gasped from a far corner.

"Trust me," Hailey muttered while tensing from the ghostly voices, "I have."

Hailey stared at the candles and put her effort into concentrating. The flames rose higher then bent toward the shackles on her wrists and ankles. Within seconds, the keyholes glowed bright red. The spirits whispered and collected around her. Their concerns were rising, and they appeared to be shielding her. Within the corridor, she heard the faint snarl of several beasts followed by sharp, shrill wails. The corridor was suddenly quiet. Lucinda stared at the chamber door almost frozen then turned toward Hailey. Her concerned look turned back to sympathetic. The candles surrounding the altar were burnt down to waxy nubs. Hailey remained shackled and watched as Lucinda approached with a thin dagger in her hand. A strange smile twisted across her face.

"No keys, but I found this--" she announced and revealed the knife.

"Is that how you killed them?"

Lucinda appeared surprised by the question then smiled and played with the dagger almost lovingly. She caressed the blade in a sensual manner.

"Pity you had to be the one sent to destroy me," she announced with a dreary sigh.

"How do you know that?" Hailey asked with surprise while attempting to read her expression in the dim lighting.

Lucinda's statement was bizarre considering Hailey didn't even know why she was commanded to the island. She hated that she was the last to know everything.

"You weren't the first," Lucinda casually replied. "Your father, the Emperor, exterminated my people nearly two decades ago. He deemed us a threat to your society."

Hailey stared at her while attempting to put it together. Strange stories were flooding her mind. It was as if her subconscious had been mysteriously unlocked and small parts of her young life were returning to her. She was only a little girl, but she remembered being told the stories by a man, possibly her uncle. They were bloody, merciless stories burned into her mind.

"Your *kind* feasts on humans," Hailey boldly announced. "Your *kind* destroyed my people."

"Only the small and the weak," she announced gleefully in true Lucinda fashion. Her playful smile turned angry. "Your father destroyed my entire family. Only a few of us escaped." Her lips curved into a scowl. "We were only children, but he would have killed us too."

"And with good reason."

Lucinda became enraged by the comment. "Enough to sacrifice his five daughters?"

Hailey's mind suddenly reeled from what she had heard. Was it true? Did she have sisters?

"Five?" Hailey suddenly gasped.

"You had four sisters," Lucinda informed her then appeared humored by the irony of the situation. "All of them with the same gifts you have and each of them failed." Her twisted smile mocked Hailey. "They had years to prepare and develop their gifts. They were the fail-safe, I assume, in case his most trusted guards failed at locating us. Unfortunately, you just realized you were different a few days ago. I assume because your uncle died, you never knew the power you possessed. If your sisters were no match for me, how can you possibly expect to defeat me?"

Hailey felt the anger building inside her. She'd just found out she had four sisters and that they were dead all at the same moment, killed by the retched woman before her.

"You killed my sisters?"

"I had to," Lucinda replied almost innocently. "There are quite a few of us living on this island, and your sisters were getting close to discovering us. Considering you knew nothing of your powers, it's baffling how you and your council were drawn here. A Numinous doesn't have that much power, and considering the one you'd picked, you're lucky he didn't blow his brains out years ago." Lucinda seemed particularly pleased with her assessment of Skyler. "Had you known your identity, we probably could have tracked you down around the same time we did your sisters."

Hailey felt her entire body twitch. The powers she contained were rising within her. Lucinda smiled with false sympathy and gently brushed the hair from Hailey's face.

"Oh, you poor thing," she cooed. "It was nothing personal, I assure you. It was them or me. You understand." Her mocking smile returned. "They went quickly, if it's any consolation. Two of them met their demise trying to find this island. One was involved in a tragic plane crash, and your other sister's boat sank a mile from the island. Your eldest sister, the first to go, never even made it that far. She died tragically in a car accident with her entire council shortly after her high school graduation." She appeared thoughtful. "Not that killing one's council really matters." She looked back at Hailey and grinned. "See, if you die, your council loses their powers, and, in most cases, their memory of the experience. That's a plus for me. For you too," she announced. "If I kill you here and now, your council wouldn't necessarily have to die. I know you'd take comfort knowing that."

"So you expect me to just let you kill me because you'll spare my council?" Hailey shook her head. "You're delusional. You always have been."

Lucinda sneered at Hailey's scathing words. "Bad news, Hailey. We're beyond all that. I intend to kill each one of them slowly and with as much pain as possible." Her hostility returned as she paced the altar. "The last thing I ever wanted was one of the emperor's daughters at my front door. But you're here now, so our only option is to exterminate. You've drawn too much attention to our way of life." She casually pointed to the ceiling with the dagger. "Everyone is gathering in the banquet hall until the hurricane passes. The roof is conveniently going to collapse from the storm, killing everyone."

Hailey's mind reeled with the new information of a mass slaughter. She couldn't allow Lucinda to get into her head. She had to stay focused.

Lucinda's mood again lightened as she smiled and became enthusiastic. "Oh, you'll be pleased to know that according to the contract Brody signed, his share of the hotel reverts back to me, his new partner, in the event of his death. Between his investment check and the insurance money, I'll be back on top." She playfully tapped Hailey's shoulder with the tip of the dagger. "Isn't that wonderful? I knew you'd be happy to hear that."

Hailey glared at Lucinda and sharply raised her brows. "Aren't you forgetting one thing?"

Lucinda thoughtfully considered the question while tapping the tip of the dagger to her chin. "You die, your council loses their powers, and we crush them like bugs." She looked back at Hailey and grinned, almost unable to contain her enthusiasm. "Nope, I think I covered everything."

The cougar suddenly leaped out of the darkness for Lucinda. She casually stepped out of its path, as if anticipating the arrival of her Protector. As it turned back for her, two beasts scurried out from under the altar and attacked the cougar. Lucinda turned toward Hailey and smiled as the creatures fought with the cougar, their snarls echoing throughout the room.

She smiled, pleased with herself. "And that includes your pesky Protector too."

They heard the faint wails of creatures being slain within the corridor. The sounds were getting closer to the chamber. Lucinda seemed annoyed, although she acted as if it was a minor nuisance.

"Your persistent council of misfits are getting through my pets," Lucinda remarked. "I don't mean to rush you, but we need to get on with this." Her look turned more serious as she gazed at Hailey with a slightly seductive look. Her hand gently caressed her face in an almost loving manner. "I'm going to miss you. I had such high hopes for a more intimate relationship."

Lucinda pulled her hand back while sighing lustfully then raised the dagger above her head. As she thrust downward with the dagger, Hailey pulled her hands free from the shackles and caught Lucinda's wrists. Having startled her former boss by freeing herself, Hailey easily knocked the dagger from Lucinda's hand. Lucinda jumped back with more surprise than anger.

Hailey quickly sat up on the altar and glared at Lucinda. "Actually, I never liked you."

"How did you get free?" Lucinda gasped while backing away from her.

"You don't give me enough credit," Hailey scoffed. "Or maybe I'm just more powerful than you'd imagined."

The cougar grabbed one of the beasts by the throat and tore through it. The second beast then attacked the cougar. It was difficult to tell who was winning. There was an urgent pounding against the crudely fixed chamber door. Hailey casually jumped off the altar and paced before Lucinda, almost mimicking her boss's actions. Lucinda continued to back away from her and toward the opposite wall.

"My misfits are knocking on your door," Hailey announced boldly as she cocked her head to the side. "Aren't you going to answer?"

The wall suddenly opened near Lucinda and she darted through. Hailey cried out as she bolted for the opening, but it closed before she reached it. She slammed her hand against the solid stone. The main chamber door burst open to reveal Rafe, Logan, and Vance. Rafe hurried to her and examined her for injuries.

"Are you okay?" he demanded.

"I'm fine, but Lucinda got away."

The cougar, although badly beaten, was victorious while panting over the two dead beasts. The cougar turned into the black cat and jumped into Hailey's arms. As she held it, its injuries immediately began to heal. The little cat purred in response. Hailey held the cat despite her alarm to the impending situation.

"They intend to kill everyone in the banquet hall and make it look like an accident to keep their secret hidden," Hailey informed them. "Skyler is unconscious, but he's been in contact with me since he was knocked out. We have to get to the banquet hall and stop them."

"Kill everyone? How?" Logan asked.

"She intends to bring the building down on them," Hailey announced. "Now that we know her plan, I'm sure they'll be ready and waiting for us in the banquet hall. We have to hurry."

"We need a plan," Vance informed them while shifting looks at his comrades.

"We'll make it up as we go," Rafe announced bluntly and stormed from the chamber.

Logan glared at Hailey and shook his head. "Your Guardian doesn't play well with others, does he?"

"No, not really," she muttered.

Hailey didn't have time to worry about her warriors not playing well together at the moment. She ran from the chamber after Rafe. Logan and Vance exchanged looks, released deep sighs, and hurried after her.

Chapter Thirty-two

$\mathcal{T}$he elegant banquet hall was large enough to host wedding receptions and other venues up to five hundred guests and still maintain enough room for a decent dance floor. Its current function, for the moment, was an emergency storm shelter for the hotel guests and employees riding out the massive storm slamming the island. One side of the banquet hall contained large windows, which were reinforced. The windows faced the garden area before the pool rather than the ocean itself. Only a small alcove faced the beach, but it contained a storm door, which could be closed in the event of an emergency. The worst storms usually skimmed the ocean side of the hotel and struck the lobby the hardest. Nearly two hundred hotel guests and almost one hundred employees socialized within the otherwise unused banquet hall. For marketing purposes, the room remained lightly decorated and contained several round tables set up for an elegant, imaginary function, so it could be shown with little advance warning to potential customers.

The bar, which was usually left empty, had been hastily set up for the 'storm gala event'. A silver, multi-tiered mimosa fountain flowed cocktails and an elegant brunch was served buffet style. Despite the rush on the banquet hall, the staff did an amazing job at keeping the guests occupied and entertained while they waited out the approaching storm. While the resort guests socialized and seemed unconcerned about the severe storm just outside, staff planned for the worst and secretly scurried about the banquet hall. They gathered supplies in the event of a power outage. The backup generator could take a lot of strain, but it too could be knocked out in extreme situations. Mel kneeled alongside a sofa on the far end of the hall, where Skyler remained unconscious.

Hailey, Rafe, Logan, and Vance entered the ballroom with their weapons raised and ready, prepared for battle. All four stopped and stared at the elegant social event playing out before them. They exchanged stunned looks.

"Where's the ambush?" Vance asked as two women passed him carrying champagne glasses.

They eyed him and the bloodstained baseball bat he held. He immediately hid it behind his back and smiled innocently. Despite what they had seen, both women eagerly smiled back and swept lustful gazes over his body. Logan and Rafe casually hid their swords behind their backs as well. Hailey studied the room, including the ceiling and shook her head.

"Something's definitely not right," Hailey muttered then looked around the room for Skyler.

"There's another exit across the room to the garden," Rafe announced while glancing at Logan. "You check it out. I'll keep watch here."

Logan placed his sword under his arm to conceal it and headed across the room. He paused before the garden side door, opened it, and looked around outside. He looked back at them from across the room with confusion on his face and shrugged. Hailey continued to scan the room then saw Mel tending to Skyler on the sofa. She hurried toward them with Vance only steps behind. Hailey kneeled before the sofa where Skyler remained unconscious and placed her hand on his forehead. Mel was surprised to see Hailey and stared at her.

"Are you okay?" Mel asked her softly then looked around. "What happened to Lucinda and Marcus?"

"They got away," Hailey replied in a soft tone, so as not to alarm the other guests. She nervously glanced around. "Anything strange happening around here?"

"Surprisingly, no," Mel remarked while attempting to mask her concern. "Everyone's in a great mood. I think most are drunk."

She stared at Hailey with a demanding look. "Are you going to tell me what happened?"

"Later," she replied.

Skyler finally woke and looked at Hailey with disorientation. She was thankful she was able to pull him out of his unconscious state. He groaned softly with relief to see her, sat up on the sofa, and hugged her.

"Hailey, thank God," he gasped.

She barely had time to return the embrace when he suddenly pulled away and stared blankly, as if sensing something. She felt alarm rushing through her. She was starting to know that look all too well. Talbert approached them and was about to speak when Skyler's expression dropped. He looked at Hailey with alarm clearly on his face.

"They're swarming," Skyler gasped almost loud enough for other guests to hear. "It's a trap."

Hailey stared at him and searched for a response.

Talbert became irritated and pointed accusingly at Skyler. "You need to stop with that--"

Skyler abruptly stood, shoved Talbert out of his path, and looked around the banquet hall. Hailey joined him and scanned for any signs of trouble, but everything seemed unusually peaceful. Rafe looked at them in silent question from the main doorway. Hailey signaled to him. He gave a general nod to Logan across the room, indicating for him to keep alert. When Logan turned back toward his door, several beasts suddenly charged into the banquet hall, nearly trampling him. He fell to the floor and the sword flew from his hand. Rafe charged across the room for the first rampaging beast as it jumped on one of the guests, tearing its sharp teeth into the man's arm. Rafe swung his samurai sword while sliding toward the beast on top of the man. The sharp blade connected with the creature's neck, decapitating its head. As the beast's head toppled across the floor, blood sprayed across the room. Rafe pulled the injured man to his feet, giving him a chance to escape.

Men and women screamed and ran from the large, snarling creatures that charged after them. Mel joined in the chaos with her own panic riddled screams while clinging to Skyler's arm. Logan sprang to his feet and slammed the door shut before more creatures could enter. Several creatures slammed against the sturdy glass doors. Logan reclaimed his sword then hurried deeper into the room to help Rafe and Vance stop the rampaging beasts. There were at least five creatures already within the room attempting to kill frightened guests and employees.

Hailey stared at the glass doors and windows with horror on her face. The beasts were swarming the glass attempting to break into the room. All she saw was a sea of black creatures slamming against the glass.

"What the hell--?" Talbert cried out in panic.

"There must be over a hundred outside," Hailey gasped and looked at Skyler, who shared her horror. "She wasn't going to destroy the hotel, she organized a slaughter."

One of the creatures tackled a woman to the floor, knocking the air from her body and leaving her defenseless. Vance swung his baseball bat for the creature's head and knocked it off her, although it didn't go down. The creature shook its large head, snarled at Vance, and charged him. Vance coiled back and swung the bat at the creature's head. The large creature was thrown backwards and struck the floor with tremendous force. It moved slightly. Guests and employees immediately pummeled the writhing creature with chairs and trays until it stopped moving. Rafe and Logan slashed at creatures with their swords, needing more than one blow to take them down. Guests and employees trapped behind the bar attempted to keep two more creatures from getting across the bar to reach them.

Mel yanked harshly on Skyler's arm, attempting to pull him toward the interior door with the heard of stampeding guests running for the exit. The first man to the door opened it to reveal another snarling beast waiting to get inside. As it attempted to plow through the doorway, several guests helped the man close the door on the creature. Everyone screamed until they had the door closed and locked, keeping the creature outside.

"We're trapped," Mel cried out while frantically looking around the room.

Several guests fended off a third creature that had followed the crowd to the main door. They were only succeeding in holding it back and quickly losing ground.

"They're going to get in," Skyler warned Hailey and immediately fidgeted, but his movements were constricted by Mel's arm tightly wrapped around his.

Hailey turned toward Talbert, who appeared to be in shock as he watched the three men at the bar fighting the beasts, which were now focused on them rather than the screaming guests.

"Is everyone here?" she asked Talbert.

Talbert didn't respond but, instead, just stared helplessly at the deteriorating situation within the banquet hall. Hailey grabbed him by the arm and gave him a firm jolt back to reality.

"Is everyone here?" she demanded.

He finally snapped out of his shock and met her gaze, fumbling for his words. "You were the last of the guests, but more than thirty employees never reported."

"That's because they're involved," Skyler remarked and looked at Hailey for their next move.

"This room is expected to withstand a hurricane, right?" Hailey asked Talbert.

"Yes, but those things--" Talbert began.

Hailey didn't bother waiting for him to finish. She turned to Skyler with a serious look on her face.

"The guys are handling the creatures already in the room and should have the situation under control shortly," she informed him. "It's important that no one leaves the safety of the banquet hall." She quickly turned back to Talbert and commanded his attention. "I need to get to the roof. Is there another way out of here other than the main doors?"

Talbert appeared surprised by her comment then considered his answer. His eyes suddenly lit up.

"There's a crawl space in the bathroom," he announced. "It'll take you to the men's bathroom just off the lobby. They're connected. It's too dangerous though. What if those things are in the lobby?"

"I'll have to risk it," Hailey replied.

As if reading her mind, Skyler stared at Hailey with a look of alarm. "Please, Hailey, don't do this," he pleaded. "You don't have to risk your life."

"Do what?" Mel gasped in terror as she gripped Skyler's arm even tighter.

Hailey's mind was already made up as she backed away from Skyler. "I'll keep in touch with you," she announced. "Just make sure this room remains sealed."

Hailey hurried into the nearby bathroom without giving him further chance to protest. Toward the center of the room, Rafe slashed the throat of the beast he fought. Trapped guests screamed and backed up behind the bar while dodging spattering blood. The second beast leaped for Rafe. Rafe somersaulted over the creature and speared it in mid flip. The creature struck the floor with a thud. Rafe landed gracefully and pulled his sword from the beast. Several feet away, Vance struck another creature in the head with his bat, tossing it toward Logan, who swung his sword and decapitated the remaining creature. As the last creature fell into a bloody heap, more creatures attempted to get inside.

"We need to reinforce the doors," Vance yelled to the panicking guests.

With the last of the creatures in the room dead, a group of men assisted Vance and helped move one of the heavier tables in front of the garden door. Rafe hurried toward Skyler, who finally managed to free his arm from Mel's clutches. Rafe looked around with concern then met Skyler's gaze.

"Where's Hailey?" he demanded.

"She said no one can leave and the room needs to remain sealed," Skyler announced, his concern clearly showing.

"What? What's she up to?"

Skyler shook his head. "I don't know what she's planning, but I can tell you it's going to be bad."

"How could you let her leave without protection?" Rafe suddenly demanded then appeared preoccupied with his concerns. "I have to find her."

He turned to walk away. Skyler grabbed his arm and stopped him.

"I'm concerned about her too," Skyler announced firmly. "She's the only friend I have, but we have to trust her."

For a brief moment, there was no telling what Rafe's intentions were. Skyler braced himself for whatever backlash was about to come his way. To Skyler's surprise, Rafe relaxed, although maintaining his disapproving look.

"Then I suppose I have no choice but trust her," Rafe muttered then turned and was about to help the others reinforce the doors. He hesitated then looked back at Skyler. "And she's *not* your only friend."

Rafe hurried across the banquet hall to join Logan by the garden side windows. Vance was already organizing the people within the room to help clear away the dead beasts and secure the area. Logan stood before the large window and studied a beast on the outside as it clawed and scratched at the thick shatterproof glass, attempting to get to him. It barely scratched the glass, which was encouraging. Rafe looked from the raging, frothing creature to Logan and raised a skeptical brow in response.

"That's not exactly productive," Rafe remarked.

Logan didn't respond. He appeared transfixed on something within the garden. Thick, thorny vines grew rapidly outside the window, crawling up the glass and the building. The creatures pricked themselves on the thorns and eventually jumped away from the window. The vines continued to spread rapidly, chasing all the beasts away from the windows. Rafe stared with astonishment while casting several glances at Logan.

"I'd like to withdraw my earlier remark," Rafe announced casually, patted Logan on the back, and indicated the plant life outside the window. "Have fun with that."

Chapter Thirty-three

*H*ailey peered out of the men's restroom and looked around the main corridor not far from the lobby. The corridor was quiet and empty. She hurried into the open elevator, swiped her keycard, and was about to press the penthouse button when she reconsidered. She pressed her own floor instead. She couldn't risk someone possibly hiding out on the twentieth floor and hearing the elevator arriving. As the doors closed, she leaned against the wall and shut her eyes a moment. She wasn't sure she was doing the right thing. Every instinct inside her screamed that her plan wouldn't work. It was a self-fulfilling prophecy of potential doom. On the short elevator ride to the nineteenth floor, she kept thinking about Lucinda's scathing remarks. She had four sisters; all who failed to destroy her evil boss. They were prepared for the challenge, and they failed. How could she ever hope to defeat Lucinda? Did she really think her misfits were up to the challenge? Had Rafe been right? Was she ultimately sending them to their death?

As the doors opened to her floor, she was still debating her plan and questioning herself. She hurried along the corridor, past her room, and directly for the stairwell. Her dilemma continued as she ran up the steps toward the roof. All she could think about were the sisters she never knew; how they must have died; and those four deluded men willing to follow her to the depths of hell just because she said so. If they died, it was on her. She wasn't sure she could live with the guilt, although if they died, she probably wouldn't outlive them by long. The thought didn't offer any comfort. She reached the twentieth floor and suddenly stopped. She looked up the steps toward the roof exit, but something was urging her to stop on the penthouse floor.

Hailey removed her keycard, which was the only way to access the penthouse stairs, and uncertainly ran the card through the slot. She gently pushed the door open and peered into the twentieth floor corridor, which was only home to Lucinda's penthouse suite and the presidential suite. Lucinda's penthouse door opened. Hailey ducked back inside the stairwell, holding the door open only a crack to watch. Twenty men and women she recognized as hotel employees left Lucinda's suite and headed for the nearby elevator. They were talking softly among themselves while they waited for the elevator to arrive.

"We'll meet up with the others in the lobby," a maintenance man announced. "When the interior door to the banquet hall is clear of snappers, we'll run to the door as if we're being chased. Once they let us in, it's necessary we take out Hailey and her misfits first. The others won't be a problem."

"And while you're keeping her council busy," a housekeeper announced, "I'll open the garden door and let the remaining snappers inside to deal with the rest of the guests."

The maintenance man chuckled, finding the thought humorous. "That's going to be a slaughter. I hope we at least get some of the leftovers."

The maid cringed her disapproval. "Do you really want sloppy seconds from a snapper?"

"We've been starved far too long," the maintenance man responded. "I'll take anything warm right about now."

The elevator door opened and all twenty men and women filtered inside. As the door slid closed, Hailey was quick to share the newly found information.

"Skyler," she announced softly aloud, even though she didn't have to say the actual words. "A group of your co-workers are on their way to the banquet hall. They're going to ambush you once they get inside. Keep them out at all costs."

Skyler responded to her warning, insisting they would make certain the staff didn't get inside. Being fairly confident the guests were safe from the murderous staff, Hailey slowly left the safety of the fire stairs and quietly walked along the corridor. She was still compelled to press onward. As she approached Lucinda's suite, she saw the busted door hadn't fully closed, since there had been no time for Lucinda to have it fixed. Hailey could hear voices within the suite. One of the voices was Lucinda's, and she was ranting like a mad woman.

"We're certain they're all within the banquet hall?" she demanded.

Within the penthouse suite, Lucinda paced the massive living room while Marcus casually leaned against the bar. Delaney and Cass were the only staff remaining inside the penthouse. Cass was seated comfortably in one of the oversized chairs while Delaney stood not far from Marcus at the bar and refilled his scotch glass with Lucinda's top-shelf liquor.

"Yes," Delaney announced as he sipped his drink. "I made sure they entered before I came up here. The snappers have them boxed in. They won't be able to escape."

Lucinda stopped pacing and stared blankly at an expensive painting on the wall. All three watched in silence as she considered her next move. She spun on her heels and looked directly at Marcus with a stern expression.

"On to more important matters. Have you found my necklace yet?" she demanded of him.

"I searched all their rooms," Marcus casually informed her. "I didn't find it. Maybe it wasn't one of them who stole it. How would they know its importance? She didn't even know who she was until two days ago. The girl knows nothing."

Lucinda folded her arms casually across her chest and strummed her fingernails on her skin while staring at Marcus. She tilted her head and suddenly smirked.

"You're absolutely right, Marcus," she announced. "There's no way she'd know about the stone's power. It would only be of value to me."

"Obviously," Marcus agreed. "It's nearly time for you to reproduce. Without the power of the stone, you'll only produce snappers. We need viable workers; not more snappers."

"Her Numinous may have foreseen its power," Delaney announced. "That could be why they stole it."

"Doubtful," Marcus remarked. "Have you met Skyler? He's a buffoon. Possibly the weakest Numinous I've come across. The boy can barely tie his shoes."

Beyond the penthouse suite door, Hailey straightened, having heard enough of their conversation to put everything together. Her conversation with Rafe about the necklace and his obsession with stealing it now made sense. Although, she was still puzzled by his instincts regarding a great many things. She needed to recover Lucinda's necklace as soon as she stopped the creatures from attacking the guests inside the banquet hall. She hurried back to the fire stairs, quietly exited through the door, and ran the last flight of steps to the roof.

Within Lucinda's suite, Lucinda again continued her pacing while rationalizing recent events. Her mind seemed to race for much needed answers.

"Let's not dismiss Skyler so quickly," Lucinda announced boldly. "I'm almost certain he was responsible for what happened here this morning. A Numinous doesn't have any real power, but you saw what happened with the snappers, and something had a telekinetic hold on your gun."

"Which had to be coming from Hailey's unconscious mind," Marcus insisted. "Telekinesis is not a characteristic of a Numinous."

"Are we certain?" Lucinda demanded.

"Absolutely," Marcus replied. "No creature on this planet possesses that sort of telekinesis." He appeared humored and allowed a laugh to escape his throat. "If he had that sort of power, that'd make him a descendant of royalty, and I can't see that idiot coming from the Emperor's bloodlines. Besides, he's too old to be some mutt love child from one of Hailey's uncles. They weren't on this planet any longer than we were."

"You're right, of course," she replied then sank back into thought.

There was an awkward silence. Cass and Delaney watched their boss attempting to come up with a more plausible explanation of her missing necklace. Lucinda studied Marcus and raised her brow with a devious look on her face.

"What about one of our own?" she asked. "Could one of ours have stolen my necklace?"

"A challenger to your throne?" Marcus demanded then chuckled softly. "Doubtful." He shot a look at Cass, who appeared rigid in her chair. "As Lucinda's closest aide, what's your opinion, Cass? Do you think any of the young females would ever consider revolting against our queen?"

"None that I would suspect," Cass replied and shot a look at Delaney by the bar. "Any ambitious females that you've noticed, Delaney?"

He shook his head without hesitation. "No, they're all perfectly content with the way things are," Delaney informed them. "There have been some comments about the last few breeding cycles having produced fewer viable workers and more snappers, but that's to be expected from time to time. I think we're going to have a good reproductive season this year."

Lucinda approached Delaney and seductively ran her hand along his chest. He didn't move or react as her hand traveled his chest to his abdomen.

"Yes," she cooed while smiling slyly. "It's going to be a fine reproductive season. Perhaps, this time, you'll put a little more effort into your duties. You seemed *distracted* last year, almost as if you were laying your seed elsewhere."

He drew a deep breath and straightened proudly. "We're not supposed to discuss reproduction in front of other females," Delaney reminded.

Lucinda and Marcus both shifted their attention to Cass, who appeared uncomfortable where she sat in the oversized chair. Lucinda chuckled softly and approached Cass.

"She doesn't mind," Lucinda replied and gently ran her hand along Cass's shoulder as she walked behind her chair. "Cass is my closest and most dependable aide." She stood behind her chair and gently massaged her shoulders in a caressing manner while looking at Delaney. "She's the only female of our kind I've ever allowed in my bed."

Cass tensed beneath Lucinda's caressing hands. Delaney attempted to show no reaction then took a large swallow from his glass. It clearly bothered him.

"I find the entire conversation inappropriate," he casually remarked as he set his glass down on the bar.

"Oh?" Lucinda questioned while staring at him as her hands caressed Cass's shoulders and moved their way toward her breasts. "I have to wonder if there's been some unauthorized breeding among my subjects. The birth of illegitimate snappers could explain the recent rash of attacks around my hotel."

"There has been no unauthorized breeding," Delaney announced with some agitation in his voice. "Each and every snapper on the island came from you and is loyal to you."

"Four women have disappeared in the last few days," Marcus snarled at Delaney. "Sure, a snapper occasionally strays and finds its own meal, but four isn't a coincidence." His eyes shot across the room to Cass, who remained uncomfortable beneath Lucinda's caressing hands. "Four random attacks sounds more like a wannabe queen building her strength for reproduction."

The look in Cass's eyes was that of alarm. She was about to protest when Lucinda's claws appeared and firmly dug deep into her flesh and tore across her throat. Cass barely had time to cry out as blood flowed from the four deep gashes through her jugular. Delaney jerked, his eyes conveying his horror. Lucinda stepped away from the gasping woman and showed no reaction for the life she claimed. She casually licked the blood from her claws. Cass thrashed slightly as the life ran from her throat. Marcus indicated the dying woman to Delaney with hostility in his hardened eyes.

"Drink her blood," he ordered.

Delaney shot looks from Marcus to Cass. He was horrified by the command.

"You'd side with that wretched girl over your queen?" Marcus demanded. "If you value your position as well as your life, you'll do it. Desecrate the female who dare betray our queen and prove your loyalty now."

Delaney slowly approached the nearly dead woman in the chair and stared into her dying eyes. She stared back at him and attempted to speak, but blood flowed from her mouth as she gurgled her words. He placed his mouth to hers and licked the blood running down her lips. He then lowered his mouth to the blood flowing from her jugular. As he slurped and lapped up her warm blood, Lucinda and Marcus exchanged satisfied grins from across the room.

"You don't know how lucky you are that it's mating season, and we're low on males," Marcus snarled at the man licking and sucking the warm blood spilling from his dead girlfriend's neck. "A great deal of having to exterminate those within the resort falls on your selfish need for power."

Delaney obviously heard him but didn't comment, instead, he continued with his duties.

"We had to cover your clumsy kills with the massacre of those playing poker in the laundry room," Marcus sternly announced. "Too many of them had come forward when Penny disappeared claiming they'd seen her in the basement." He shook his head with disgust while watching the man hovering over the blood-soaked dead woman. "I'm very disappointed in you, betraying your queen like that. You're lucky she doesn't have your head for this."

"He's forgiven," Lucinda announced with little concern. "He's proven his loyalty. Too often, young males fall victim to a younger female lobbying for her chance to be queen. They feel a younger queen will produce more workers and less snappers. I don't hold it against him." She casually crossed the room toward Marcus and seductively caressed his chest. She gave him an approving once over then looked back at Delaney. "Once you've finished your meal," she boldly announced while waving her hand with disgust, "kindly discard the carcass from the window into the garden below. My pets need their nourishment."

†

*H*ailey, slightly out of breath, appeared on the roof from the stairs and stopped to stare at the raging storm nearly upon them. There wasn't any rain, but the sky was almost black, and the wind blew violently. She hurried to the half wall and looked out to the ocean. The surf was rough, crashing violently to shore, and appeared even less friendly than the sky. Hailey drew a deep breath and tried to focus on her task. She briefly considered what she was doing and again questioned if it was the right thing to do. It seemed odd that she could almost hear the screams coming from the banquet hall, although she knew that was impossible. Strange premonitions kept sweeping her mind. It was almost as if she could feel what Skyler felt. Their connection to each other seemed to be growing stronger, and it was frightening.

"Skyler, I'm on the roof," she announced aloud. "How's it looking down there?"

†

*A*t the same time, within the ballroom, the creatures vibrated the garden side door despite the barriers. Guests were screaming at Skyler and Vance, who prevented them from allowing thirty or more employees from entering the banquet hall through the main entrance. They could hear them screaming and see their panic-filled faces through a small window on the main door. They were pleading to be allowed inside. Skyler kept his body against the door while Vance yelled and swung his baseball bat at the furious guests. It was only when the guests saw the creatures attempting to break open the door without attacking the staff outside, that they understood what was really happening. Creatures and traitorous employees together attempted to break through the main door.

The windows on the garden side appeared secure with their thorny shield over them. Despite the mass chaos outside the banquet hall, the guests and remaining staff gathered toward the back corner and attempted to remain quiet. Several sobs and sounds of mass hysteria occasionally broke the silence. Hailey's warriors moved closer to the center of the room with their weapons securely in hand and kept watch on both sets of doors. Skyler suddenly clutched his temples and zoned out. Rafe and Logan eyed him and awaited whatever news he had to report.

"Hailey, thank God," Skyler gasped aloud and looked around the banquet hall. "The doors are holding but not for long. Whatever you're going to do, do it fast."

Rafe took two quick steps toward Skyler and appeared demanding. "Are you talking to Hailey?"

Skyler held his temple, frowned, and waved off Rafe like a mother to her child while on the telephone.

"I'll let you know if they start breaking the doors, but what does that matter?" Skyler asked.

Vance and Logan exchanged concerned looks. Logan looked at Skyler, who now concentrated on his telepathic conversation.

"What's she saying?" Logan asked.

Skyler waved him off as well and concentrated on what Hailey was telling him. Logan was clearly offended.

"The necklace?" Skyler asked with a puzzled look then glanced at Rafe. "Hailey needs Lucinda's necklace."

Rafe appeared impatient and motioned demandingly. "Let me talk to her."

Skyler stared at him with surprise then appeared annoyed. "Sorry, I must've misplaced the handset."

Chapter Thirty-four

Hurricane type conditions were pushing their way along the beach and ocean. Palm trees were bending to the point of breaking and palms lie scattered along the once immaculate beach. Hailey stood on the roof before the half wall while staring at the ocean. She breathed deeply several times then held out her hand. The water crashed to shore in large, violent waves then rolled back out. A tremendous thundering sound was heard as the water continued to roll further and further into the ocean. The ocean floor was exposed, revealing the sunken remains of a large ship from decades past embedded in the sand. The water receded further and further back, causing the thundering rumbling sound to escalate to near deafening levels. Beyond the desolate ocean floor, there was a massive wall of water rumbling and rolling backwards. Hailey kept her trembling hand extended and stared out to the ocean with shock and dismay at the horror she was creating. It wasn't a nightmare! She had foreseen her own psychic prophecy.

"Oh, my God--" she gasped softly while watching the massive wall of water off in the distant horizon. It rumbled and rolled on itself as if awaiting her command. Her hand trembled while holding the wave in place. "Skyler, batten down the hatches!"

t

$\mathcal{B}$ack within the banquet hall, Skyler suddenly came to an abrupt stop, touched his temple, and appeared horrified at what he was hearing. He looked at the three men, who stared back at him with shared concern to his frightened expression.

"What's happening?" Vance asked slowly, appearing uncertain that he wanted to know the answer.

A mutilated, blood-soaked body suddenly dropped outside the vine covered windows behind the creatures. Mel, who was standing near the window at the time, screamed at the sight. Several creatures immediately turned toward the body and tore into its dried out flesh in a frantic feeding frenzy. Mel moved away from the glass and held her stomach. A strange sound was heard in the distance. Mel suddenly looked around with alarm on her face.

"Do you hear that?" she gasped.

Everyone within the banquet hall could hear the loud rumbling of rushing water. The sound grew louder. All five hurried to the vine covered windows within the alcove with a limited view of the ocean. A massive wave over sixty feet high was almost certainly awaiting to strike the beach and the resort, preparing to hit them head on. The sound of the distant wave was almost deafening. Rafe turned to Skyler and grabbed his shoulders, panicking for the first time.

"Is she insane?" he exploded. "The hotel will collapse under that pressure."

"Actually, given the distance and velocity--" Vance casually announced.

Rafe released Skyler and pointed a warning finger at Vance. "Skip the lecture, professor," he growled then looked around. "We need to somehow reinforce the doors and windows. They'll never hold!"

The sound of the wave grew louder now. The frightened people within the banquet hall bravely moved closer to the windows in the alcove and attempted to look outside. Despite their situation, they wanted to know what was happening. The creatures were now forcing their way through both sets of doors, alarming everyone further. Mel was the first to notice the creatures breaching the door on the garden side.

"They're getting in!" Mel cried out.

Skyler appeared alarmed and touched his temples while shouting aloud, "Hailey, abort! The creatures are breaking through. The seals won't hold!"

"We need to do something or we're going to drown," Vance cried out.

"Like what?" Logan demanded.

Vance shook his head then looked at the other three with enthusiasm. "Maybe we can do that thing where we combine our powers and stop it."

Rafe casually waved them off, returning to his relaxed, emotionless state. "We're dead. Accept it and move on."

The garden door was suddenly thrown open, and a creature bolted inside. Everyone screamed and ran from the charging creature. Rafe and Logan raised their swords and were about to fight it when the creature was suddenly catapulted backwards and propelled out the open door. The broken door slammed shut on its own with a thunderous crack. The entire room suddenly vibrated harshly, reminding them that the wave was about to hit the hotel. Everyone looked around, clinging to anyone close to him or her. Mel stood before the glass, stared out the window, and looked at the others with horror in her eyes.

"The wave is coming!" she screamed.

Rafe, Vance, and Logan looked around the vibrating room, as if simultaneously realizing it wasn't the wave that was causing the room to vibrate. According to Mel, it hadn't even reached the hotel yet. Their eyes fell upon Skyler. Skyler held his hands out while staring at the broken, shut door. He appeared motionless and fixated. Everyone fell silent to the deafening sound of the enormous wave and the vibrating room. All eyes were soon upon Skyler. Everyone stepped away from him.

†

The massive tidal wave hit the shore and crashed into the resort with tremendous force and a thunderous slap. Doors and windows shattered simultaneously under the pressure. Water crashed into the lobby in a massive flood and rushed through the main hallway and secondary corridors. The entire lobby was under water within seconds, allowing furniture to float haphazard. The lights flickered and went out throughout the entire hotel. The massive flood of water struck the creatures and non-human staff before slamming against the banquet hall doors with tremendous force. Water engulfed the entire corridor.

†

*T*he banquet hall continued to vibrate causing bottles of alcohol to fall from the bar and shatter. Heavy chairs danced along the floor in rhythm with the rumbling. The sound of rushing water echoed throughout the room. As the lights flickered and went out, everyone gasped and looked around. The walls, doors, and windows creaked loudly as massive cracks appeared. Water poured in through the cracks but remained beyond an invisible force field. The doors and walls bulged and groaned loudly. There were more terrified gasps and screams from the frightened men and women. Skyler remained still and fixated with his hands out in front and behind him. His hands began to tremble, the veins on his temples bulged, and blood ran from his nose. The room continued to vibrate and creak loudly as the echo of water pressure could be heard just outside the walls. Mel looked at the water beyond the window and watched dead creatures float past. The water was too high even to calculate. They were completely submerged under water in their protective, waterproof bubble.

The water rushed back into the ocean as furniture and creatures were carried out with the tide. Every window up to the sixth floor was shattered and the rooms were undoubtedly flooded beyond repair. Debris from the lobby and the garden littered the beach and resort grounds.

Within the banquet hall, everyone stared at the cracked walls and ceiling in silence as the water rushed away as quickly as it had arrived. Skyler slowly lowered his hands, gasped, and collapsed to his knees. He touched his bleeding nose then looked at the small pool of blood that had collected on the floor near where he had stood. Rafe, Vance, and Logan hurried toward Skyler to check on him. Vance and Logan helped him to his feet, although he remained weak and unsteady. Rafe stared at Skyler with some disbelief and shook his head.

"Not half bad," Rafe casually announced. His look immediately turned serious. "Where's Hailey? Is she okay?"

Skyler slowly nodded. "Yeah, she's fine. She's pretty drained after her little water show. She's on her way back to her room to retrieve Lucinda's necklace where you hid it."

197

Rafe hurried across the room toward the broken door, which now lie on the floor, and ran from the banquet hall. Vance and Logan stared at Skyler while shaking their heads as they marveled with disbelief.

"It's always the quiet ones," Vance remarked then chuckled while slapping him on the back.

Skyler grimaced from the back slap. Mel handed Skyler a cloth napkin and offered a warm smile. He gratefully accepted the napkin and dabbed the blood from his nose.

"Thanks," he said gently.

"No, thank you," Mel announced then kissed him quickly but firmly on the lips.

As she pulled away, Skyler stared at Mel with surprise and his cheeks immediately reddened with embarrassment. Vance and Logan snickered softly to each other.

Chapter Thirty-five

*T*here was still a foot of standing water remaining within the once elegant lobby, which contained the carcasses of several dead creatures sporadically lying about. The water continued to recede, leaving the need for extensive repairs from the damage. The elevator doors opened to reveal Lucinda and Marcus. Both stared at the remaining water as it flooded into the elevator to greet them. Lucinda saw one of the dead creatures lying within the water across the hall. They heard laughter and cheering coming from the banquet hall. Her precious pets and her entire colony had been destroyed, yet the humans survived their extermination. Lucinda glared at Marcus with a venomous look that almost matched his.

"I want her and her council dead!"

She violently hit the penthouse button until the door closed, taking her and Marcus back upstairs to the twentieth floor. As the water receded from the lobby, a flood of guests passed through and marveled at the damage before heading outside. Vance, Logan, and Skyler followed the guests into the water-damaged lobby. They stopped and looked around, nearly awestruck by the amount of damage it had sustained.

"What a mess," Vance casually remarked.

Talbert entered the lobby behind them and looked around with horror. "Look at my hotel! This will take forever to restore!"

After his initial outburst, Talbert seemed at a loss for words. He looked at Skyler as if sizing him up for the massive undertaking of cleaning the lobby.

Skyler caught his look, snorted a laugh, and threw his hands in the air. "Don't look at me," he announced callously. "You fired me, remember?"

Skyler casually cast himself onto a nearby sofa. It sloshed beneath him, soaking his pants. He shut his eyes and groaned softly to what had to be a very uncomfortable feeling. Talbert displayed his annoyance and continued across the lobby to survey the damage. Every window was broken, furniture was displaced, and anything lightweight that fit through the door had been taken out to sea. The desk seemed to be the only piece of furniture still in its original location. Vance and Logan looked at each other and grinned in silent celebration.

"How about a drink?" Logan suggested cheerfully.

"How about several?" Vance teased while holding his arms out with enthusiasm.

"You're on," Logan replied then looked at Skyler where he remained on the soaked sofa. "You coming?"

Skyler didn't seem in the mood for celebrating just yet, and it probably had little to do with his wet pants. "No, you go on ahead. I'll wait for Hailey."

They nodded in response and headed down the hallway toward the lounge. If they were lucky, they'd be able to find some booze stored behind the bar, providing it hadn't all been sucked out into the ocean.

t

*H*ailey slowly entered her suite while half clinging to the wall for support. She was completely drained. Her legs were so weak; she didn't know how she made it down the stairs from the roof. She slowly crossed the room to the fireplace, took a moment to catch her breath, and then moved to her knees before the opening. She felt around inside the chimney, but every small movement was an effort.

She didn't know how long she'd feel drained and wiped out, but she had to find the necklace. Her fingers touched a smooth stone. Hailey breathed a sigh of relief and removed Lucinda's soot covered stone necklace from the chimney. She brushed some of the soot from the stone and grimaced at the sight of it. It truly was a hideous looking thing. She then heard the sound of a gun being cocked behind her. Hailey tensed to the sound and slowly turned on her knees to face Marcus, who stood over her with his gun aimed at her head. He snatched the necklace from her.

"You've ruined everything we've spent nearly two decades to achieve," Marcus snarled with a look on his hardened face that frightened her. "I can't wait to be rid of you."

Hailey slowly stood and stared at the gun aimed at her face. She didn't exactly like her predicament. She was powerless and weakened while alone in her suite with Marcus. Although, she was never truly alone. As if on cue, the cougar mysteriously appeared from alongside the sofa and leaped for Marcus. Marcus saw the cougar, showed little emotion, and casually shot it in the head. He watched the cougar fall bloody and limp to the floor. He then turned his attention and his gun back on Hailey, but it was too late. Hailey had already set her counterattack in motion. With every ounce of strength, she swiftly kicked Marcus in the groin. She was getting a little tired of everyone killing her cat! Although she nailed Marcus firmly between his legs, he barely flinched and immediately backhanded her across the face in response. Hailey was thrown against the fireplace. It was a surprisingly hard slap, which felt more like a punch. She attempted to straighten while plotting her next move. She summoned her powers, but felt nothing building inside her.

"Stupid girl--"

Marcus aimed the gun at her and tightened his finger on the trigger. Rafe was suddenly alongside Marcus and knocked the gun from his hand. As the gun flew across the floor, Rafe punched Marcus in the face. The necklace fell from his hand and slid beneath the coffee table. Surprisingly, Marcus didn't go down from the powerful hit. Any normal man would have been unconscious on the floor.

Marcus glared at him and smiled evilly. "I've been waiting a long time for this day, Rafe," he snarled. "It's going to be a pleasure tearing you apart."

"Give it your best shot," Rafe growled in response.

Razor sharp claws appeared from Marcus' fingertips. He then smiled to reveal sharp, cat-like fangs. Rafe was almost as surprised as Hailey was.

"That's not good," Hailey gasped as her body twitched, but she was still unable to summon her powers.

Marcus didn't take his eyes off Rafe. "You really have no idea what you're dealing with," he snarled.

He slashed at Rafe, who leaped out of the path of the claws. Hailey scrambled to the floor for the discarded gun. It was just within her reach. The gun was suddenly kicked away from her fingers. Hailey looked up and saw Lucinda standing over her with an evil, fanged smirk beyond her plump red lips.

"I don't think so, my dear," she hissed.

Lucinda grabbed Hailey by the throat and pulled her to her feet. Claws appeared from her fingertips as well and nearly pierced Hailey's neck. Hailey stared into Lucinda's yellow cat eyes and attempted to struggle against the clawed hand that held her throat. Hailey needed her powers to return, but she could do little more than grasp and clutch at the woman's wrist in an attempt to loosen her grip.

"Numinous!" she gasped with all her breath even though she didn't need to speak aloud at all.

Lucinda seemed humored by the cry for help and added a throaty chuckle. "Your little friends can't help you," she remarked. "Not anymore."

✝

*S*everal hotel guests returned from gawking at the exterior damage to the resort and now milled around the lobby, surveying the water damage to the ceiling. Most were fascinated by the events that had unfolded. Some even took selfies with the few dead creatures lying scattered about the room. Skyler now paced the lobby while waiting for Hailey to return from her suite. Mel leaned against the desk and watched him marathon pace as he alternated shaking his head and running fingers through his hair. He suddenly gasped and placed his hands to his temples almost as if in pain. His eyes were wide with horror as he turned to Mel.

"Hailey's in trouble," he cried out. "Go to the lounge and tell Vance and Logan to meet me in Hailey's suite!"

Mel nodded and both ran in the direction of the corridor. Skyler turned toward the elevators and suddenly stopped. He clutched his temples and doubled over with surprise. Mel suddenly stopped, turned, and looked back at him.

"Are you okay?" she asked.

Skyler stared blankly a moment longer as if unable to speak. His body twitched as if going into a seizure. There was a flash of Rafe lying motionless and bloody followed by another image of Hailey being shot. Skyler jerked out of his twitching trance, gasped for air, and then looked back at Mel while straightening.

"I saw Hailey and Rafe dead," he cried out in panic. "I have to get to them!"

Skyler ran for the elevator and punched the button roughly. The door immediately opened as if on command. It was possibly the first time in his life anything ever went his way when he needed it to. He darted inside as Mel ran down the hallway the reach the men in the lounge.

Chapter Thirty-six

Lucinda tightened her grip on Hailey's neck. Her hard fingers were crushing her throat and the tips of her claws now pierced the skin, allowing droplets of blood to run down her neck. It would be a race to see whether Lucinda would slice her jugular or crush her throat first. Hailey clutched Lucinda's wrist and summoned every ounce of strength she had left within her. Nothing happened. The cougar's lifeless body twitched, catching both women's attention. Lucinda groaned lowly with annoyance, although it had no effect on her viselike grip on Hailey's throat.

"Why won't that damned thing stay dead?"

From a few feet away, Rafe saw Lucinda holding Hailey by the throat, but Marcus wasn't about to let him through to rescue her. Rafe leaped into a fast, hard kick, struck Marcus in the chest, and sent him flying backward into Lucinda. Lucinda and Marcus crashed to the floor, taking Hailey with them. Hailey was tossed further away from the other two. Despite being momentarily dazed, she looked across the floor and saw the necklace within her reach just beneath the coffee table. Hailey grabbed the necklace. Before she could get to her feet, Lucinda saw her with the necklace, violently tossed Marcus off her, and leaped for Hailey. Hailey saw the menacing woman about to pounce on her and rolled out of her path. Lucinda struck the coffee table with enough force that it should have seriously injured her, but it barely slowed her down. Hailey realized she was seriously outmatched in her weakened condition against her inhuman boss. She scrambled to her feet as Lucinda slashed at her, narrowly avoiding the sharp claws. Rafe looked across the room at Hailey as Marcus came back at him.

"Hailey, run!"

As Hailey looked back at Rafe, Marcus slashed him across his abdomen, leaving bleeding scratches. Hailey cried out, fearing for the worst. If Rafe knew he'd been injured, he didn't show it. Instead, Rafe spun into a roundhouse kick and struck Marcus harshly across the face.

Rafe met Hailey's concerned stare across the room. "Go!" he shouted his orders.

Lucinda leaped for Hailey with her claws slashing for her face. Hailey gasped and, against her better judgement, bolted for the door, leaving Rafe to his own devices. Lucinda grabbed the discarded gun from the floor and ran after her. The black panther suddenly emerged with renewed vigor from the cougar's pelt. The pelt disintegrated. Marcus lunged for Rafe and both crashed onto the coffee table. The table broke beneath their combined weight, leaving Marcus on top of Rafe. The panther ran across the suite for the door, momentarily stopped, and slashed Marcus across the back before running from the room. Marcus cried out from the deep gashes across his back. That split second was all Rafe needed to get out from under Marcus. Both men jumped to their feet and prepared for another round of punishment. Rafe kicked Marcus in the chest as his claws slashed Rafe's leg.

Rafe cried out from the sudden surge of pain, caught his balance, and kicked with his left leg, nailing Marcus in the mouth. Marcus flew backwards several steps but still didn't go down. Rafe clutched his bleeding leg, sneered, and approached Marcus. Marcus again slashed at Rafe, aiming for his throat. Rafe attempted to block his claws and received four gashes across his lower arm. He cried out and clutched his bleeding arm. Despite his injuries, Rafe kicked Marcus in the groin so hard it elevated him from the floor. Marcus clutched himself and fell to his knees. Rafe attempted to catch his breath and slowly approached Marcus on the floor. He crouched over him and grabbed him by the throat with blood-covered hands, prepared to deliver the deathblow. Marcus suddenly came to life and slashed Rafe across the chest, slicing him to the bone. Rafe cried out and fell onto his backside on the broken coffee table while clutching his bleeding chest.

Marcus slowly moved to his knees, maneuvered over Rafe, and was about to slash him across the throat. Rafe raised his free hand, which held the broken coffee table leg, and impaled Marcus through the chest with the thick shard of wood. Marcus gasped and slowly moved to his feet while clutching the jagged wood in his chest. Rafe weakly moved to his feet, now panting to catch his breath. Marcus attempted to pull the wood from his chest. Despite his weakened state, Rafe delivered a hard kick, driving the wood deeper into Marcus' chest. Marcus gasped as blood ran from his mouth while staring into Rafe's determined, hateful eyes. Marcus remained standing a moment or two then collapsed to the floor. Rafe clutched his bleeding chest, almost as if feeling the enormous pain for the first time, looked at the massive amount of blood spilling onto his hand, and frowned his annoyance.

"This day officially sucks," he muttered.

"Rafe," Vance was heard calling out from across the room. "Where's Hailey?"

Rafe slowly turned toward Vance in the doorway and weakly shook his head. "I don't know."

Vance saw Rafe's blood-soaked body and appeared horrified by his injuries. "Rafe--?"

"Hailey needs you," he announced nearly out of breath. "I'll be along shortly. I need to rest a moment."

Vance stared at Rafe's severe injuries with concern then slowly backed away. They both knew the inevitable outcome, but neither said it.

"Yeah, you've got it," Vance said softly, almost choking on his words. "I'll look after her."

As Vance ran from the suite, Rafe slowly collapsed onto the sofa and rested his head against the back.

†

*T*he sky remained dark and threatening as the wind continued to whip. The creatures were no longer a threat, but the storm was still sideswiping them. Lucinda silently walked along the roof looking for Hailey. She tapped her claws together then looked at the helicopter still positioned where she had landed it several days ago.

She grinned, exposing her sharp fangs as she approached the helicopter. She ran her claws along the side of the helicopter, making a hideous grinding sound as she left scratches along the glossy exterior. She threw open the back door to reveal Hailey hiding on the floor. Lucinda maintained her evil smile and extended her clawed hand. Her bloodstained claws were long and sharp, commanding Hailey's attention.

"I'll take my necklace now," Lucinda snarled while smiling victoriously.

"You mean this?" Skyler's voice was heard shouting from behind her.

Lucinda turned with surprise to see Skyler standing several yards away with the necklace dangling from his fingers. His smile mocked her.

"You want it?" he asked while taunting her with it. His smile twisted into a sneer. "Come and get it, bitch."

Lucinda aimed Marcus' gun at Skyler. Hailey no longer pretended to be the frightened victim and kicked the gun upward from Lucinda's hand. The gun flew back at Hailey, who attempted to catch it, struck the inside front windshield, and fell to the floor with a distinctive clatter. Lucinda glared at Hailey but was obviously less concerned with her at the moment and turned for Skyler. When Skyler saw her claws and fangs, his mocking smile immediately dropped to that of horror.

"Okay, no one mentioned claws and fangs!"

Lucinda lunged for Skyler. He cried out and bolted from her path, literally running up the half wall and flipping off it like a deranged ninja. Lucinda didn't have time to stop and struck the half wall with tremendous force. She slammed her palms on the ledge, snarled her displeasure, and spun toward him with rage in her yellow cat eyes. Skyler was momentarily intimidated by her animal like eyes but quickly rebounded. He backed up several steps, dangled the necklace, and grinned.

"Here kitty, kitty, kitty--"

Lucinda snarled with rage and lunged for him, slashing with her claws. The black panther suddenly leaped past Skyler and snatched the necklace from his hand with its mouth. The panther stopped not far from them, arched its back while looking at Lucinda, and growled as the necklace dangled from its teeth.

"Oops, wrong kitty," Skyler remarked.

Lucinda cried out and slashed at Skyler with her claws, nearly slicing him. He managed to leap out of her path with his own cat-like reflexes then nervously smiled.

"Gotta go!"

Skyler ran across the roof for the door and collided with Delaney, who mysteriously appeared almost out of nowhere. He slashed Skyler's arm with his own claws. Skyler fell against the closed door, clutching his bleeding arm, and stared helplessly at Delaney. Skyler's look then turned angry.

"Owe, that hurt, you son-of-a-bitch!"

Lucinda glared at the growling panther. "I'll be back to claim my necklace once I kill your reason for existing."

She turned toward the helicopter, about to collect her prize, when she came face-to-face with Hailey, who stood directly behind her. Hailey swung a metal pipe for Lucinda's head. Lucinda caught the pipe with her claws, surprising Hailey, and casually cast it aside. Hailey backed away from her without taking her eyes from her. Now would be a good time for her powers to return.

"Never mind the freak, Delaney," Lucinda called back while staring at Hailey. "He'll be dealt with easily enough once this one's dead."

Skyler stared past Delaney at Lucinda and appeared offended. "You're one to talk, hairball!"

"Get my necklace," Lucinda ordered her man without taking her eyes off Hailey. "I'll deal with the princess." She cocked her head slightly and gave Hailey a quick once over. "Once she's eliminated, her council loses their powers."

Delaney turned his attention from Skyler to the panther with the necklace in its mouth. The panther growled at him. Skyler still clutched his bleeding arm and looked at Hailey across the roof from him.

"Hailey, do something!"

Only one thing came to mind as she helplessly watched the scene about to unfold.

"Kitty, run!" Hailey cried out.

The panther turned and ran with the necklace. Delaney attempted to pounce on the panther but missed and hit the roof floor. The panther leaped onto the half wall and dived into a nearby tree. The tree swayed and the panther was no longer seen. Delaney didn't hesitate and leaped into the tree after the large cat. Skyler stared at Hailey across the roof with a dumbfounded look.

"Not exactly what I had in mind, Hail."

"It's the best I've got," Hailey called back.

Lucinda turned to Hailey with rage clearly in her yellow cat eyes. "I've had enough of you and your pathetic council. It's time to end this."

She raised her clawed hand to slash her throat. The roof door was suddenly thrown open, casting Skyler carelessly across the roof, to reveal Vance in full 'knight in shining armor' mode. Even Hailey couldn't deny his dashing charm with the way he stood in the doorway like some medieval savior.

"Not another one," Lucinda cried out with frustration. "You're like bugs crawling out of the woodwork!"

"Or better yet," Vance announced as he grinned, "bats from a belfry."

Vance held his hands in the air. There was a strange sound against the stormy sky. A large, dark swarm rapidly closed in. Lucinda appeared bewildered and took a step back. She seemed frightened for the first time. A huge swarm of exceedingly large bats flew toward them.

Vance laughed evilly and waved his arms wildly in the air. "Fly my pretties--fly!"

Lucinda cried out as the bats swarmed around her in a black tornado. She shielded her face and screamed while attempting to keep them away.

After Vance had his moment, he looked at Hailey and turned serious. "Hailey, Rafe's been injured pretty badly. You need to, you know, do your *touchy* thing."

"My vision--" Skyler gasped.

Hailey hurried for the open roof door and nearly ran over Logan, who was just arriving. Logan took a moment to catch his breath, having run up the stairs, and then stared with surprise at the swarm of large bats flying around Lucinda. He smiled while nodding his approval.

"Now *that* is cool."

"Delaney is trying to get the necklace from kitty," Skyler announced and finally released his injured arm once the bleeding had stopped.

"Where?" Logan asked.

Logan, Vance, and Skyler approached the edge of the roof and looked into the swaying trees. Logan held out his hand and concentrated. The tree branches bent and vines rapidly grew along the trees. They heard Delaney screaming.

"I wouldn't worry," Logan announced cheerfully. "Delaney is a little tied up right now." He then looked around and appeared curious. "Where's Rafe?"

There was an awkward silence as Vance and Skyler exchanged concerned looks.

"He's been injured," Skyler reported in a timid tone.

"It's pretty serious," Vance added.

Logan's expression dropped.

t

*H*ailey hurried into her suite and suddenly stopped just inside the doorway. Rafe was reclined on the sofa with his feet crossed at the ankles on the broken coffee table and his eyes were closed. Blood soaked his torn shirt, and she could see more blood surrounding the gashes on his thigh. Hailey hurried to the sofa, sat alongside him, and gently touched his face. His eyes slowly opened and a smirk crossed his face.

"You should see the other guy--"

Rafe gave a slight mocking nod to Marcus lying on the floor, impaled through the chest with a wooden table leg. He attempted a laugh, clutched his bleeding chest, and cringed with pain. Hailey placed her hand on the deep gashes.

"Oh, Rafe--"

He looked at her and offered a tiny smile. "It's too late for that, Hailey. We both know it."

Hailey met his gaze with tears in her eyes and a determined look. "I can save you."

"You already have," he replied gently and offered a tender smile. "I can't think of a more noble cause then dying for the woman I love."

She stared at him and could almost feel her heart stop beating. It couldn't be possible. He couldn't die. Could he? He suddenly appeared humored and attempted to laugh, although it was obviously too painful.

"Hey? Isn't this how we first met?" he teased. "You standing over my bloody carcass?"

She felt the irony, but it suddenly gave her hope. "I brought you back once," she replied softly. "I can do it again."

"I don't think I get nine lives."

She shook her head with conviction and fear that resembled anger. "I won't let you go, Rafe."

"Be as stubborn as you want, but you really don't have much choice."

Hailey fought her tears and kissed him warmly on the lips. Rafe pulled her closer for a more passionate kiss. She returned his kiss as tears ran down her face. She kept her hand on his wounds without breaking off the kiss. Rafe's head slowly fell against the back of the sofa. Hailey pulled her head back and stared at him with tears streaking her face. She kept her left hand firmly on his chest wound and placed her right hand to his temple. Her look conveyed her determination.

"I won't let you go," she whispered.

Chapter Thirty-seven

Skyler and Logan stood by the half wall and stared at the motionless tree containing the panther and Delaney. Delaney could still be heard yelling, although his struggling against the vines wasn't doing any good. With little warning, the black panther leaped from the tree, tackled Logan to the roof floor, and sat on him with the necklace dangling from his mouth.

"Awe, he likes you," Skyler teased.

Logan stared at the panther sitting on his large chest, having knocked the air from him. "Yeah, well, us brothers got to stick together," he gasped.

Skyler took the necklace from Kitty's mouth and pushed the panther off his friend. Logan groaned. Several feet away from them, the large bats still swarmed around the crouched and cowering Lucinda. Vance stood nearby and allowed one of the larger bats to dangle from his hand. He turned his head upside down to study the creature.

"Who's the pretty little bat?" he cooed. "You're the pretty little bat."

Lucinda slowly lowered her arms from her face and looked at Vance through the swarm. Her claws and fangs were now gone. Her eyes seemed darker and almost innocent.

"Make them stop," she pleaded softly to him. "I give up. You win."

Vance allowed the bat to fly away and looked at Lucinda with arrogance. "I guess you should have thought about that before you got all rowdy."

"I never knew that beneath that handsome exterior was a man of great power," she said in a seductive tone. "I submit to you, Vance. You are superior to me."

He laughed at the comment. "If you weren't such an evil bitch, I think I'd be turned on."

Their eyes only met briefly, but that was all Lucinda needed. As she stared into his eyes, Vance stared back. His smile faded and he appeared almost helpless to her hypnotic gaze. Lucinda maintained her seductive smile despite the swarming bats.

"A characteristic flaw of the Charmer is the inability to refuse *my* charm. That makes you my slave," she informed him. "Now, my love, call off your pets."

Vance waved his hand, allowing the bats to fly away. Lucinda straightened with a satisfied smile. Logan and Skyler saw the bats flying past them then turned to see Lucinda free.

"Vance, no!" Logan cried out.

Vance pointed to Logan and Skyler. The bats took their cue, changed direction, and swarmed around them. Both men ducked and shielded their faces from the tornado of bats

"What's wrong with him?" Logan cried out, displaying his fear of the mammoth, flying creatures.

"He appears to be under some sort of spell," Skyler announced while attempting to get a closer look while shielding his face. "Hailey! We have a problem!"

Lucinda casually approached the men and their swarming bats. Her devious grin was frightening. Vance obediently followed in his trance-like state.

"The necklace, Vance," she ordered sweetly.

Vance reached through the swarm and snatched the necklace from Logan, who reluctantly released it. Lucinda took the necklace and seductively touched Vance's face.

"Come along, handsome," Lucinda announced. "We have a helicopter to catch."

Vance followed Lucinda to the helicopter. Hailey ran through the open doorway from the stairs in time to witness Lucinda and

Vance heading toward the helicopter. Lucinda opened the helicopter door, looked back at Hailey, and smiled sweetly.

"Vance, darling, *kill* that woman."

Vance turned toward Hailey and approached her. Hailey uncertainly backed away. The black panther attempted to come to her rescue but the bats kept it low to the ground. Kitty hissed at the bats and even swatted at a few.

"Vance, what's wrong with you?" Hailey suddenly asked with concern while avoiding his approach.

"He's under her spell," Logan cried out. "She did something to him!"

Hailey stared at Vance, although he avoided looking directly into her eyes. Despite the spell he was under, that part of him still remained. The helicopter started, alarming Hailey. She had to do something fast or Lucinda would get away. Hailey took a quick step closer to Vance and placed her hands firmly on his face.

"No, Hailey, run!" Skyler screamed.

Vance grabbed Hailey by the throat. Hailey gasped as he applied pressure, cutting off her air. Despite his grip, she forced him to look into her eyes. His grip tightened, and she was having a difficult time catching her breath. They stared into each other's eyes for only a few seconds. His expression suddenly dropped, and he pulled away from her as if she'd sent lightning through him. Vance clutched his head and dropped to his knees. Hailey slowly kneeled before him and gently touched his shoulder.

"Are you okay?"

Vance lowered his trembling hands and looked at Hailey. He stared helplessly into her eyes for the first time and appeared almost horrified.

"What happened?"

"A mild case of impotence, but it's only temporary, I promise," she replied.

Vance looked at his shaking hands and appeared too weak to stand. The helicopter began to lift from the pad, alarming Hailey. She quickly straightened.

"Vance, release the bats!"

Vance weakly lifted his hand and the bats flew away. It was all he had. Logan and Skyler quickly straightened. Vance remained kneeling on the roof floor unable to move and stared helplessly at his trembling hands. The helicopter lifted a few feet from the ground and was about to take off. Vines suddenly entwined around the rungs. The helicopter pulled up and easily snapped the vines.

"Damn it," Logan cried out.

The helicopter suddenly jolted but remained hovering in place. Hailey and Logan looked at Skyler, who held his hand out and kept the helicopter in place with an invisible force. Hailey jumped onto the half wall, teetered a moment to catch her balance, and then hurried along the wall toward the elevated helicopter.

"Hailey, no," Logan called after her.

Logan leaped onto the half wall near him and skillfully ran along it from the opposite direction for her. Lucinda pulled sharply on the controls. The helicopter jolted from the throttle and Skyler's hold. The back end of the helicopter spun slightly and headed directly for Logan. Logan cried out and plummeted over the edge. A vine entwined around his ankle and stopped him from falling to his death. He dangled from the vine while screaming. Skyler's eyes narrowed and his hand trembled. The helicopter's engine was heard revving loudly, but the helicopter remained held in place by Skyler's invisible force. Hailey made her way along the half wall just near the helicopter. Lucinda attempted to pull away from Skyler's telekinetic hold. The helicopter bucked. Skyler gasped and closed his fist. The helicopter remained steady. Hailey opened the passenger side door to reveal Lucinda aiming Marcus' discarded gun at her. Rafe suddenly appeared and tackled Hailey to the roof as the gun fired, narrowly missing her. Skyler sneered and violently released his telekinetic hold on the helicopter.

The helicopter suddenly jerked from Lucinda's pressure on the throttle, spun wildly out of control, and dropped over the side of the building. The helicopter crashed through several trees as it plummeted toward the ground twenty stories below. It struck the ground and exploded into flames. Skyler fell harshly to his knees and wiped the blood from his nose with disgust.

"Never underestimate a freak, bitch," Skyler muttered.

Rafe moved off Hailey, helped her into a sitting position, and then pulled her into his arms with a gentle groan. She clung to him and laughed softly.

"You sure know how to make an entrance," she announced as relief swept through her.

Rafe kissed her forehead then grinned and helped her to her feet. Vance placed his hand on Skyler's shoulder and weakly collapsed alongside him.

"Very effective, Numinous, but remind me never to fly with you," Vance announced.

There was a faint voice from over the side of the building. "Uh, could someone give me a hand?" Logan was heard outside the building just below the wall.

Everyone hurried for the half wall and looked over the side. Logan swayed back and forth by the vine attached to his ankle. The panther stood on its hind legs with its front paws on the half wall, watched Logan sway, and playfully batted at him.

Chapter Thirty-eight

The storm had passed, leaving the beachfront hotel virtually untouched. Unfortunately, plenty of damage had already been done earlier that day. The moonlit night on the terrace was calm, and the guests were having a good time despite all that had happened. It was unclear if anyone was sober by that point. The soft sound of music soothed guests' frayed nerves. Tam tended the makeshift bar, hastily nailed together. Logan sat before a portable keyboard attached to speakers and played a romantic melody while Hailey and Rafe slow danced in the shadows just beyond the terrace on the sand. Vance sat at a severely bent table sipping one of many fruity drinks. Brody pulled out a chair and joined him at the wobbling table. Both steadied the table until it no longer rocked.

"This was my first day as partner of this lovely beachfront property," Brody cheerfully informed Vance.

Vance snorted a laugh as he worked on finishing his fourth drink. "Certainly one vacation no one will forget," he replied while hiding his grin.

"I know I never will." Brody nodded toward the couple dancing in the shadows. "My 'all work' bodyguard just resigned in favor of 'all play'."

"Yeah, nearly dying can change a man," Vance remarked while grinning. "Third time's a charm."

An attractive woman passed them and smiled at Vance. He met her gaze and flashed his own smile in response. So began the pre-foreplay dance. He looked back at Brody.

"I think I'm being paged," Vance cheerfully informed him. "Was there something I could do for you, Brody?"

He sighed heavily with defeat. "According to the terms of the contract, I inherit Lucinda's half of the resort. Unfortunately, I also inherit the hotel's debt, which will potentially bankrupt me. I'm in desperate need of a partner." He stared at Vance and his agenda surfaced. "I took the liberty of having you checked out, and learned you're a man of considerable wealth with no real estate investments. I thought you might be interested in trying the hotel industry. You might like it."

Vance considered the idea, tilted his head, and then grinned in response. "Life in paradise?" he suddenly asked. "How much of a good thing is too much?" He chuckled softly. "I think I'd like to find out."

Vance extended his hand to Brody, who eagerly shook it, sealing their deal. Vance smiled and stood, indicating the woman who'd just passed.

"Now, if you'll excuse me," Vance announced. "I have to make sure I haven't lost my touch."

Brody smiled and laughed as Vance hurried after the attractive woman. Skyler appeared on the terrace from the side door, approached Logan at the keyboard, and sat next to him. He set the manuscript down near him. Logan eyed the manuscript and appeared curious.

"Did you actually read that?"

"Yeah, but I didn't care for the ending," Skyler announced with little interest.

"What was wrong with the ending?" Logan suddenly demanded, appearing insulted.

"It didn't make sense," Skyler replied. "It seems like there should be more."

Logan stopped playing his portable keyboard and snatched the manuscript. "Everyone's a critic."

Talbert approached Skyler and looked around with disgust. "Considering the circumstances, I guess you can have your old job back."

Skyler stood with his head held high and looked Talbert in the eyes. "Sorry, but I already have a job." He grinned proudly. "I'm Numinous."

Mel approached Skyler and affectionately clung to his arm. "You promised me a moonlit walk on the beach."

Skyler grinned and walked away with her. Talbert watched him leave with Mel and frowned. Logan flipped though the ending of the manuscript with a puzzled look on his face. Talbert glared at Logan and indicated the keyboard.

"Play something, will you?" he snarled with annoyance then walked away.

Logan glared after Talbert, sneered, and gave him the middle finger. Hailey and Rafe continued to slow dance in the sand despite the absence of music.

"What now?" Rafe asked while hiding his humor. "It seems we're both unemployed."

"According to Skyler's latest psychic analysis, Vance will become Brody's partner here at the resort," she informed him. "They will mutually agree to fire Talbert and hire Skyler as hotel manager. Brody will then beg you to be head of security."

He laughed at her analysis then turned serious. "What becomes of the princess?"

"The princess falls in love with the new head of security and, strangely enough, becomes Brody's assistant."

"I think all that power has gone to Skyler's head," Rafe remarked and grinned. "He's losing his touch."

"Actually, I already accepted the position," Hailey informed him then shrugged.

Rafe grinned and pulled her against him as they stopped dancing. He looked into her eyes and gently touched her face.

"Tell me more about happily ever after."

Hailey smiled warmly and brushed her lips past his. He eagerly moved his mouth closer to hers to accept her teasing kiss.

"Hailey--" Logan called out.

Hailey pulled away from Rafe as if caught doing something wrong.

Rafe groaned with disgust. "Next time we leave the kids at home."

Logan hurried toward them with the manuscript in his hands. Vance and Skyler heard the odd urgency in his voice and approached as well.

"You're not going to believe this," Logan announced.

"Is something wrong?" Vance asked and cast a glance at his lady-in-waiting to make sure she was still waiting.

"It's the ending," Logan informed them.

Hailey grinned lustfully and moved closer to Rafe, gently running her hand along his chest. Rafe eagerly pulled her into arms and against him.

"We've already figured that one out," she teased.

Logan shook his head while staring at her. "No, there's more to the story..."

The End

Other books by Holly Copella!
Reviews left on Amazon are appreciated!

"The Battle for Andrea Maria"

A cruise ship attack turns six survivors into overnight celebrities after they take credit for the heroic act of a stowaway who died saving them.

The cruise is just what Jess needed--a bit of harmless fun far from her daily grind. But what begins as a relaxing vacation turns into a desperate fight for her life when terrorists take over the ship and start piling up bodies. Teaming up with a mysterious stowaway, Jess attempts to send out a distress call but knows they cannot wait for help to come. If she or the few remaining passengers have any hope for survival, Jess must act now. The papers dub it "The Battle for *Andrea Maria*," but to Jess it is the moment she fought side-by-side with her enigmatic Romeo, saving the ship--and losing him. She thinks the story ends there, but really, the nightmare is just beginning...

"Insanely Deadly"

When the dead return to life, it's up to an admiral's daughter and a mildly insane, former war hero to save their small town.

Jetta Cross, a Navy Admiral's daughter, is tasked with keeping her father's comrade, a former war hero turned town crazy, grounded in the real world. Capt. John Hunter is still fighting the war in his head, where imaginary dead people are part of his world. When a viral outbreak brings about a zombie uprising, Hunter is left to his own devices. He must resume his role as a one-man commando unit in order to destroy the ravenous undead. With Hunter still fighting his own inner demons as well as the undead, the townspeople fear their zombie neighbors may not be the only threat. Stranded at the island's luxurious resort with a handful of workers, Jetta is forced to live up to her father's reputation and take charge of the deteriorating situation at the hotel. She must wage her own war against the infected before the government declares her hometown a total loss.

"Deadly Institution"

A town recluse suspected of killing his wife teams up with a young woman in order to stop a killer.

After being accused of murdering his wife, Konrad Asher turns his back on the town that once adored him. Ten years later, he still holds his grudge and the title of the most feared man in town. With the reopening of the burned mental institution, where his wife had died, former employees are now murdered one-by-one, throwing suspicion back on Asher. A young local reporter, Jacey, is forced to reveal her long-time friendship with the infamous recluse in order to clear his name not only in the recent murders but to exonerate him in the death of his wife as well. Will Jacey's relationship with Asher invite the killer closer to her? Or is the killer already in her life?

"Screenplays: The Island Collection"
"Jungle Princess", "A.L.F. Resort", "Brighton Island"

Discover how romance and fun in the sun can be downright *chilling*!

"Jungle Princess" is a romantic/thriller that leaves a teenage girl stranded on an island with two male shipmates and a creature of "unknown" origin. She soon discovers the island is home to an abandoned prison with several prisoners roaming free. What really killed over one hundred prisoners? And is it still out there--?

"A.L.F. Resort" is a romantic/thriller set on an island resort with Artificial Life Forms as the main draw. At this resort, all your fantasies come true...until a malfunction removes safety inhibitors on the A.L.F.'s. Zombies, biker gangs, and mobsters run amuck, turning fantasies into nightmares. A young reporter gets more of a story than she anticipates, but will she survive long enough to write the story?

"Brighton Island" is a romantic/thriller set on a private island. When the owner's niece brings her psychic friend to the mansion, his presence awakens the spirits' tortured souls. As the psychic attempts to solve the old murders, the niece is confronted with the possibility that she's next to join the mansion ghosts. Stranded on the island with a crazed killer, her uncle wages his own war to save them. Will his "shock and awe" tactics actually save them or get them killed?

"Reaper of Souls" A fantasy short story

A young woman must outwit an evil sorcerer in order to save her brother or become one of his minions forever.

Unwilling to believe her brother is dead, Reggie discovers an underhanded deal made with Kahn, a less than ethical sorcerer, who collects humans to serve as slaves in his kingdom. In order to rescue her brother from his horrible fate, she must complete his failed task or be forced to serve Kahn forever. After being transported to his world, Reggie realizes that even if she beats Kahn at his own game, she's at his mercy for him to uphold his end of the deal. All seems lost until Kahn's discontented, self-serving brother, Helsing, arrives. Can Reggie convince Helsing to help her? And at what cost?

"Death Displacement"

A grief-stricken man travels back in time to seek revenge on the woman who murdered his girlfriend but inadvertently falls in love with her.

Kane is about to marry the woman he loves. His life is perfect. A few weeks before the wedding, a vindictive woman from his girlfriend's past mysteriously arrives and kills her. He learns of a traumatic accident that happened five years earlier, which triggers Riley's hatred for his girlfriend. Distraught over his girlfriend's death, Kane uses an antique time machine to travel into the past in order to find and destroy the woman responsible. When he runs into Riley's younger self, he realizes she's not the monster she later becomes, and he can't bring himself to destroy her. With a little help from his oddball friend from the past, they formulate a plan to prevent the accident that sends Riley down her destructive path. Kane's plan backfires when he falls for the younger Riley. His new tortured existence is further complicated when future Riley, his girlfriend's killer, shows up with her own devious agenda that doesn't include him. Will he be able to stop the time ripple, which ultimately ends with his girlfriend's death? Or will future Riley take him out of the timeline forever--

"Dead Village"

After strange happenings isolate a small resort town from the rest of the world, nearly one hundred residents seek refuge at the closed hotel. Only eight survive the night. And that's just the beginning...

One day after the entire population of Fox Ridge Village disappears, a car wreck forces several unsuspecting crash victims to seek help at the closed summer hotel. Within the hotel, they discover the grisly aftermath of a brutal slaughter. Crash victims Vander and Devon, a reluctant clairvoyant, team up to solve the riddle of the "haunted hotel" and the mass hysteria plaguing the remaining survivors. By the time they discover the hotel's secret, they're already drawn into the hysteria. As the body count continues to climb, it's a race to isolate the source and bring everyone back to reality before they kill one another. Will Devon be able to communicate with the traumatized spirits before their fate becomes her own?

"Basement Dwellers"

A viral outbreak at a hospital leaves a mortician, sheriff, and coroner fighting for their lives against a horde of undead and the CDC.

After a massive car wreck leaves several survivors in critical condition at the local hospital, a surgeon uses experimental drugs on his critical patients and accidentally causes a zombie outbreak. When local mortician, Lexx, receives an infected corpse as her client, she becomes stranded in the hospital basement during CDC quarantine along with the local sheriff and the coroner. The infamous surgeon struggles to find a cure for his infectious blunder by using the other survivors as test subjects. Meanwhile, Lexx and the sheriff attempt to locate his missing sister, who's stranded somewhere in the battle zone that once was the emergency room. It's a race against time and the ravenous undead. Can they survive the undead before CDC sanitizes the hospital of all infection?

"Town Darling"

After surviving a brutal attack that claims the lives of those she loves, a young woman seeks revenge on a corrupt town.

Going back home is never easy, but for Casey, it means returning to her corrupt hometown where she barely survived a brutal attack. Accompanied by two *family friends*, she seeks justice for the night that destroyed her life. Her physical scars are nothing compared to her emotional ones, forcing the local sheriff to believe that the town darling is back for revenge. As the conspiracy for her revenge appears to be leading up to the coveted town fair, the sheriff is determined to stop her from fulfilling her vengeful scheme...but guilt over his role on that fateful night continues to haunt him. His desperate need for Casey's forgiveness could be his undoing.

"Witness Protection"

After witnessing an execution, a resourceful young woman attempts to disappear while being pursued by a hitman and a handsome federal agent.

A helicopter pilot, Jackie Remus, reluctantly agrees to go on a date with one of her clients, but her date is unexpectedly cut short when she witnesses a man being murdered. After narrowly escaping with her life, she is placed into protective custody. When the safe house is breached, Jackie makes a daring escape from both the hired killers and the handsome FBI agent, who wants to return her to protective custody. With a little help from her sly and crafty friend, Monroe, Jackie is convinced she can disappear until the trial. While on her journey to meet with her friend, she solicits help from a few shady but lovable characters along the way. Although she manages to stay one-step ahead of the hired killers, the federal agent remains in hot pursuit. Will Jackie reach Monroe before she's captured by the FBI and returned to protective custody? Or will the hired killers silence her first?

Coming Soon!
"Unconditional"

A young woman puts her life on hold to care for an unstable, highly skilled combat soldier, who believes someone is trying to kill him.

A botched military coup leaves a team of elite fighters injured with one clinging to life in a coma. When Harlan wakes from his coma, he's left with no memory of his past life. His commander's daughter, Indy, takes it upon herself to care for the fallen war hero. She's challenged with more than just his physical care as she combats with not only his memory loss but also his newly found desire for her. His infatuation with her becomes the least of her worries when he sinks back into his role of a combat soldier. Believing his life is in danger, his fighting skills surface, turning him into an unpredictable and dangerous man. Will his memory return to him before Indy is forced to commit him? Or will he finally find his nemesis, "the coyote", and possibly claim the life of an innocent person?

Coming Spring 2016!
"Witness Protection 2"
"The Return of Whiskey Tango Foxtrot"

ABOUT THE AUTHOR

Holly Copella has been writing since the age of twelve when her frustration at a book's poor plot drove her to author her own story. Over the last decade, she's written a number of screenplays, some of which she's now adapting into novels. Her fascination with zombies and other darker material lends an edge to her writing, which tends to lean toward horror. As a fan of Agatha Christie, she appreciates the craft of a good plot and the importance of creating significant characters.

Hailing from Pennsylvania, Copella lives in the Endless Mountains on a farm with her rescue horses and other animals. In addition to writing and reading fiction, she enjoys riding horses and traveling to Las Vegas and Disney World.